Time Twist
by

Jeanie R. Davis

Time Twist

Cover Art by *Kristian Norris*

The Wild Rose Press, Inc.
PO Box 708
Adams Basin, NY 14410-0708
Visit us at www.thewildrosepress.com

Publishing History
First Paranormal Romance Edition, 2018
Print ISBN 978-1-5092-2253-7
Digital ISBN 978-1-5092-2254-4

Published in the United States of America

Christopher was certain his father had been using his device to travel back in time, committing more crimes to increase his fortune. Criminals such as his father were never satisfied—the desire for money never fulfilled, the thirst for power never quenched and the urge to spill blood never quelled. Christopher didn't know how extreme his father's lust for power and fortune had become, but in his heart, he feared the worst.

His own memories of the machine were hazy, at best. He hadn't seen it, but he'd never forget the loud vibrations it had caused just before he'd slipped into complete darkness, back in London, then heard again vaguely when they'd landed in Colorado.

He and his partner drove to the address from the 911 call. His heart sank. This house, so near the city center, couldn't possibly have anything to do with his father. It was probably a complaint about noisy kids or something. No. Christopher was certain Father had built the mansion—his family's future home, Arianna's current worksite—outside of Pueblo, where no one would be bothered by such noises.

New fear for Ari's safety prickled his skin. What if the device was at the home already? What if she was there when Father decided to use it? What if he did something to Ari, then transported her to another time? Worry gnawed at him.

Dedication

My daughters, Cassi, Kiera, BrieAnne and Ashlyn, who helped inspire this story

Chapter One

London, England—April 1814

Christopher tugged a ragged curtain open, letting the full moon light his room. He pulled out his pocket watch and discovered it was nearly two o'clock in the morning. Why he was fully dressed at this hour, he couldn't say. A feeling? An omen, of sorts.

Movement outside caught his eye. He watched his father stumble up the cobbled drive, no doubt foxed.

No. Not foxed. Christopher peered more closely. He may have had a few drinks, but a large bundle on his back appeared to weigh him down, causing him to stagger.

Christopher's impulse to rush to Father's aid was quelled when a ray of light from a streetlamp glanced off his waistcoat. The coat, finely tailored for the son of an earl, had seen better days, but had never been soiled. Now it was. In what? In blood? Surely not his own. Christopher scowled, and his pulse quickened as bitterness oozed through his consciousness. The time had come.

How could Father have fallen so far? He was a man once. With property. With dignity. Now what had he become? Had he no concern for his family?

Christopher began to pace. How should he proceed? If he could slip from the townhouse unnoticed

1

and fetch a constable... No. Protecting his mother, sister and brother must be his top priority. He couldn't leave them. It had been too long since Father had been kind to any of the family.

The front door slammed shut. His father wheezed loudly enough to hear through the thin walls of the small townhouse they shared. Christopher stopped his pacing and cracked open his door to observe the scene in the candle-lit room.

"I need your help, Bea!" Father barked. His breath came out in loud puffs. For a man who'd divided his time between drinking and scheming, whatever he carried on his back obviously weighed him down.

Mother, clothed in a threadbare nightdress, rushed toward her husband, arms outstretched. "Oh, Benjamin, I have worried so." She stopped short when her eyes landed on his stained fingers. "Your hands!" She dropped her arms and rocked back. "Your coat! Is that blood?" She sucked in a breath. "Are you injured?" Her face wrinkled in concern. It was all Christopher could do to rein in his impulse to jump to action and instead wait. He needed more information about Father's scheme before charging forward. His heartbeat picked up a notch.

Ignoring her question, his father stomped his foot. "I said I need help!" A flame sputtered, causing the shadows to quiver.

Her gaze flew from his bloody hands to his face. "Help with what? ...And what have you got in that bag?"

"That, my dear, is our future." He dropped the bag onto the kitchen table, where the contents clinked and tinkled. Mother's mouth gaped open, but before she could say anything more, Father cleared his throat. "Pay very close attention." He waved a finger in her face. "You need to gather the family and meet me in the bookroom. We are leaving this shabby existence—forever."

"But—"

Father raised a hand, quieting her. "If there are items of value, or anything you or the children wish to see again, I suggest you bring them." He pushed past her, exiting the room. "What are you waiting for, Beatrice? Pick up your feet and move!" he hollered back at her.

Shadows of worry, mingled with confusion, crossed Mother's face.

Christopher had heard enough. The anger flowing through his veins threatened to choke him. He must stop his father before someone got hurt. Reaching under his bed, he jerked out a satchel plump with his belongings. Uncertain of Father's scheme, he had prepared for anything imaginable—including protecting his family. He tucked a sheathed dagger into his waistband.

Through the door he'd left ajar, he glimpsed Mother—a candlestick in one hand, a large bag in the other—rousing his brother and sister. She moved like a puppet, blindly obeying her husband's demands. Christopher wondered for a moment why she retrieved his siblings first. After all, he'd acted as the man of the house for months now. Then the angry words he and Father had exchanged earlier hit him like a wall of ice crashing through his head. Mother had every reason to worry about his reaction. He let out a breath to calm his racing heart.

Sarah and Joshua were easily maneuvered, as if they were sleepwalking. Once they were out of his vision, he watched Mother scan their room, grabbing an armful of clothing; a miniature drawn of their family, which Joshua especially treasured; Sarah's journal; some remnants—that hadn't been auctioned off yet—from their former life at the estate; and a few other items.

Christopher nudged his door open, nearly running into his mother. "Christopher! I—I thought you were asleep. Your father wants—"

"I know, Mother. I heard him."

"Why are you awake, son?"

"Never mind that. What has Father planned?"

Judging by the bewilderment on Mother's face, she knew nothing of what his father had been up to. She was innocent—had always been innocent. Through all Father's failures, drinking and conniving, Mother had remained in the dark.

"I do not know, Christopher. Only that it involves jewels which I'm certain were stolen. And"—she let out a shuddering breath—"there is blood on his coat." A sob escaped her throat. "Oh, Christopher, I fear he has committed a grievous crime." The floor creaked, warning them that Father wasn't far away.

Christopher's heart sank at his mother's words. She didn't deserve this. It must be the liquor causing Father's lapse in judgment. He'd once treated his wife with respect.

"Son, your father will be angry if we tarry. Come. Bring anything you value."

"I have it right here." He patted his satchel, then followed Mother. As they neared the bookroom, his father stepped out, stopping them in their tracks. Christopher met the challenge in Father's piercing gaze.

He would not be cowed by this man.

He gripped the handle of the hidden blade beneath his coat—his intentions were not to willfully injure, but protect.

"What have you done, Father?" Christopher stepped around his mother, shielding her.

"Do not take that tone with me." Father sneered. "You were so piously unwilling to help me with my plan to save our family. You'll have no say in matters now."

"Unwilling? Unwilling to rob? Unwilling to murder?" Christopher moved closer to his father, his blood boiling. "Unwilling to save our family? What about the responsibilities you fell short on, plunging us into bankruptcy? Have you forgotten I *have* been helping? I've been the wage earner at this address. I left Cambridge prematurely to pick up the pieces you let fall—just as your very reputation has plummeted!" His voice hit a fever pitch.

Father's crimson face twitched. A maniacal gleam entered his eyes, yet he spoke with an eerie calmness, raising the hair on Christopher's skin. "You are a Somerset. My son." He rubbed the onyx ring his late father had given him as if to send a message. "Sons aid their fathers. Had you helped me, spilling blood may have been avoided."

"Do not use me to justify your actions." Christopher held his ground, his heart beating thunderously.

"My invention has made us rich." Father took a step toward Christopher, a crazed expression on his face. "No man's mind is as clever as mine." Christopher had once believed those words. Pain shot through his chest as if his father's sins and failures and what he had become sailed on an arrow, piercing his heart. "And you will not defy me!"

Christopher tugged out the knife, ready to defend. Mother gasped, breaking his concentration and his eye contact. He caught movement from Father as the blunt force of something hard slammed down on his head. He groaned and fought for consciousness, wielding the knife futilely until his world darkened to black.

Chapter Two

Denver, Colorado—Present Day

Arianna Miller watched the red Corvette speed away, stunned. *He loves me?* Why would Zach say it if he didn't mean it? And he couldn't possibly mean it so early in the relationship. So taken off-guard, she'd opened her mouth, but couldn't choke out the words. They'd come out something like: "I—I...lo—like you...a lot." Sigh. *Lo—like you?* Horrible time to be tongue-tied. When and if she ever felt sincerely ready to say those three words, it would be to someone she'd shared her hopes and dreams with; shared good times and bad. Someone who would move heaven and earth to help her, if need be. And she'd do the same for him. Perhaps it would be Zach. Only time would tell. She was excited at the possibility.

She swung the door open to Johnson and Tate Design Firm. The smell of potpourri lightly scented the air of the century-old, cottage-style house-turned-office complex. She glanced around the empty waiting area and couldn't imagine having a better job. She smiled at the meticulous detail of the furnishings—professional, yet comfortable.

Before she found her desk, Maggie's head popped up. "How was lunch? How is Zach? Did you—"

Arianna laughed. "Yes, I brought you a soda. What are friends for?"

"Good. That's all I really cared about."

"I don't believe you for a second." Ari handed Maggie the drink. "And your pregnancy cravings change every day. Yesterday it was pretzels."

Maggie shrugged and took a sip. "Yeah, and I used to go running with you in the mornings." She patted her swollen belly. "Now I'm a hippo with cravings." Her eyes twinkled. "So, tonight's the art fair benefit. Is Zach still taking you?"

Ari frowned. "He had to cancel. Work meeting." She scooted up to her desk. Perhaps that's why he'd said he loved her—guilt.

Maggie's eyes narrowed. "Dentists have work meetings at night?"

"That's what he said." Ari shrugged. She didn't know why Maggie always acted suspicious of Zach. She was lucky to have such a perfect boyfriend—rich and handsome.

"Your phone's buzzing." Maggie pointed at Ari's purse. "Maybe he's reconsidered."

Arianna plucked her phone from her bag and read the text. *Hey babe. My night freed up. I'll be over at seven. Wear that slinky number you wore last weekend.* For a split-second Ari stared at her screen, confused. Then realization dawned, and nausea threatened to send her to the restroom. This text wasn't meant for her. She didn't even own a "slinky number." She wanted to scream.

"You're pale, Ari. Is the text from Zach?"

"It's from him, all right." She handed Maggie the phone. Tears stung her eyes, but she willed them away. Zach didn't deserve them.

"I don't get it." Maggie's eyes scanned the text a second time. "He's free now? Slinky number? But I thought you two were taking things slow—" She clapped a hand over her mouth.

"He doesn't call me babe and I didn't see him last weekend, either," said Ari.

Maggie gulped. "He thought he sent this text to someone else!"

Ari's voice rose the angrier she became. "We were just together ten minutes ago. He even told me he loved me! I wonder how long he's been seeing this...this tramp!"

A red-faced Mr. Johnson stormed through the room, glaring at her. "Do I need to remind you that this is a place of business, Miss Miller? Keep your personal life at home, and never raise your voice in front of our customers." He stomped into his office.

"How does he do that? He comes in here ranting and raving, and nobody takes notice. Whereas I raise my voice once, and the whole state of Colorado hears me," she whispered. "Besides, there's nobody in the waiting—"

Maggie motioned toward the front.

Ari peeked up to see several seated clients, staring in her direction. She let go of a sigh. It had been empty after lunch—ten short minutes ago. "Did I really just lose it in front of everyone?"

"You really just did, but you were justified." Maggie flicked a lock of auburn hair over her shoulder, her eyes still on the text. "Wait—he said he loved you?"

"Yes, not that it meant anything. But seriously"—keeping her voice low, she motioned to the words on the screen—"can you believe that?" She tilted her head to urge a response from her friend.

Maggie handed back the phone and turned to face her. "Zach's scum. You know I've never trusted the guy." She appeared to have more to say.

"But?" One thing she loved and sometimes hated about Maggie was her honesty.

"Well, do you realize that you've been dating him for a month now and the most you'll give him is a kiss?" Her eyebrows drew up in an arch. "In fact, with your super-model looks you could have your pick of all the bachelors in Denver. But none of them are good enough."

"What's your point, Mags? Just because I have higher standards than some doesn't mean I should settle for less, does it?" She returned the pointed look.

"Some girls? Try every girl we've ever met." Her voice had begun to rise. She cleared her throat and lowered it again. "Honestly, Ari, I hate what Zach did, but you're becoming a prude. I think you've read way too many of those books, those—what do you call them?"

"Regency romances." Ari loved history and had even minored in it in college. She spent any spare time reading and had developed a fascination with the romantic English stories. "You mean when the men were gentlemen and girls were ladies? When it wasn't even proper to kiss until you were practically married?"

Maggie rolled her eyes. "Yup, those books. Two hundred years ago, Ari! You are living in a dream world from over two centuries ago! They've made you delusional."

"Have you ever considered that maybe—just maybe—I haven't met the right man for me?" What was she saying? Only moments ago, she'd wondered if Zach might be the man she'd share her future with. How could she have been so blind? She wouldn't tell Maggie she'd been right, Zach *had* pressured her weeks ago to "put out," as he called it. Love should be more than that. When she'd explained her feelings to Zach, he'd seemed to understand—even acted as if he admired her for her values. Evidently, he'd found a way to get what he wanted—without her. Ari was determined to find a man with the same ideals—if such a man existed.

"Miller." Arianna looked up, expecting another set-down from her angry boss. She respected Mr. Johnson, but he wasn't the reason she loved her job. Decorating, and Maggie, made her job the best. "Come into my office." His voice sounded firm, but unemotional.

Arianna crossed the room, carefully avoiding those customers to whom she'd divulged too much personal information and slipped into Mr. Johnson's office. Nerves made her heartbeat accelerate.

"Sit down, Arianna." Mr. Johnson pushed his hand back and forth across his balding head. Graying tufts of hair fringed the sides around his ears. *No wonder he's losing his hair.* She stifled a grin, then remembered she hadn't been called into his office for good behavior.

She sat down and began her appeal. "I'm really sorry, Mr. Johnson. It won't happen again. I didn't realize I was talking so loudly. I really need this—"

"That's not why I called you in here, Ari." His face softened. "It seems I have an assignment for you. A job that will require you to be away on location." He pushed some papers toward her. "You are talented, but I'm not sure you're ready for something of this magnitude, as this will be your first solo job. However, Zoe and Evan both have projects underway, and our friend Maggie will be on maternity leave soon, as you well know. I have no other options. This project is a big one and will take a lot of time." His hand wandered back up to his thinning hairline.

Fingers trembling, she fumbled with the papers. Arianna, the new designer on the block, having only worked for Johnson and Tate for a year and a half, was good—anyway, she thought so. She just needed a chance to prove herself. Up to this point, she'd only been assigned to partner with the other three well-seasoned designers. But this could be her chance to demonstrate what she could do.

She pointed at one of the papers. "Mr. Johnson, it says here the home is near Pueblo. Isn't that a bit of a drive?"

He leaned forward on his desk. "That's what I mean when I say it's away on location. It's a few miles south of the city of Pueblo—just a couple of hours from here. You can commute and we'll cover your gas, or you can find an apartment there for the duration of the project, which the company will pay for. It's your call."

"I think I'd like to live there." Arianna said, after only a few moments of pondering.

A thousand questions flooded into her mind, and evidently Mr. Johnson could read it because before she could ask the first of many, he stood, motioning her to do the same. "Everything is in there." He pointed to the scattered papers in front of her. "Read through them and let me know tomorrow if you feel you're up to it. And Ari, I don't need to remind you how important this job is to our firm. We need all the business we can get right now. You will find, while reading the paperwork, that this client comes across as somewhat eccentric, but he also appears to have deep pockets. We could use a few deep pockets right now."

"Yes, sir." Ari backed out of the room. She felt like hugging Mr. Johnson, or at least saluting him. She settled on giving him a nod and a smile as she mumbled, "Thanks."

She plunked the papers on her desk and scooted close to Maggie. "Mags, Mags, Mags, I got my first solo job. And it's on location in Pueblo." And seriously couldn't have come at a better time.

Maggie didn't look sufficiently impressed as she cocked her head to gaze at Ari. Rather, she seemed puzzled. "What in the world is in Pueblo, and why would you want to leave me to go there?" She scrunched her nose.

"Oh, come on, Maggie. You know how long I've been waiting to be the lead designer on a job. This is my chance to prove myself. I know I can do it. Say you're excited for me." She widened her eyes expectantly.

"I'm excited for you." Maggie glanced down at some paperwork while twirling a few strands of hair through her fingers.

Arianna frowned. "Seriously, Maggie, I can move to Pueblo for a few months and get a fresh start. You know how hard it is for me. Everywhere I go in this city there are memories that haunt me."

"Memories of Zach?" Maggie raised her head to meet Arianna's gaze. "I'm dying to know how you're going to respond to him, now that you know what he's been up to."

Ari couldn't think about Zach right now. She'd formulate a reply later, when the mere mention of him didn't make her sick. "Yes, Zach." Just saying his name hurt. "…And memories of my family." She'd eventually get over Zach, but her family was gone forever.

A shiver ran down her spine when she thought about the cold, winter day her world had turned upside-down. She'd noticed a series of missed calls on her silenced cell phone during class. She'd quickly excused herself only to find someone from the college administration headed straight for her with the message that her mother, father and younger brother had been killed in a car accident. She still felt numb inside and out, even though two and a half years had passed. She had picked up the pieces as well as she could, but she would never fully recover from the shock of that dreadful day. Born and raised in Denver, it had been natural for her to return after her four years away at Colorado State, but she didn't feel the need to stay there forever. It was a home without family, and that was hardly a home.

"Oh," Maggie said in a more reverent tone. She placed a gentle arm around Arianna. "I'm so sorry.

Sometimes I forget how painful it must be for you to even get through a day with those reminders."

"They're mostly good memories, but it still hurts knowing I'll never see the people I love most again."

"Not to mention, the driver who hit them is still roaming around on Denver asphalt." Maggie fisted a hand and hit her knee. "I'm still upset so little was done to find the creep."

"I'm sure they did all they could." Ari swallowed a lump growing in her throat. Maybe they had, maybe they hadn't. Dwelling on it never helped. She generally avoided the subject. "This could be a fresh start for me. Even if it's in Pueblo." She smiled as a tear trickled down her cheek.

"Arianna's at her desk. Go on back," the receptionist said from across the office. Ari perked up immediately. Who would be here for her?

Zach.

Chapter Three

Think, think, think. Ari wasn't ready to confront Zach yet. But ready or not, here he came. He waved and made a path toward her desk. Why was he here?

As if to answer her question, he raised a doggy bag of food she must have left in his car.

Maggie whispered in her ear, "Well, if it isn't your two-timing boyfriend now."

Ari winced. "Go with me on this, Maggie."

He approached her desk. "I got all the way back to my office before I noticed you'd left this." His perfect smile—gleaming straight, white teeth, and all—did nothing to soothe Ari's angst.

"Oh, hi *babe*." She watched as Zach's smile faltered for a split-second. "You didn't need to bring the food back to me. Next time, just throw it away."

"It was the least I could do after bailing on you tonight."

"Yeah, your work meeting." She glanced at Maggie, then back at Zach. "What time will your meeting be over? I'm thinking of cutting out early from the benefit. I'll stop by your place."

Maggie jumped in. "Make sure to take that slinky number you just bought, Ari. He'll love it."

Zach's face paled. "What?" He took a step back, as if he'd been slapped.

Ari stood and walked up close to him so no one else could hear. "Next time you arrange to meet up with someone other than me, you'd better check the number you're texting."

"I—I don't know what you're talking about."

Maggie held up a folder. "Ari, Mr. Johnson wants you to check on this."

"Goodbye, Zach." Ari turned, took the file from Maggie, and walked away. She had no destination in mind—perhaps the ladies' room—she just couldn't stick around and listen to Zach lie his way out of his blunder.

****

Three days later she had her little red Subaru packed and ready to begin her adventure in Pueblo. She'd ignored text after text from Zach, still unwilling to consider any explanation he might come up with. He was a cheater. She'd wasted enough time on him already. Her heart ached, but not for Zach. It ached for a future with a man who loved and respected her.

Sitting in Mr. Johnson's office, she waited to meet the owners of the house she'd been commissioned to decorate. The file her boss had given her left much to the imagination. While it brimmed with opinions on colors and style, there were gaping holes where personal information should have been about the owners. Curious.

Mr. and Mrs. Benjamin Somers were scheduled to arrive at eleven o'clock. The meeting would entail Arianna receiving specific instructions and a key to the new home. Tension had her stomach tied up in knots as she waited to meet them. It was her first solo job. She hoped she wouldn't lose her breakfast or faint right in front of them. That would *not* inspire confidence.

"Mr. Johnson and your designer, Ms. Miller, are this way." Ari's head snapped up as she heard the receptionist's voice. The knots tightened. She turned to watch through the open door as the couple followed the receptionist into the room. Arianna sucked in a breath. Something about the way the man carried himself, or maybe his eyes, put her on edge. She sat a little straighter, needing all the confidence she could muster.

Mr. Johnson stood to greet the Somers. "Welcome to Johnson and Tate." He extended his arm to shake first Mr. then Mrs. Somers' hands. Mrs. Somers didn't respond for a moment. Her husband gave her a not-so-gentle shove, and she lifted a limp hand to Mr. Johnson's. That was odd. "May I introduce you to our designer, Arianna Miller?" Ari also stood and held out her hand but was met with a questioning stare before a hesitant handshake. She couldn't help but notice the ring Mr. Somers wore. It glowed black and shiny, just like his eyes.

"She looks young," mumbled Mr. Somers.

This wasn't helping her nerves. Ari shifted her weight. She recognized his cologne as sandalwood. She should know since her mom used to dabble in essential oils. Mom had used it as an antiseptic. Interesting. She'd never known a man to wear it as cologne.

"Oh, I assure you that Arianna is a top-notch designer and will do a great job for you." He tugged a page from Ari's file and handed it to Mr. Somers. "In fact, she is quite familiar with the Victorian Era and, as your new home is Victorian, she is the right person for the job." Mr. Johnson sounded nervous. She didn't blame him, every inch of Mr. Somers screamed intimidation.

The couple appeared more distressed than reassured by Mr. Johnson's pitch. Arianna, however, found it refreshing to hear her prickly boss sing her praises—even if it was his job. All the more reason for her to do her most impressive work. Mr. Johnson hurried on to say, "If you find her performance lacking in any way, please, just let me know and we will arrange for a new designer. Mr. Somers seemed to relax a little, knowing he could dismiss her at any time. Ari tamped down her rising anxiety—and her breakfast.

A large man, Mr. Somers had graying black hair and eyes that seemed to pierce a hole right through his target. He sported a black three-piece suit—definitely overdressed for the occasion. He looked stodgy, almost as if he could be wearing a bowler hat and a cape. Ari suppressed a smile at the image. Mrs. Somers, however, with her crystal-blue eyes, had her brown hair swept gracefully back and wore a flowing muslin skirt. Arianna imagined her to be quite pretty in earlier times. Now, though, she looked sad. Intriguing. At first glance, the woman didn't seem the type to agree to lavish décor in their new home, but now she wondered if Mrs. Somers ever voiced her opinion at all.

Mr. Somers analyzed the file paper, which, from what Ari could see, listed her credentials. "The girl looks to be qualified," he said, shoving the page back at Mr. Johnson.

"You're British," Ari said with more exuberance than intended. She had always loved an English accent, and theirs was thicker than any she'd heard. Her pronouncement didn't appear to impress or please either of the Somers, as they exchanged worried glances.

"Yes, Arianna," Mr. Johnson cut in. "The Somers relocated to Denver from London just four years ago."

She gulped down her fears and took a breath. Even though the Somers seemed less than enthusiastic about her, she was thrilled to be decorating their home—that is, if they didn't fire her before she had a chance to work her magic.

"Miss Miller, is it?" Mr. Somers turned his frosty gaze to Ari.

"Yes. Arianna Miller—you can call me Arianna, or just Ari, if you'd like."

"Miss Miller—"

Or not. Miss Miller works, too. Geez.

Mr. Somers cleared his throat.

She straightened her posture under his scrutiny, certain his glare might set her on a fire.

"Please take your time with this job, as we prefer to have our new home decorated as authentically as possible. We intend to move our belongings in slowly, as time permits. For the most part, we will be coming to the home on weekends to check your progress, as well as deliver our personal items."

Arianna was intrigued with his thick English accent to the point of distraction. Mr. Johnson gave her a nudge, which brought her back to the conversation at hand.

"Oh, of course. I completely agree about the authenticity. I minored in history and have a fascination with England and the Victorian Era, the Regency Era, and—" She felt another little nudge. "I—I assure you, I will do my best to please you, Mr. Somers."

That seemed to satisfy the Somers—or at least Mr. Somers. Mrs. Somers never said a word and rarely looked up.

After a few more instructions, Mr. Somers gave Arianna the key to the house along with the alarm code.

"The builders assured me that now is the optimal time for a designer to commence decorating. They have a few minor touches which should only take a week or two more. After that, they will notify the alarm company and the house will be armed, so it is imperative you use the code when entering and reset it when you leave." Mr. Somers' stiff smile didn't reach his eyes. The cool undercurrent in his demeanor caused a shiver to snake down Ari's spine.

"No problem." Arianna's smile was genuine. She couldn't let this man get under her skin—not if she planned to work for him.

Organizing the Somers' items and placing them into her bag, Ari watched as her new, eccentric employers departed the building. She met Maggie in the hall and gave her a long hug as she secured a promise for generous updates. Ari didn't want to be in the dark about office gossip, after all. Not to mention, the impending birth of Maggie's son.

"And you'd better send me pictures of everything you do at that house in Pueblo, Ari. The owners seem a little creepy. I bet the home is fascinating."

"I know, right? I hope it isn't haunted. I'd better get on the road so I can get there before dark."

Arianna left the office and pointed her packed-to-the-roof Subaru south, heading toward her future.

Time flew by as she drove. The radio set on the oldies station cranked out one of her favorite songs. She anticipated pulling up to a quaint little Victorian neighborhood on the outskirts of town. Victorian houses were not generally being built any more, having fallen out of vogue several years before, but Arianna loved them and couldn't be more excited to decorate one.

She changed lanes. The car behind her followed suit. Was it her imagination, or had the same vehicle been tailing her since she'd left Denver? Speeding up, she changed lanes again. The car behind her stayed in its own lane but kept pace with her. Neither the car nor the driver looked familiar. *Why would anyone follow me?* She tried to shake off the eerie sensation prickling her skin.

Chapter Four

A loud noise startled Ari, and her car began to fishtail. Her imagination ran wild. Had someone shot a gun at her? Then she heard it: the thump, thump, thump of a flat tire. *Not now! Not here!* She pulled over, but stayed in her car and watched the vehicle behind her. It continued past her. Relief!

Thankful her dad had taught her some basic mechanics, she located the spare, then set to work changing the tire. Images of every horror show she'd ever seen ran through her mind. *Girl alone on the side of the road, while crazed axe murderer stalks her.* The notion made her fingers shake as she loosened the lug nuts.

"Need some help?" a raspy voice asked.

She jumped and spun around. It was the man who'd followed her. He must have exited the freeway and circled back. She lifted the lug wrench to wield as a weapon. He raised both hands. "Why are you following me?"

The man hesitated before speaking, tilting his head in question.

"Well?" Ari shook the wrench.

"I'm not following you. I live in Pueblo but had meetings in Denver today. When your tire popped, I was going too fast to stop, so I came back to help."

Trembling, she lowered the wrench, but kept a tight grip on it. "I'm sorry. I—I thought you were...never mind." Mr. Somers must have done a number on her to make her so paranoid.

The man's phone rang. "Hi, Bonnie. Yes, I'm almost home. Just stopped to help a lady with a flat tire. Sure thing. Love ya." He hung up. "My wife's expecting me. Do you want my help?"

Chagrinned, Ari allowed the man to help her. Making small talk as they worked, they had the spare tire on in minutes.

The man retrieved a towel from his car and cleaned his hands. "So, you say you're an interior designer and your job is to decorate that mansion outside of town?"

Ari nodded. "I'm excited to get started."

"Well, be careful. I hear the owner is running from the law. Why else would he build his fortress way out there?"

Ari shivered. "What?"

The man chuckled. "Small towns and their rumors. I'm sure there's nothing to worry about."

She offered to pay him, but he refused, muttering something about old-fashioned values becoming obsolete. Ari couldn't agree more. She waved to the stranger as he sped away.

Guided by her GPS, she continued southeast through Pueblo and beyond until she thought she'd left civilization. Her phone service faded in and out, forcing her to pull over and retrieve the paper map from the Somers' file. She examined it, then studied the vast expanse surrounding her. Nothing. No one. The feeling of complete isolation nearly had her turning around, but she took a deep breath and pressed forward. Back on the road again, a few turns off the highway took her to an abandoned shack here and there, but certainly not the quaint neighborhood she'd anticipated. One more turn led her to her destination.

Her breath caught, and she could think of no words to adequately describe the house that sat on the slight slope before her, giving it a "castle on a hill" appearance. She'd studied the pictures in the Somers' file, but to see it in person was indescribable.

It was the most beautiful, authentic Queen Anne-style Victorian home she'd ever seen. She swallowed and slumped down in her seat. The house loomed enormous and the detail meticulous. No wonder the Somers seemed to doubt her ability. Arianna shook herself, trying to reawaken the confidence she'd had just a few hours before in Mr. Johnson's office.

The mansion was dove-gray, but when the sun hit it just so, it appeared to be a lovely shade of light pink. Constructed mostly of wood, it had several stone inset walls and was trimmed in white. To top it off, there were turrets reaching to the sky on both the east and west sides. A reverent sensation settled over her as she observed the fine craftsmanship employed to construct this incredible home.

Why build something this beautiful in the middle of nowhere? They must really miss England. Not to mention, they don't seem to like people. Eccentric is an understatement.

She decided to take a stroll around the grounds first, while it was still light outside. It looked as if the landscapers had recently been working, as fresh sod covered the terraced front yard. A vast array of rose bushes lined the walkways, and newly planted saplings preparing to grow into huge oak trees framed the perimeter. As she worked her way to the rear of the house, she was surprised to find a corral and stalls for horses.

It felt as if she had been transported back to another time and place.

The grounds went on and on, but the landscaping did not. The landscapers would probably be there for much of the time that she was. She let out a slow breath, relieved she wouldn't always be out in the middle of nowhere alone. So alone.

She circled back to the front of the house and mounted the porch stairs. A massive hand-carved door towered before her. The key slipped easily into the lock, and as soon as she stepped into the foyer she stopped—eyes popping and mouth agape. She breathed in the rich smell of wood as she scanned the highly polished walnut floors and the rich wood-trim moldings along the walls and up the grand staircase. Then her eyes were drawn to a glistening chandelier overhead. She almost heard the butler asking her to follow him into the parlor to have some tea while he "collected" her wealthy British friend. She laughed at the notion.

She commenced a self-guided tour, beginning with the bedrooms upstairs. Every space was equally beautiful. *My entire apartment in Denver could fit into one of these rooms*. And there were so many of them. She wondered why a family of—what had she read—oh yes, four—needed such a large home.

Leaving the bedrooms, she descended the grand staircase and entered the kitchen. She gasped as she observed the spacious cooking and dining areas. Somehow the architect had been able to capture the past with wood trim, floors and moldings, antique lighting, and etched glass cabinetry, then combined them with top-of-the-line, modern appliances to create a fabulous kitchen.

She suddenly wished she weren't the only designer on the job.

Maggie needed to hear about this house. She reached for her cell phone. As she began dialing, her phone beeped at her. Oh man! No bars. Apparently, cell phone service wasn't the greatest out here. She frowned at the thought of no phone conversations with Maggie during her breaks. Another thought forced its way into her mind: *I'm in a house in the middle of nowhere, by myself—alone with no phone service.*

Continuing her tour, she moved to the study. The Somers had already begun moving in their belongings. In fact, on the floor in the middle of the room lay a beautiful Persian rug. Whoa, a Tabriz. Maggie would never believe this. Ari had only seen these in catalogs. Entering the room to take a closer look, she let out a deep sigh. The Somers certainly spared no expense on their home or their furnishings. She scanned the room, taking it all in. The walls were adorned with several beautiful art pieces, as if someone had already occupied it—well, except for the lack of a desk. She wondered why the Somers hadn't waited for her professional opinion on placement before hanging the art. She shrugged. Perhaps she'd rearrange them later.

Originals? No way; they couldn't be. She narrowed her eyes at one. Digging deep into her memory, she recalled learning in Art History that there had been a heist. The details were foggy. Oh yeah, it was back in 1990 in Boston. She tapped her head. The Isabella

Stewart Gardner Museum. A few Rembrandts, a Degas and a Manet were taken, if she remembered correctly. She cocked her head examining the painting more closely. It sure looked like Rembrandt's *Storm on the Sea of Galilee*. But that was ridiculous, right? A chill ran down her spine.

Besides the beautiful rug, art and a few pieces of small furniture, Arianna noticed a boxful of miscellaneous items. On top was a leather book. An avid reader, and curious by nature, she picked it up to scan. First, she breathed in the aroma of the leather cover. *This isn't a book.* She fanned the pages. *This is a journal.* A very old-style journal at that—positively antique, yet in perfect condition. She knew to keep out of other people's belongings—especially journals—but her curiosity piqued, getting the best of her, and she had to read at least one page. It couldn't be anyone's current diary—it was just too old.

One page turned into twenty before Arianna realized she'd broken her own just-one-page rule. But this was fantastic reading. The first half had been written in the most elegant cursive. It appeared to be from an actual quill pen. Then, the latter half had been written in similar handwriting, but by an obviously modern pen—perhaps ballpoint.

This journal had definitely been written by two different people, although, the handwriting was similar.

Arianna perused the book, searching for the page where the quill pen writing ended and the ballpoint began. Strange. It continued as if it were the same person. Even stranger were the phrases that jumped out at her.

> *Father is a drunk. He forced us to move to this horrid land and will not let us out of his sight. Even Mother is afraid of him.*

Ari shivered. She wondered who this poor soul was. She kept reading.

> *Father brought a television home last night. I've seen nothing like it. Colorful moving pictures are both frightening and mesmerizing.*

Ari shook her head at the absurdity of what she read. It couldn't possibly be real. TVs had been around for decades.

She flipped a few pages and continued.

> *My brother and I received clothing from the mail coach today, although, I believe it's no longer called a coach. I can see it from my window. It has black wheels and is very loud. I do not know where we are, but there are no horses here. Father lets us choose whatever clothing we want from a picture book. He said we have enough money to buy the entire catalog of gowns—however, dresses are scarce in the book. Instead, the ladies in the pictures wear trousers. My friends in London would think I'd gone mad if they could see my wardrobe now. So unladylike. I wish to go home.*

Ari wondered where home for this girl was. Most people considered Colorado quite beautiful. But then, nothing she'd read made much sense.

She skipped ahead several pages.

I celebrated my nineteenth birthday yesterday. As Mother puts it, Father was in his cups, so we did nothing but sing a few songs. I miss my friends in London. Mother tutors us here, so I haven't met a soul in nearly four years.

Four years? She sounded like a prisoner.

The last entry made Arianna squirm.

Father hit Mother last night, then, to make up for his cruelty, promised to build her a home worthy of a son of an earl. Ha! I think he's become daft. Perhaps he was reared by an earl, but his actions would alarm my dear grandfather. I don't know how much more of Father's abuse this family can take.

Worst of all was the phrase,

I broke a glass last night and plunged it into my chest. I am obviously as weak in body as I am in spirit, as the razor-sharp glass only served to make a bloody mess. If only...

The entry ended there.

"She attempted suicide." Ari shivered. "If only what?"

She flipped back to the beginning, where the mood had been completely different. There, this girl from the past spoke of young men she liked, gowns being designed for her, and practicing the pianoforte. Gradually her writings became dark and depressing. Ari's flesh crawled. What had happened to her? Maybe her abusive father had caught her with a boy, or something. She gazed up at the ceiling. *What am I thinking? It absolutely cannot be the same person.*

A door slammed shut, and Ari jumped, her heart thudding. Someone must be upstairs. Chills prickled her skin. But that couldn't be; she'd just been up there and had seen no one. Perhaps it had come from the garage. Willing herself to move, she forced herself to search the house. Surely, she was alone. Before she'd reached the second floor, another door closed with a bang. Warm air hit her face. *The heat registers.* Even though the spring days were pleasant, evenings in Colorado were chilly. Air shooting from the vents must have changed the pressure, forcing the doors shut. She took a calming breath and glanced at her watch. Nearly midnight. Where did the time go?

Weariness made her eyelids droop, and she still needed to drive back to Pueblo and locate her new apartment. She snapped a few pictures so she could start sketching ideas—the sooner the better. She also wanted to text some photos to Maggie. After all, she'd promised to call every day and give her more details about this mysterious family.

Thinking about Maggie made her homesick. Her friend had been in tears when Arianna had said her goodbyes, until Ari had promised she wouldn't miss her baby shower. Initially Ari had been the party planner, but things changed once she'd received the Pueblo assignment. Tasha Tate, Mr. Johnson's partner and wife, took up the shower planning reins. Ari swallowed down a lump growing in her throat. All those ideas for games, finger-foods and invitations had been filed away for another time. *Maggie understands.*

Maggie was the closest thing to family she had left in this world.

Ari soon left and found her furnished apartment in Pueblo without any problem. It was older construction, but in a good part of town and, best of all, clean. Pleased she now had cell phone service, she texted a few pictures to Maggie, then retrieved her notepad to scribble down some mental notes she'd taken while in the house. Without internet service at the project, the notepad was going to get a lot of use.

She'd brought a few boxes of necessary items from home, along with a cooler so she would have something to eat in her devoid-of-food apartment, not knowing how soon she'd get to a market. She dug out a TV dinner, which left much to be desired; but did the job. All the excitement of the day settled hard, making her extra sleepy. She climbed into bed, appreciating the soft pillow and mattress that came with the place, then gave in to the drowsiness.

****

The sun peeked through the blinds early the following morning, waking Arianna. The fragrant smell of lilacs and the cool breeze wisped through the window she'd left cracked open the night before. Clearing the cobwebs from her head, she smiled as she recalled the reason she had awakened in a strange bed, in a strange room.

She dressed quickly to get on the road. Thankfully, she found a drive-through restaurant nearby where she could grab a bite to eat. *Note to self: leave the job earlier tonight to pick up some groceries. TV dinners and fast food will not do.* She wasn't a health-food nut, but did steer clear of fatty foods. She'd not return to

Denver all lumpy with fast-food bulges. She shuddered at the thought.

Arriving at the house just after eight o'clock, she stood outside for a few moments to take it all in again. Once more she felt its majestic beauty. A perfect rose growing in a dustbowl. She shoved the key into the lock and turned the knob. Before she cracked open the door, sirens began to sound.

Chapter Five

Oh, no! The house wasn't supposed to be armed until next week. Fumbling around in her purse, she realized she'd left the alarm code in her car. After retrieving the papers from the front seat, she sprinted back to the house and pushed the appropriate buttons to silence the shrieking noise. She sank down on the Persian rug, grateful there weren't any neighbors in the vicinity.

It wasn't ten minutes later when she heard banging on the front door. Startled, she froze for a second. The door burst open, and there stood a tall man a few years her senior, with dark brown hair and piercing blue eyes. She stared, struck by his good looks.

The puzzled expression on his face made her wonder if he had expected to find someone else inside the home. "Who are you?" she finally choked out, scanning the room for any sort of weapon. Gorgeous or not, she didn't trust someone who burst through the door without warning.

He held up his hand to show her his badge. "I'm Officer Flemming. Sorry to frighten you. The police department gets dispatched when the security alarm on this house is triggered. Is everything okay?"

His British accent caught her off-guard. "Of course. Your uniform." She motioned to his attire. "I didn't know the alarm was set until it scared me senseless." She laughed until she realized he wasn't smiling. "The owners told me it would be a week or two before it would be armed. Would you like to step in?"

He shook his head. "Why are you here?" Officer Flemming asked, a little too curtly, almost as if he were put off by her presence in the home.

Wow, she hoped all Puebloans, or whatever they called themselves, weren't this frosty. "I've been hired to decorate this house. It's beautiful, isn't it?"

He looked around and gave a slight nod. "Where are the others?"

"What others?" Arianna wrinkled her forehead in confusion.

"Surely there's more than one decorator for this," he waved his hand, "monstrosity of a house." He grimaced as if the house itself put a bad taste in his mouth.

Even wearing a scowl he was handsome, but Ari could do without the attitude. "Nope, just me. I'm working solo, which will take much longer than if I had a partner, but I was the only designer available to relocate to Pueblo for the job." Nervous rambling took over where good sense once resided. "It's okay, though; the owners aren't in any hurry to move in. They're all about quality—not speed."

"Four years. I've waited four years," he mumbled under his breath.

"What?" Arianna had heard him but wondered why he'd say such a thing. His cold demeanor made her uneasy. She clutched the door frame, grateful he'd declined her invitation to step in.

"Oh"—he cleared his throat— "it's nothing,

Miss—"

"Miller. Arianna Miller. My friends call me Ari. My mother named me after a character from one of her favorite books." Which was probably more than he wanted to know, but he made her edgy.

Edgy or not, she kept talking. "Are you from England?"

"Yes, originally. But that was a long time ago." He shifted his weight, rocking back on the porch.

"The owners of this house are also from England. Your accent is a lot like theirs."

"Miss Miller, you really shouldn't be out here working alone. It is not safe."

Arianna frowned and narrowed her eyes. "Why isn't it safe? I'm fine. There aren't any neighbors nearby, and it's quite peaceful working out here on my own." Last night's fears about being alone reared their ugly heads. She ignored them.

"Precisely. You are alone. Should something happen, I don't believe there is even cell phone service out this far." Officer Flemming's brows lowered, making him appear put out and frustrated—or maybe he was worried. Her heart flipped, thinking he might care. Ridiculous. He wouldn't care. They'd just met.

"Yes, I noticed that the phone service is sketchy out here. But"—Ari raised her hands—"what's going to happen way out in the middle of nowhere? I'm sure I'll be safe." Her voice wobbled a little. "Plus, there'll be workers coming and going once my project is in full-swing."

"Well, as a police officer, this area is part of my route, so I hope you won't mind if I stop in now and then to check on you." His face softened.

"Of course not. That's fine."

"But, really, Miss Miller—"

"Arianna. Please, you're making me feel old."

"Very well. Arianna." She loved the way he said her name. It sounded so beautiful in that British accent—or maybe it was prettier coming out of his perfect mouth.

She shook her head, irritated with herself. She didn't know why she'd have such an attraction to the man. He wasn't very friendly.

"Miss Mill—Arianna?"

"Sorry. Go on."

"Please keep the doors locked while you are working, and get to an area where you can alert me immediately if anything"—he shrugged—"unusual happens. Here's my card. The phones might not work out here, but they do when you drive a little closer to the city."

A shiver ran down her spine as she took the card. She wondered if he was trying to spook her, or just thought she was a helpless girl. "I can't imagine anything unusual happening while I'm on the job, but rest assured, Officer Flemming, I will be careful."

He gave a satisfied nod, but his eyes betrayed his concern before he turned to leave.

Ari gazed at the intricately engraved door that closed behind him, still puzzled about the encounter. She was sorely tempted to set the alarm off again, just to have another conversation with Officer Flemming.

Chapter Six

Christopher Flemming returned to the station and sat at his desk. He steepled his fingers and rocked forward in his chair, a feeling of foreboding nearly choking him. When the call had come in from the alarm company alerting him to the house, he'd expected his mother, brother, or sister to answer the door. Not a designer. He'd waited months for his family to occupy the ridiculously large house on the outskirts of Pueblo. Now he'd have another long wait.

Four years had passed since his family had been catapulted from nineteenth century England to twenty-first century America. Four years had passed since his father had banished him from his home and family. Four years he'd monitored their movements, watching for a way to rescue his mother and siblings from his dangerous father. What was another few months? He wadded a piece of scrap paper and tossed it into the trash. Likely, his family had given up on him; thought him dead, even.

And as if to complicate the matter further, there was a designer—someone else to worry about. *She is not safe there,* he couldn't help thinking over and over. *She is too young, and too vulnerable to be working alone on the house of a dangerous criminal.* Since he'd been unable to communicate with his family, he didn't know his father's current status. Perhaps he'd changed.

More likely he hadn't. Christopher's occupation in law enforcement exposed him to criminals of all varieties—it was rare to find an offender whose behavior improved with time.

His thoughts flitted between fear for the foolish girl, determined to do her job, and delight at how attractive she was. He had never seen such golden hair and dancing green eyes—or were they blue? They seemed to change with her mood. And her skin, he let out a breath, flawless.

"Flemming," another officer called across the room, jolting him from his thoughts. "How's about we grab some lunch?"

"Sounds good—I'll be right there."

****

Christopher watched bubbles sputter and pop in his soda. Sweet, carbonated beverages were among the many commonplace twenty-first century indulgences he'd discovered since his arrival four years before.

Yellow curtains dangled over a window next to him. Abby's had become his favorite diner in Pueblo. Its warm atmosphere and home-cooked food filled an empty place in his heart. He missed his mother.

"I'll be back with your meals in a jiff." The waitress twinkled her brown eyes at Christopher and his fellow officer, Joe Wilson.

"No rush." Joe winked.

Christopher shook his head. "Must you flirt with every girl you meet?"

"No. Only the pretty ones." Joe's grin was infectious and Christopher chuckled. "One of these times, I'll find the girl for me—someone who isn't starin' at you all the time. Is it your dashing good looks, or that accent of yours women can't resist?"

"What are you talking about, Joe?"

"You know. You don't flirt, yet everywhere we go, all eyes are drawn to you. Do you even date?"

"Of course I date." He took a slow drink of his soda.

Joe's eyes wandered to a brunette sitting alone at the bar. "You mind if I—" He motioned his head toward the girl.

Christopher nodded. "Go ahead." Relief replaced the anxiety he'd begun to feel when confronted with Joe's questions. He couldn't be completely honest. After all, meeting and forming relationships with females differed vastly in the twenty-first century compared to the nineteenth century. Until he found a girl open-minded enough to believe and accept the fact he'd been transported through time—very unlikely— he'd remain a bachelor.

"I'll be back when the food gets here." Joe sauntered over to the bar and sat on a red vinyl-covered stool next to the girl.

Christopher's attention returned to the popping bubbles.

"Hey handsome, your friend said you could use some company."

He startled. A woman wearing cutoffs and a tight shirt slid onto the seat across from him. She batted her lashes. He stared at the thick coating of mascara on them, wondering how she kept her eyes open.

"Extensions and Lashbody mascara." She giggled, making a high-toned trilling noise.

It was all he could do not to cringe. Instead he nodded and wondered what else on her was fake.

"You acted confused." Another giggle. "Everyone wonders about my long lashes. It will be our secret." She winked.

He shot a look at Joe, who had glanced back at him from the bar. Joe waggled his brows. Christopher suppressed the urge to roll his eyes.

He liked Joe—even when he felt like throttling him. His friendly disposition drew people in. While most officers were referred to by their last names, Joe was simply Joe. It suited him. They'd become fast friends just days after Christopher had transferred from Denver to Pueblo—a move he'd requested once he'd discovered his father's plans to build a house there. Although he'd not been able to see or know what was going on in the new family residence, he was determined to be nearby if ever needed—thus the transfer. What he hadn't anticipated was that designer he'd met earlier. He thought his family would have relocated by now.

"You must be shy. I like the shy ones." The woman batted her lashes a few more times. "My name is Charlotte. You can call me Char." She held a hand out for Christopher to shake. Long shiny, red fingernails fluttered before him.

He shook her hand, cursing Joe more by the second. "I'm Christopher."

Charlotte giggled. Christopher ground his teeth to hold his tongue. The shrill sound of her laugh shot through his head like a bullet.

"You've got an accent. Let me guess; I'm good at this." She tapped a red nail to her head. "Are you from Mexico?"

Really? "I'm from Engla—"

"Shh." Her finger jerked from her head to his lips. He gently pushed it away. "I said I wanted to guess." Her red mouth fell into a pout. "Oh, well. You spoiled it; you're from England. That was gonna be my next guess. Why'd ya move here?"

Christopher took a long look into Charlotte's gray eyes. He'd never told a soul his story—the honest version. He'd wanted to, but he doubted anyone would believe him. Perhaps he'd take the truth for a spin with Charlotte. Foreseeing no future meetings with her, he really had nothing to lose. So what if she thought him delusional?

"Well, my handsome Brit, what's your story?"

"You want to know why I came to America from England?"

"That's what I asked. I want to know every single thing about you." She tapped his nose with each word, as if he were a child.

He wanted out. Away from her batting lashes and her red nails. He glanced at Joe once more. Joe's head was bent toward the brunette's, both chuckling. Christopher would get no help from him. "Very well. Here's my story. It's quite unbelievable."

"Two hundred and four years ago, my father, who is an inventor, committed a jewelry heist in London." At least, that's what he'd gathered from the pouchful of diamonds his mother had slipped into his satchel.

Charlotte's eyes widened. "Oh my! Was he caught? What happened next? Wait! Did you say two hundred and four years ago? That's not possible!"

"I'm getting to that. He was not caught. You see, he'd built a time travel machine, of sorts." He wished he could describe it, but he'd never seen it. The only thing he could say about the machine was that it made a rumbling noise. He'd heard it before his father knocked him out cold. "He forced me and my family to travel two hundred years into the future, so he could escape the law." He watched her eyes closely. They only widened further, looking like the moon pies he sometimes bought from the department's vending machine. Her mouth dropped open. *Here it comes.* This is where she'd laugh at him and stomp off.

"What was it like traveling through time? I've always been fascinated with time travel, but you're the first person I've met who's actually done it." She licked her lips.

He narrowed his eyes. How could she believe him? He cleared his throat, then continued. "I don't know what it was like. My father rendered me unconscious before loading me onto the machine."

Horror crossed Charlotte's face. "He knocked you out? Why?"

He shrugged. "Let's just say he didn't like my attitude."

"So why not just leave you in London?"

Christopher had wondered the same thing many times. "I think he wanted me to help him with future heists."

"Wow! When you landed here, what did you think of the future?"

The story had sounded ridiculous, even to him. But as long as she'd listen, he'd keep talking. He found reciting his tale therapeutic. "I thought it was too bright. I'd awoken in a modern twenty-first century house with overhead lights shining in my eyes. I'd seen nothing like it. No candles—just lightbulbs."

She threw her head back and trilled long and loud. "Oh, that's funny. We have candles, silly." She slapped Christopher's arm. "What about your dad? Was he still mad at you when you got to the future?"

"He, in fact, pulled a pistol on me and told me to get out of his sight." The memories bubbled up, as if they'd happened yesterday.

Chapter Seven

Charlotte kept talking, but Christopher's focus waned, stolen away to a night he would never forget.

He'd found himself in a bed—not his bed in London—and when he'd opened his eyes, his mother hovered over him protectively.

Disoriented, Christopher had squinted to adjust to the blinding light shining overhead. Never had he seen anything like it. He'd clutched his mother's arm. "What—what happened? Where are we?"

He'd never forget the fear on her face. "Hush now, Christopher. Your father mustn't hear you."

His hazy mind had begun to clear as the memory of his father's face, distorted by desperate anger, entered it. His father had knocked him out with something. His hand wandered to the large bump. Hundreds of questions had floated to the forefront of his aching head. "Where is Father?"

His mother had tried to calm him by laying a gentle hand over his mouth, but to no avail. Father had come booming into the room. He'd peered down at Christopher, eyes narrowed.

"What have you done, Father?" He threw off the bed-covers.

"I have done something you would never have had the spine to do. I have transported my family to a better place and time. Now our possibilities are endless."

Christopher remembered sitting motionless as his father continued gloating about how his remarkable invention had saved their family.

"You should be singing my praises, son. I've altered our future." His father's chest had puffed up like a peacock's. "Now, we have all the money we will ever need. I always said one of my inventions would pay off someday, and today is that day."

"At what cost, Father?"

Silence.

"At. What. Cost?" Christopher had roared. "How much blood was shed? From whom did you steal so that we might have this better life?"

"I do not have to explain myself to you or anyone else, for that matter. If you had helped me when I'd asked, then you would know. But you have always thought yourself better than I. Is that not true? Who cares what the cost was? It happened two hundred years ago—they would all be dead now, anyway!"

The words had begun to bleed together until Christopher snapped. Grabbing his father by the front of his shirt, he'd pulled himself up to his full height and shoved him against the wall. "Enough! I have heard enough of what you have done for this family. You are nothing but a common criminal."

As the horrible argument escalated between the two of them, twelve-year-old Joshua tried to intervene, wedging himself between Christopher and his father. "Leave Christopher alone!" he'd wailed.

"Oh no, Joshua. I'll not have another son dishonor me."

The next thing Christopher remembered hearing was the sound of Joshua's body careening into the wall, ugly red welts forming on his frightened face. Sarah and Mother had huddled together with pale, wet cheeks. The argument had ended when his father pointed a pistol at Christopher. "Get out! You are no longer part of this family. I never wish to see you again."

Mother had leaped up. "No, Benjamin, he's our son," she pleaded, but had been pushed aside by Father. His very being sparked with anger.

"It's all right, Mother. I have no desire to see him any longer, either."

After the argument, Christopher had witnessed Mother slipping a small pouch into his satchel before handing it to him. With tears in her eyes, she'd embraced him tightly and choked out her goodbye. He'd scarcely had time to hug his siblings and whisper in their ears that he would be watching over them, as best he could, before his father told him to get out of his sight.

Christopher had no complaints about steering clear of his father, but the rest of his family he'd worry about. Father had not been kind in England, and Christopher was certain he'd not be kind here. He wouldn't approach him again if he didn't have to, but he knew he must watch over the rest of the family.

Discerning where to go in an unknown land and time had been a monumental challenge. Surely Father had expected him to fail, making banishment a death sentence. He'd not give him the satisfaction. Nothing but the sun above and the ground below resembled life in the nineteenth century. Cars he'd noticed immediately. No horses—just cars. The fast-paced vehicles were both exhilarating and frightening—an indication of what his new existence would become.

"So?" Charlotte snapped Christopher from his thorny hike down memory lane.

He stared at her blankly.

"Well, if you don't want to tell me, forget it." She stood up, spearing him with a glare. "And I don't believe a word you said, anyway!"

"Sorry. I was distracted. What did you ask?"

"Humph!" Charlotte spun on her heel and walked away.

"What's up with you, Flemming?" Joe ducked as he passed Charlotte, as if to avoid her spewing venom, and reclaimed his seat across from Christopher. "Did she ask you how much money you make? She's a gold digger. She should know police officers don't make much." He shook his head. "She sure was mad." He motioned to Christopher's plate. "You haven't even touched your food."

Immersed in thought, Christopher hadn't realized his food had arrived. "Yes, I have," he lied, as he shoved a forkful of potatoes into his mouth.

Joe's eyes stayed on Christopher. "Something's up with you, man. If you're not thinking of Charlotte, then what is it?"

Neither wishing to divulge the conversation he'd had with Charlotte, nor the one he'd had in his head, Christopher took a different tack. "I guess I was just thinking about a girl I met at a security alarm call I made this morning." That was partly true. While his family occupied most of his thoughts, he had to admit that Arianna Miller had been a diversion.

Joe lowered his voice and glanced around. "So that's what got Char so hoppin' mad. Was the girl hot?"

Christopher gave a slight nod—still unaccustomed to the language of this century.

"She must be." A grin spread across Joe's boyish face. "Because you love Abby's pot roast and you've barely touched it."

With a fraction of Christopher's burden lifted, after sharing his story with gold-digging, not-so-bright Charlotte, he felt a tiny bit of relief. He dug into his lunch without further comments to Joe. One day he hoped to disclose his story to someone who truly believed him. Someone he could share his past, present and future with. Someone he could love.

He wondered what Arianna might be eating for lunch. Surely, she took lunch breaks, but her worksite was miles from town. Too bad it wasn't closer. Shaking his head, he gave himself a mental reprimand. He shouldn't be daydreaming about a girl he'd just met.

But perhaps he should call on her to rectify his behavior. He was certain he'd made her feel unwelcome, which was not his intention. She'd just taken him by surprise. Still, he'd been rude. It was only proper that a gentleman and grandson of an earl make a complete apology. Now if he only knew what constituted an apology to a beautiful woman in the twenty-first century. A letter? A phone call? Something simple. It was only an apology, after all. Nothing more.

Chapter Eight

Arianna watched Mr. Somers march from room to room, analyzing, scrutinizing, examining…what? She didn't know. She'd only been working in Pueblo for a couple of days; not long enough for anything new to have arrived. He'd told her to expect Friday visits. Evidently, he was a man of his word.

He stood in the kitchen. "You do know what colors I…er…we expect to have in this room?" He peered down his long nose at her.

"Yes, unless you've changed your mind. I have an itemized list in here." She motioned to her notebook. "The painters come next week."

"Changed my mind?" He shook his head. "I've no changes." He darted a few glances at her while fumbling with something in his pocket. She didn't know what he expected. Should she continue measuring the rooms upstairs for furniture orders, or stand at attention until he dismissed her?

"Is there anything else, Mr. Somers?"

He glared at her, as if she'd asked an impertinent question. What did he want from her? Crazy man. She ignored the look and pressed on. "If not, I'd like to finish taking some measurements upstairs."

He grunted. "I have work to do in my office. Do not disturb me." He did an about face and left the room.

He had work in his office. Strange. Would he be sitting on the settee or the floor? A desk had yet to arrive. Ari shook her head and wandered up the stairs.

Mr. Somers' very presence gave the once warm house an eerie feeling. And, though she tried to hide it, his cold demeanor intimidated her, causing her to second-guess her choices of patterns, fabrics and textures. She even measured everything three times—just to be sure. By the end of the day, she was exhausted. Thank goodness it was the weekend.

****

Officer Flemming stood at the front door of Ari's apartment holding a bouquet of daisies. "I owe you an apology, Miss Mil—Arianna."

Ari stared in disbelief. Officer Flemming looked like a different man in his casual denim shirt and jeans. No longer the intimidating policeman wearing a scowl. And he smelled good. Like spicy freshness. "It's really okay. You didn't need to—"

"Yes, I did. I was rude. It's just"—he shifted his weight—"finding you—or anyone—in that house took me by surprise. I didn't know construction on it had been completed. You've most likely received warmer welcomes than the one I gave you." He chuckled but sounded nervous. "Will you let me make it up to you with a picnic lunch?"

She appraised him through narrowed eyes, unsure of what to think. *Picnic lunch. Huh.* That was a new one. "How did you know where I live?"

"I am a police officer; I know where everybody lives. There are no secrets at a police station." His mouth spread into a grin.

She hesitantly returned his smile. "I guess that makes sense. And you want to take me on a picnic?" Flustered, she looked down at her bare feet and the worn jeans and sky-blue t-shirt she'd pulled on after her shower. Saturday mornings meant sleeping in and reading a book—her favorite pastime. She hadn't even finished the first chapter before Officer Flemming had shown up.

"Uh"—he ran his hand through his dark hair—"if I have caught you at a bad time, I understand." He pushed the bouquet toward her. "We can talk another day." He took a step back.

"No, no. I'm just surprised to see you. And I'm not dressed to go anywhere." She waved him in. "I should probably change my clothes."

"No need, you're perfect. That is, you're dressed just right for a picnic." She noticed a hint of red spreading across his cheeks.

She looked at the bouquet in her hands and walked a few feet to the kitchen to grab a vase, not knowing whether to be nervous or excited. She shrugged and decided to throw caution to the wind. *Excited it is—for now.* Officer Flemming remained in the doorway. She called over her shoulder, "Do I need to make sandwiches, or something?" She couldn't recall the last time she'd been on a picnic.

"I suppose I was being presumptuous, or perhaps just hopeful, that you would be willing to go with me today. I brought food. It's in the cruiser." He motioned to the squad car in front of her apartment.

She scanned the room for her purse and shoes. "We're going in your police car? Can you do that when you're not on duty?"

"My only other vehicle is a motorcycle, and it is rather difficult to carry a picnic basket on one of those. And to answer your second question, Pueblo is pretty—what would you say"—he raised his eyes upward for a moment—"laid back. There is only one thing I am not allowed to do in the cruiser when I am not on duty."

"What?"

"Drag."

"Drag?" Her mind could take her in several directions with that.

He chuckled, but his posture stiffened. "Sorry. That's what Joe calls racing. We didn't call it that in England."

"Oh, you mean drag racing. You can't drag race in your squad car." She watched his dimples pucker and his face turn red. "Yeah, it's probably a good idea to avoid racing, unless you're chasing a criminal." She smiled.

He let out a breath and his shoulders relaxed a fraction.

"But, there's one thing I must know before I agree to this picnic." She lowered her brows to appear serious.

His forehead creased in a look of concern. "And what is that?"

"I don't think I can spend the afternoon calling you Officer. Is there any possibility you have a different name—when you're off duty, of course?" She cracked a grin.

"As a matter of fact, I do. My name is Christopher."

"Hmm, Christopher." She looked at the ceiling before meeting his gaze. "I like it. It suits you. I suppose I'll go with you." She slipped into her sandals and grabbed her bag.

"I shudder to think of what you would do if my name were Horace, or Rudolph." She pulled a sour face. His laugh, rich and warm, made her heart skip a beat. "In that case"—he held his arm out for her to take—"let us be off then, shall we?"

She took his arm, enjoying a tingling sensation in her fingers, as they walked to the waiting squad car. He opened the door and she slid onto the vinyl seat. She felt a little awkward riding in a police cruiser, but she definitely enjoyed sitting next to the handsome, spicy-fresh smelling officer at the wheel.

"I didn't realize I live so close to a park. I guess I spend all my time driving away from the city." She glanced around as they approached the beautiful green expanse. Elm trees stood as sentinels around the perimeter, providing patches of cool shade. She breathed in the smell of spring in the air—fresh cut grass and blooming flowers.

There were several families at the park with the same idea—enjoying a picnic. Sudden tears sprang to her eyes. She never considered that something as simple as a family picnicking together would invoke sadness. In that moment, the two and a half years her family had been gone felt like only a day. She blinked back the moisture, willing her memories away from the surface. She glanced up to see Christopher staring at her. His cobalt blue eyes focused on hers.

"Are you well, Arianna?"

"Yes. Allergies." She gave him her brightest smile. She wasn't about to unload her grief on a nearly perfect stranger.

His face relaxed as he led the way to a lovely spot in the shade. He laid down a blanket, opened the picnic basket and removed a bounteous spread of sandwiches, fruit, potato chips, water bottles and even some French pastries for dessert.

Her stomach rumbled. Embarrassed, she remembered she hadn't eaten breakfast. "Working on the outskirts of town works well for my starvation diet." She rubbed her growling middle, hoping to hush it. "This is so nice. Thank you." She reached for a piece of fruit. Grocery shopping was on her to-do list. It really was—right after she finished reading a few chapters in her book, and maybe taking a nap. Her stomach growled again. Christopher may have just saved her life—or fostered her procrastination.

"I wondered if you were skipping your lunches. The project you're working on is miles from civilization. As far as a diet goes, however"—he shook his head—"I didn't show up a minute too soon. You look as if you might blow away with the next gust of wind."

Arianna laughed and bit into an apple. He was definitely saying the right things—so far. In her experience, men would say everything she'd want to hear to get her out on that first date. Then their true colors would appear. By showing up unannounced, Christopher Flemming was messing with the order of things. Interesting. She liked it.

Conversation came easily once they'd hurdled the initial awkwardness. He was starkly different from the police officer who'd shown up at her project site on Tuesday—very congenial. She found herself thinking of clever things to say just to watch his blue eyes sparkle and his face dimple.

They sat lazily eating as if they'd known each other for years. Ari hadn't realized how homesick she'd become in the few short days she'd been away from her friends in Denver. Now she had a friend in Pueblo.

When the last sandwich had been devoured, a Frisbee crashed down between them. Two kids rushed over to retrieve the errant toy. Christopher grabbed the disc and flipped it around, as if he were examining it.

"It's just a Frisbee, Christopher." Ari motioned with her head to toss it back to the children.

The kids waited patiently. Finally, the boy said in a voice of authority, "Don't you know how to throw it? I'll show you." He took the disc, turned it to the proper position and gave it back to Chris. "Now tuck and throw." He mimicked the motion with his empty hand.

Christopher followed the boy's directions and sent it gliding through the air in perfect form. Ari shook her head. Christopher had obviously thrown a Frisbee before.

Only seconds later the Frisbee returned, sailing closer to her this time. They both jumped up and she successfully caught it, but her foot snagged on an exposed root, lurching her forward. Warm arms closed around her waist, steadying her. "You all right?" Christopher's voice tickled her ear. His musky aftershave smelled so good. Electricity sparked through her.

For a split-second, she wished to turn around and gaze into his eyes, but she tamped down the longing and stepped away. "Yes, thank you." She glanced back at him and saw a shadow of desire mirrored in his eyes.

She returned to the blanket and the French pastry she'd been eating. After the thrill of being in Christopher's arms, the goody lost some of its appeal.

Enamored with Christopher now, the kids wanted to keep up the fun and games.

"I'll tell you what," he said to the pair when they returned the Frisbee for the third time. "How about I take this delicious pastry, filled with whipped cream, and split it in half for the two of you, and you can return to your family picnic? I believe your parents are becoming a bit jealous of my friend and me."

Nodding their heads, they each took their half of his pastry and made off to their parents' blanket.

Feeling more than a little guilty, Arianna lifted her own half-eaten pastry. "Do you want the rest of mine?"

"No, thank you." His mouth quirked into a grin. "I'd rather watch you eat it—or, you know, wear it." His smile broadened, and his dimples deepened.

"What?" Ari grabbed a napkin and began dabbing her lips. He pointed to her nose. Oh, no, she knew the pastry had been messy, but her nose? She swiped at it. "Better?"

"Perfect."

Heat rose to meet Ari's already warm cheeks. "Oh my goodness, how long was that there?"

"Just long enough." His eyes sparkled.

After a while of relaxing on the blanket, he stood up and held out his hand to Arianna. "I do believe I should take you home before it is time for supper."

Reluctantly, she allowed herself to be pulled to a standing position. She never wanted the picnic to end. He was different than other men—such a gentleman.

Christopher drove her to her apartment and walked her to the door. He politely thanked her for spending the afternoon with him, took her hand, and pressed a kiss on her fingers.

Her heart thumped erratically, as if it might leap from her chest. Before she had time to react, he was gone.

"This simply will not wait. I have to call Maggie." She pulled out her phone and dialed, eager to spill every detail of the picnic, from the perfect way Christopher looked, to his impeccable manners.

"Don't get too excited, Ari." Maggie dowsed Arianna's enthusiasm by her reply but didn't snuff it out. "You don't want to jinx anything. This guy sounds too good to be true."

Ari had to agree. After all, he hadn't been exactly pleasant on their first encounter. Still, she couldn't stop thinking about the tender way he'd gazed at her, his warm arms around her waist, and the kiss on her hand, which she'd permanently etched into her memory. Even so, first dates were too early to form an accurate appraisal. She needed more data. More dates.

Chapter Nine

Christopher sped away from Ari's apartment, the fragrance of her tropical shampoo still hanging in the air. He inhaled deeply and smiled—then scowled. Irritated with his good mood, he pounded the steering wheel. What was he thinking? He couldn't fall for this girl. He couldn't fall for any girl. His past wouldn't permit it. His goal today had been to rectify a wrong— an apology picnic. He'd only wished to welcome her properly to Pueblo. Let her know he was friend, not foe. He needed her trust. Instead he found her consuming his thoughts.

Admittedly, he couldn't help comparing her to other women. Charming and naturally pretty, she was real—so unlike Charlotte. Sure, Ari wore makeup, but very little. Her beauty came from an inner glow and sparkling eyes.

He had hoped to become better acquainted with her and earn her confidence while on the picnic. The idea had been a good one, and seemed to work. Yet, it had also backfired. *She's one more person for me to feel responsible for.* A twinge of guilt pinched his conscience for thinking of Arianna as a burden, but his father gave him every reason to worry for her safety.

In any other circumstance—well, back in the 1800s, that is—he would love to get to know her on a more intimate level, but now he just needed to see that she did her job and returned safely to Denver. It had shocked and made him feel uneasy to find her working in his family's house. And to top that, she was a vulnerable young lady—working alone. Why couldn't the designer be a muscle-bound, weightlifting, Harley rider? He grinned at the image. It was a fleeting emotion, however, as he flattened his lips to a frown.

He didn't know exactly what his father had been up to over the past four years, but he had pieced enough of the puzzle together to know Benjamin Somerset had not transported himself two hundred years into the future to live as a choirboy.

****

Christopher ducked into Riverside Bar and Grill, where he met up with some guys from work. He wasn't much of a drinker, but he enjoyed the company of his friends and Riverside's great food. He'd never made it a secret that his father had been an alcoholic, and by not drinking, Christopher knew he'd never become his father. Sometimes his friends ribbed him, but for the most part, he'd earned their respect. He took it all in stride, held firm to his convictions and didn't even mind the title he'd earned as the "Pueblo PD's Designated Driver."

"Heard you met Charlotte," Luke Cahill shouted over the din of the bar. Several men groaned. "Did Joe do that to ya?"

Christopher shot Joe a mock glare. "Indeed, he did."

"Don't worry. Charlotte only wants your money." Cahill bit into a chicken wing.

Joe lifted his drink, motioning to Christopher. "Well, she seems to think Flemming here's got some stashed away. She stormed out of Abby's screamin' that he wouldn't tell her where the diamonds were hidden, or some nonsense." The men roared with laughter. "And Flemming's just starin' at his food like he didn't know what hit him. That Charlotte's a loon."

Christopher chuckled with the guys, relieved to learn of Charlotte's low credibility. For the life of him, he couldn't figure out why he'd shared his unbelievable tale with her. It had seemed like a good idea at the time.

"Let us know if you find that stash of jewels, Flemming. I want in," jibed Cahill. More laughter.

A baseball game on TV took their attention off Christopher. He finished his burger, then stared into space.

"Flemming, you have that dazed look on your face again. Could you be thinking about a certain designer?" Joe slyly punched him on the arm.

Christopher shook his head and took a sip of soda. In truth, he was thinking about Arianna, but he would never hear the end of it if he admitted it to this group. He'd thought of little else since their picnic earlier in the day. Her warm personality had been refreshingly sincere. And, still, every time he pictured her pretty face, his heart thudded erratically. He'd wished to reach out and grab her where she stood in the doorway, with her eyes twinkling—blue today—and wearing that beautiful smile. Of course, he'd never do that. His father may have made a mess of his life, but Christopher, reared by his mother to be a gentleman, showed restraint. Then in the park, the way she'd looked sitting in the sunlight with her golden hair cascading gently down her back—it was a sight he'd not soon forget. The kids playing Frisbee thankfully knocked him from the trance she had him in before he said anything foolish.

Nights were lonely for Christopher. But he'd learned early on that courting in the twenty-first century wasn't in the cards for him. After a few attempts, he'd realized he could never be completely honest about his past, and a good relationship required honesty. Therefore, he avoided forming attachments altogether.

Arianna seemed different from other women, however. She had an innocence he found appealing which brightened her countenance—a true inner beauty. And there was that sparkle in her captivating blue-green eyes he'd found irresistible.

The problem he faced now was how to protect her from his father without becoming too attached—if it wasn't already too late. He patted his phone. Good thing he'd gotten her number so he could check on her now and then.

Chapter Ten

Arianna checked her phone for at least the twentieth time. She knew she shouldn't be waiting to hear from Christopher, but he'd occupied most of her thoughts ever since their picnic on Saturday. She never imagined she'd be happy to see Monday arrive, but she loved her job and welcomed a reason to push thoughts of Christopher aside.

Once back at the Somers' house, she became absorbed in decorating. She still had rooms to measure, colors to coordinate, and textures to blend. Designing was an art; that's why she loved it. Plus, this week, two of the special orders were scheduled to arrive—pieces the Somers had picked out before hiring her. Being surrounded by new decor made her happy. On her days off, she often spent hours walking through showrooms. The different configurations in which store designers arranged furniture intrigued her—plus, she loved the smell. *There's nothing like breathing in the scent of new sofas, table, chairs; all of it.* She closed her eyes and smiled.

Finally, on Wednesday, she had some down time. She wished she could leave early and begin placing more orders, but there was still a delivery due to arrive later that afternoon. She sighed.

Walking from room to room, she assessed what still needed to be done—which amounted to quite a bit.

She ran her hands over the engraved wood of a baroque mirror waiting to be hung above one of the fireplaces. She jotted some notes about paint color, then moved to the study. "Ah, I love this room." She straightened one of the many paintings. "It feels like an art gallery in here." Her eyes fell on the leather journal still resting on top of a boxful of the Somers' belongings.

Arianna frowned. She remembered what she had read before in the ancient-looking book and desperately wished to read more of this girl's tortured thoughts. Pushing guilt aside, she picked up the journal. She didn't care that it was wrong to read a few more pages, since she had nothing else to do while she waited for the deliveryman. This time she began reading toward the end of the book—the last of the modern penned pages. The words on the well-preserved paper unnerved her and compelled her to continue.

> *We are hostages here—prisoners in our own home. Not only are we held captive, but we are trapped in a foreign land and time. Will we ever be free from the cruel dominion Father has placed us under? I wish to go home.*

Ari couldn't wrap her mind around what she read, so she flipped back a few more pages.

> *None of us are allowed to leave our home without Father. And when he is with us, he watches our every movement. I am nineteen years of age, yet he treats me as if I am a child. I fear I shall grow old never knowing anything beyond these four walls.*

"Can this possibly be real?" Ari asked herself. "Maybe someone was writing a novel—a horror story, even." That was it; it had to be. Nothing else made sense. It started out as a journal. Someone must have found it and decided to write a story in its remaining pages.

A sharp knock at the door startled Arianna. Self-reproach nagged at her, realizing she might be invading someone's private thoughts. Her hands shook as she closed the book and shoved it back into the box. The furniture had finally arrived. Disappointment and relief warred with each other. She shouldn't have been reading that book, anyway, she scolded herself.

She opened the door, excited to welcome the new arrivals, when her heart began thudding in her chest. Christopher greeted her.

"Hello," she squeaked out, hoping he couldn't read her thoughts, which were in a severe tangle. She regained her composure. "I was expecting a furniture delivery."

"Sorry to disappoint. I was just in the neighborhood and thought I would see how things are going in the world of design."

"Uh"—she tilted her head—"in the neighborhood?" She knew she stammered, but her nerves were again getting the best of her.

"Yes, as I think I mentioned before, this area is part of my beat." His eyebrows drew together as though he worried he'd made a misstep by coming. "But if you're busy, I can check in on you another time."

"I'm not—busy, that is. In fact, I've been kind of bored waiting for the truck." Her nerves began to calm. The late afternoon sun set him aglow. He looked striking and a bit intimidating in his uniform. "Please, come in."

Christopher stepped inside, his eyes appraising the place. The study sat to the right of the foyer. Ari had left the door open when she'd answered his knock, putting the room in full view. His gaze stopped on the box containing the journal. He motioned to it. "What is that?"

"Oh, just some personal items brought over by the Somers." Guilty heat rose to her cheeks, but he seemed genuinely interested.

"Have you looked through it?"

She bit her lip and twisted her fingers together, trying to think of how to answer. "Uh, I have to admit, I've been tempted to go through the entire box. After all, this family is such a mystery to me. But I only got to the book on top." There, she said it, and she hadn't lied. She hoped he wouldn't arrest her for snooping.

She went on, "It reads like a journal—at least in the beginning—probably from a long-ago relative. Then, near the end, it sounds like some kind of scary novel."

His face drained its color. What in the world? Why would he care about some old book? She glanced at him again. Either he'd recovered, or his reaction had been her imagination. "Do you want to see it?" There was no turning back now. Either he would say no, and probably think less of her for reading it, or he might find it as intriguing as she did.

He glanced at his watch. "I think I have time to do a little light reading." His laugh sounded forced.

She exhaled, relieved he wasn't judging her. She sat down and patted the spot next to her, inviting him to join her on the settee—so far, the only seat in the room—to read the mysterious relic.

His musky cologne made it hard for her to concentrate. She exhaled and pointed to the writing. She showed him how it began in a calligraphy-like pen. "Then, about halfway through, it changes to a modern pen."

He was listening, but mostly he was reading, so she pushed the book toward him. He hesitated for a moment, then took it in both hands.

In the meantime, she decided to explore deeper into the box. There, she found antique knick-knacks, some unfinished embroidery work, and a framed drawing. The picture fascinated her the most—obviously a rendering of the Somers family, but completely off-center, giving it a lop-sided appearance.

"Look at this." Ari moved back to sit by Christopher. When she glanced at him, she realized how totally engrossed he'd become in the journal, one hand pressed against his forehead. Before responding, he sat for a moment, seemingly collecting his thoughts. As he moved his hand down across his face, Ari caught a glimpse of his distraught expression. She wondered why he would get emotional over an old journal.

He cleared his throat and examined the drawing, acting as if nothing strange had passed. Again, a tortured look crossed his face. She didn't know whether to ask him, or just act as if she didn't notice anything. She opened her mouth to ask when he spoke. "Who are they?"

"It's the Somers family. They are dressed up in old-fashioned clothing for some reason—probably a photo booth at a fair, or something. But don't you find it odd that it is so off-center? It's as if there should be one more person on this end." She pointed to the side of the picture crowding the frame. "I wonder what happened. Why would they intentionally cut someone out of the picture?"

Without warning, Christopher stood, gave the journal back to her, looked at his watch mumbling something about being late for an appointment, and left.

Arianna stared at the closed door. She touched her face. For some reason, she felt as if she'd been slapped. His behavior had gone from happy warmth to stone cold.

Chapter Eleven

Christopher drove aimlessly around the uninhabited expanse beyond the Somers'—his family's—home. He knew his abrupt departure would raise questions, but it'd been more than he could take. He felt as if his heart had been wrenched from his chest.

First, to read Sarah's journal and realize what she and the rest of his family had been subjected to—which turned out to be worse than he'd ever imagined. His father treated them as hostages in their own home, no doubt to keep his device and their nineteenth century origins secret. Then Sarah's pain-filled words about Father's abuse toward the three of them. The thought sickened him. "I must help them." He swallowed down the rising bile in his throat. "I've waited four years to help them, only to be invited into a house devoid of family yet haunted with Father's presence."

Then, as if to add insult to injury, Arianna had held up the drawing of his family, which had once rested atop the mantel of a long-forgotten home. It was all too much. He'd needed to get out of that house. His hands trembled as his anger flared. He gripped the steering wheel tighter as his frustration mounted.

He wondered what Arianna thought of the boxful of Somers' mementos, and most of all, what she'd thought of his abrupt departure. She had seemed to sense his discomfort, as she couldn't look directly at him, or he at her, but she couldn't possibly know what kind of torture he'd experienced by going through that container of memories. He wished so badly he could tell her everything. He nearly had. She seemed different from other people in this age. Something about her put him at ease—as if he wouldn't be judged if he were to open up to her. But no, his was a burden that had weighed heavily, and for so long now, on his shoulders alone. *If I could just explain it to Arianna—to share this burden.* He shook his head and let out a breath. What was he thinking? He barely knew the girl. No one with an ounce of intelligence, would believe him. He wiped his sweaty palms on his pants.

The home itself brought back memories of England—the good times, before his father had become a drunk. The Somersets had resided on a modest but lovely estate, where Christopher grew up with kind parents. He'd attended Eton first, then studied law at Cambridge for two years before his life had unraveled. His family evicted and his education cut short, he had been forced to take a job just to keep food on the table. Thankfully, he'd been able to find work as a barrister's clerk, which at least bore a resemblance to what he'd been training for.

In the twenty-first century he'd chosen law-enforcement as his occupation. He needed to help his family and had believed he could best accomplish his goal by becoming a police officer. He'd worked hard and passed the physical and academic tests with ease, which allowed him to become one of Colorado's Finest.

Sometimes he had vivid dreams about his seemingly charmed life when he'd idolized his father instead of despised him. A time when his family had loved and supported each other through pleasure and pain—they'd always been there for him, and he for them. After such a dream, Christopher expected to wake up at Cambridge, happily continuing his education. But no matter how much time had passed, reality always lurked in the shadows, waiting to swallow him whole. He refused to dwell in the past. He'd decided four years ago that looking back only caused pain. Moving forward was his only option.

This balancing game he played with Ari was turning out to be more complicated than anticipated. He *must* have her trust to keep a foot in the door so when his parents began occupying the home, he could have access to it right away. He sensed the answers to his questions—the path to rescuing his family—were in that home. And yet, he'd just made another error by abruptly leaving. One more thing to rectify—if he could.

Chapter Twelve

The quiet solitude of the Somers' house began driving Arianna crazy. She craved human interaction. The landscapers had been there several times, but they'd kept busy and never bothered her. She hadn't seen Christopher since his mysterious visit a couple of weeks ago. Mr. Somers—well, he was hardly human. However, he'd emailed her to say he would be bringing his entire family today. Ari felt almost giddy with the anticipation of having someone to talk to.

She flipped through some papers, certain she'd seen the children's names and ages listed. Oh yes, on the upstairs floorplan. Their bedrooms were labeled. Joshua was sixteen—the same age her brother had been when he died. A lump formed in her throat. She shook it off. It wouldn't do to be teary when her guests arrived. After Joshua's name came Sarah's. Nineteen. Ari's heart lightened. Surely Sarah would need a friend, being new to the area.

At ten o'clock the Somers arrived in their black Cadillac Escalade. *Of course, how fitting. Mr. Somers drives a hearse—or close to it.* Through the window, she watched as each family member walked up the drive. Mr. Somers entered first, his beady, black eyes darting from wall to wall like a ping-pong ball. Joshua walked in next, looking like a typical teenager. Except for his coloring, he could be a miniature of his father.

Everything just a few shades lighter—his eyes; his hair. Ari wanted to introduce herself, but he sped past her, keeping pace with his dad.

Then came Mrs. Somers. And that's who the boy got his complexion from. Arianna smiled at her. Mrs. Somers ducked her head and studied the box she carried. Her reaction shouldn't have surprised Ari, after the way she'd acted during their first meeting. But it had. As Mrs. Somers swished by, Ari thought she had to be old-fashioned to wear skirts when she came to work at the house. Finally, a pretty, raven-haired girl walked in, also carrying a box. Sarah.

"Hi. I'm Arianna." Ari gave the girl her brightest smile, happy to finally meet another young woman in Pueblo.

Sarah flinched, nearly dropping her box of linens. She righted herself, mumbled something indiscernible and hurried to catch up to the others.

Ari's heart sank. Any hope she'd had of making a friend today had vanished just like that. Or, perhaps it was Mr. Somers' presence influencing the rest of the family. She wouldn't give up yet.

She observed as Sarah wandered from room to room. Her blue jeans and peasant blouse seemed comfortable enough, but those shoes—they looked like slippers. Heavenly. She wondered where she got them—perhaps a boutique. She would have to ask her once they were better acquainted—*if* they became better acquainted. Sarah's eyes scanned every box and shelf. "May I help you?" Ari asked when nobody else was within earshot. "You look like you've lost something."

Sarah dropped her gaze, as if she were hesitant to speak.

"It's okay. You don't have to talk to me. I just thought I could—"

Sarah cut her off with a whisper. "It's my journal. I believe it ended up in a box that it ought not to have. As I have been unable to locate it, I thought it might be here somewhere. Have you come across anything like that?"

A chill made Ari's blood run cold. The journal was indeed a journal. Not a novel, but a journal. Sarah's journal. Passages from the book made her skin prickle all over again. She eyed the girl carefully for signs of abuse.

"Never mind. I'll keep searching." Sarah jolted Ari from her inspection and turned to leave.

"Wait. Have you checked the study? I think I saw a box with random items in there." Arianna tried not to let on that she had not only found a journal but had also read most of it.

Sarah gave her a puzzled look, then recovered, saying, "Oh, the bookroom." She smiled. "In England we called them bookrooms."

Arianna let go of a nervous breath. She warmed to Sarah immediately. She had a beautiful smile. It was too bad she rarely showed it. Ari led her to the study and pointed to the box. Sarah snatched up the journal as if it were a lost treasure. Guilt pinched Ari's conscience. She could only hope Sarah had embellished her dark writing.

"It's beautiful," Arianna said, as if she were seeing it for the first time. "I don't believe I've seen such an exquisitely embossed leather journal before. It looks quite antique."

Sarah beamed at the compliment, then immediately stiffened. Mr. Somers had entered the study, probably after hearing any voice other than his own. He demanded that Sarah leave the room immediately, as he needed to speak to Miss Miller. Sarah wasted no time. Clutching the journal to her chest, she quickly fled.

"You want to speak to me?" Arianna looked Mr. Somers straight in the eye. He didn't appear to like this direct approach, as his gaze suddenly went everywhere but to her face. For a man who seemed to thrive on his powers of intimidation, he was certainly acting cowardly.

"Yes." He cleared his throat in an obvious attempt to regain his tone of authority. "I wish to enquire about the draperies."

Arianna pulled out her notebook, found the tab marked "Window Coverings" and readied herself to answer the many questions she anticipated. He did not disappoint. Mr. Somers marched her from room to room, demanding details about every curtain, valance, shade, shutter and blind. "What color did you order for this room? How soon will they arrive?" It was as if he wanted her to give him an incorrect answer. She silently congratulated herself for not allowing him that type of satisfaction.

He hemmed and hawed over the details, but still found no criticism. Last of all he asked, "Have you been successful in finding high quality products suitable for a home of this caliber?"

She wanted to ask him if anyone would actually be allowed in this home to observe the quality of its furnishings. She didn't. Instead, she provided the credentials of each company from which she'd ordered furnishings.

Mr. Somers let out a satisfied grunt as he gave a curt nod. He turned and left the room while bellowing to his family, "Finish your dawdling and prepare to leave."

Arianna closed her eyes and sighed. Her shoulders relaxed, and she leaned against a wall as the family exited.

Mr. Somers paused before closing the door. "Miss Miller." Ari tensed again. "Under no circumstance are you to speak to my daughter." Arianna turned to fully face him. Sparks of anger burned in her chest. "I was only being courteous."

"Coming here from England has been a little traumatic for my family. They need time to adjust to their new lives here." His voice sounded calm, but Arianna could sense a fierceness bubbling beneath his cool veneer. Time to adjust? They'd been here four years. That sure seemed like ample time to adjust.

"I would think their new lives would include friends. That's all I am trying to be to Sarah."

"Miss Miller, listen to me carefully." His coal black eyes locked onto hers and his face hardened into a series of rigid, hard planes. "I hired you to do a job. That is all I expect or desire from you. Please, keep your distance from the rest of my family." No hint of a friendly admonition rang in his voice. Arianna felt the full impact of a threat.

"Never speak to my daughter again."

Ari narrowed her eyes. "Excuse me?"

"You heard me."

****

Arianna awoke to her phone ringing Saturday morning. Maggie's picture flashed on the screen.

"Maggie, it's so good to hear your voice." She unscrewed the cap of a water bottle sitting on the nightstand and tried to swallow the early morning frog that croaked in her throat.

"Sorry, Arianna. I didn't mean to wake you. You've always been an early riser."

"Yeah, well, I don't usually work until three in the morning, either."

"Why on earth are you working so late? Especially on a Friday night?"

"I don't get internet service at the Somers' house, so I have to place all my orders here in town. And if you knew Mr. Somers, you'd understand how crucial it is that I make no mistakes." She let out a sigh.

"I'm sorry, Arianna. That sounds painful. I wish I were there to help you out."

"That would be wonderful, but it's okay. I'm getting to use everything I've ever learned in school and on the job for this project. It's a fun challenge."

"You always have looked at the bright side of things. I admire that about you."

"Thanks, Maggie. I'm sure you didn't call to talk about my lack of sleep."

"No, what I really called for has nothing to do with work."

"Good. I could use a break. What's up?" Ari took another sip of water and opened the shutters on the window next to her bed.

"Do you remember my upcoming baby shower?

Arianna choked. "Um"—she glanced at a calendar perched on her dresser—"of course I remember. It's in two weeks, right?"

"Nice recovery, girlfriend," Maggie teased. "You obviously forgot. I know you've been busy, so it's okay, but I hope you can still come."

"I'm coming, Maggie. You know I wouldn't miss it." She closed her eyes, grateful Maggie had reminded her, so she wouldn't miss it. "I'll drive out on Friday night so I can help with the preparations." Their boss, Tasha Tate, Reese Johnson's wife and business partner, had taken over plans for the shower. Besides supporting her friend, Ari needed to help Tasha out with the event.

"You can bring your hot new boyfriend, too, if you want. I'd love to meet him. He's not invited to the shower." Maggie laughed. "But maybe we can do something together later."

"He's not my boyfriend, Maggie." She didn't even know if he was her friend. Things had been a little weird between them. She just couldn't get a read on him. At times he had gazed at her like she was the most important person in the world; then, the next thing she knew, he wouldn't even look her in the eye. "I haven't seen him for a while." He'd made himself scarce since the day he'd stopped by to check on her.

"I'm sorry. I wanted him to be the one. He sounded like a perfect match for you—British and old-fashioned manners and everything. We all know how much you love those old British romance novels with the proper manners in them. No pressure, but you seemed happy when you talked about him, and I just want you to be as happy as Jason and I are."

Arianna was glad Maggie couldn't see her red face through the phone. She really did know her type— British and everything. "Hey, there's a lot of history in those British romance novels you tease me about. But you're correct. Christopher seemed like the perfect match for me. Someday I'll find Mr. Right. I'm happy, just confused about Christopher at the moment." She frowned at her image in the dresser mirror. She would love for Christopher to be the man for her. Tugging sweats from a drawer, she put the phone on speaker so she could dress.

"You know I love you, even though I think you're a prude." Maggie sounded sisterly. Arianna knew that tone well. Maggie used it when she thought Arianna needed comforting—and it worked.

"Yes, I know." Ari padded down the hall and into the kitchen in search of nutrition. She settled on a protein shake.

"Don't listen to her when she jibes you like that." Jason had obviously overheard their conversation. His voice sounded like he was hollering in the background.

"Jason?" Ari smiled, imagining the tussle happening with the phone. She sipped on her shake while Jason and Maggie bantered.

"You're not a prude. Maggie tells me all the time she looks up to you for your high moral standards, Ari. So, don't let her teasing get to you."

Arianna cleared her throat. "I think you two need to continue this conversation without me. I can't wait to see you both in two weeks." After she hung up and sank into the puffy recliner that had taunted her all week, she realized her heart hurt. How she missed Maggie.

She stared at the phone, still in her hand. She wished it would ring and this time have a deep British voice on the other end.

Chapter Thirteen

Christopher opened a window in his bedroom to let the stale air escape. A floral scent from the bushes outside immediately improved the air quality. Then he took a seat in an armchair next to his bed. He had been in something of a stupor ever since the day he'd read Sarah's journal. He punched at the nearest pillow. It wrinkled in the middle where his fist had connected, creating a saggy, white, smiling face. He took another swing and punched the smile right out of it.

Thoughts spun round and round, never finding a secure place to land. He eventually digested the twisted reality of it all. He could truly never live a normal life while his father lived. And to that, Christopher had no solution.

Thinking about Arianna was the only thing maintaining his sanity right now. He'd kept his distance the past week or two. His feelings were still too raw and unpredictable. She most likely did not want his company, either, after he'd practically lost his composure right in front of her when he read Sarah's journal. Furthermore, he could never explain it to her. He ran his fingers through his hair. And now she might believe she was to blame for his behavior. Ridiculous, of course, but there it was again—he'd given her no reason to think otherwise. He hated this.

He'd allow a few more days and maybe check on her the following week. By then, she may have been able to forget their last encounter. Doubtful, but he had to see her, and see to her safety. After all, he was certain his father had paid his precious mansion a visit or two by now. A chill made him shudder, thinking about his father alone in the house with Arianna. Father wouldn't do anything to Ari...would he? No. Then again, if he felt cornered there's no telling what he'd do. If history were any indication, he'd stop at nothing to protect his money or his secrets—even murder.

He wondered about Ari's impression of the great-in-his-own-mind Benjamin Somerset—make that Somers. Christopher had noticed on the property deed his father had filed with the city, he'd shortened the family name. Good. Somerset belonged to Christopher's grandfather—the honorable Earl of Hemington—not his criminal son. So disgusted by his father's behavior, Christopher had changed his own surname to Flemming—his mother's maiden name.

****

After a somewhat torturous weekend with his thoughts flip-flopping between his family's situation and Arianna, Christopher decided to call her. He'd try to reach her before she left for work to see if he could manage a decent conversation.

She answered on the third ring. When he said who it was, he couldn't tell whether her voice reflected surprise or disappointment. He pressed forward. "Can I interest you in lunch? I am certain there are no eating establishments near your worksite. I would hate for you to dwindle away to nothing during your stay here in

Pueblo." He attempted lightheartedness to balance out their last encounter.

Ari laughed, putting him at ease. "I do work up an appetite, walking from one end to the other in that giant house."

He held the phone away and let out a long exhale. "I can pick you up—"

"Don't be ridiculous. Unless you're planning to be near my jobsite anyway, I'll meet you there. No need wasting your lunch hour driving unnecessarily."

"Very well, then." After some brief instructions of how to get to Abby's diner, he hung up the phone. His shoulders slumped as he let his rigid body relax. Maybe he could act like a normal human yet. She must think he had multiple personalities—a Jekyll and Hyde sort, perhaps. And he would not blame her.

Chapter Fourteen

Arianna ended the call. She frowned—not because she didn't want to see Christopher again—she did. It just took her by surprise to hear his voice on the other end. He sounded so, she shrugged, normal. It was easier to push thoughts of him out of her mind when he acted strange. Oh well, she was happy to have someone to go to lunch with, and maybe she could at least find a friend in him.

Scanning her closet, she picked out a casual but attractive outfit, red blouse and white capris, and headed to work. Before long, lunchtime had arrived and she found herself sitting across from her British gentleman turned American policeman. That's how she'd come to think of the enigma that was Christopher.

Ari loved Abby's diner. Everything; from the yellow café rod curtains to the country-themed art and music; made her smile. And the smells of home-cooked food were heavenly.

As she popped the last bite of meatloaf into her mouth, she looked up to see Christopher grinning at her. "I told you Abby makes the best meatloaf in Colorado." He winked.

Her heart thudded against her chest. Those dimples. She had never seen any man so absolutely gorgeous. She wiped her lips on a checkered napkin. "You were right about that. Now I won't have to eat any dinner. I don't think I've eaten so much since high school when I lived with Mom's home cooking." She took a drink and tamped down the memories of her family she had inadvertently invoked.

Lunch on Monday turned into lunch on Tuesday, Wednesday, and Thursday, as well. Arianna enjoyed every moment spent with Christopher. He was a fantastic listener, not to mention gorgeous.

During Thursday's lunch, she twirled too many pasta noodles around her fork before trying to fit it into her mouth.

"It seems your mouth is not quite large enough." Christopher's dimples appeared.

"You must think I have no manners." Her cheeks warmed with a blush. "I haven't done that since I was a kid. I just wanted to see if I could."

Christopher's blue eyes twinkled. "Hold still." He reached up and held Ari's chin with one hand while he wiped marinara sauce from the corners of her lips with the other. When he finished, his fingers lingered on her chin, sending shivers down her spine.

They both looked up when a waitress put a basket of steaming breadsticks on their table. The aroma wafted through the air, making Arianna's mouth water.

"I need bread." Ari eyed the basket.

"I believe that is what they call this." Christopher picked up a breadstick and motioned for Ari to open her mouth.

"No, I mean I'm out of bread and a few other groceries. Sorry. The breadsticks reminded me that I haven't been shopping in a while. I'll go tonight after work. I'll still take that breadstick, though." She pulled his hand closer to her mouth and took a bite of the bread, then hesitated before releasing it. The fact that he didn't pull his hand away wasn't lost on her.

"I could use a few items as well; would you like some company?" Christopher took a bite of the same breadstick.

"That would be nice."

"Then I will pick you up at seven."

"Sounds perfect." Ari's heart thudded. She ducked her head to hide a smile. She didn't know why grocery shopping sounded like a fun date. Maybe because it was such a domestic thing to do. Kind of like having a boyfriend.

****

That evening, Arianna glanced out the window and saw Christopher pull up to the curb promptly at seven. She'd never known a man as punctual as he was.

They leisurely walked each aisle together; Ari grabbing an item here and there. She noticed Christopher had yet to put anything in the basket they pushed. "I thought you needed food."

"I do. We just haven't found the items I'm looking for yet."

She stopped pushing the cart. "Do you have a list?"

"Yes, I have a list." Christopher tilted his head. His lips tugged up into a lopsided smile.

"Let's see it." Ari reached a hand toward him.

He surprised her by closing his own hand around hers instead of providing the list. Sparks of energy traveled up her arm, settling in her chest. She didn't want to let go of his hand but wanted to see the list to make sure they hadn't passed anything he needed. Hmm. What to do.

As if reading her mind, he grinned. "No worries, I've not missed anything on my list yet." He put her hand back on the basket and covered it with his, then began pushing again. It made for an awkward gait, but a wonderful sensation.

As they rounded the corner to the dairy section, he stopped and picked up a dozen eggs. He slipped a small paper from his pocket and examined it. "I only need three more items."

He did have a list. She didn't know why she'd doubted him. Maybe because most men she knew made mental lists, then forgot half the items by the time they reached the market. Curious, she peeked over his shoulder to read it. "Eggs, sausage, bread, and lard?"

He stuffed the paper into his pocket. "Is that so very strange?"

She shook her head. "No. I just didn't know people still used lard to cook with."

He shrugged. Animal fats taste better than oils when I make Scotch eggs. More authentic."

Ari gazed at him. "Sometimes I think you are an old soul. I like it."

He squeezed her hand and they began walking again.

The last lane was the catch-all aisle. The lane that didn't have a title because it contained a variety of items. "Look at this." He held the box out for Arianna to see it. "I didn't know they sold games in a market."

"Do you like Scrabble?" she asked.

He shrugged. "I don't know. I've never played."

Arianna looked at him as if he'd said he'd never heard of pizza. "You have never played Scrabble? What about Uno?" She picked up the game next to it.

"Uh, we did not have these games where I grew up."

"In England? You didn't have these games in England?"

"No, I suppose not. We played a card game called Whist."

"Seriously? They still play Whist in England? I thought that was just a game they played a couple hundred years ago. It's in all the books I've read from that era."

"You enjoy books from hundreds of years ago?"

"I love 'em—especially the British romances. Things were so…proper back then."

"Yes, they were—" He shifted his weight. "I meant to say, I'm certain you are right about that." He swallowed and took a breath. Ari thought he seemed tense. Strange. "So, you like to read about what England was like in the past?"

She nodded. "I guess guys don't get into that kind of stuff, but I'm fascinated by the whole Regency era— you know, all the royals, princes, dukes, earls—"

Christopher's smile faltered for a second. "No. You're right." He cut her off. "Guys don't get into that sort of thing. But we do like a little healthy competition." He waved the game box in front of her.

"Well, you, my friend, are going to learn something new tonight, then."

Christopher tilted his head. Arianna realized what she'd said and felt warmth rise from her feet to her head.

"I mean the game." She grabbed the Scrabble box, ignoring the innocent look on his face, and put it in her shopping cart, then turned away so he couldn't see her blush. Evidently her accidental innuendo was lost on him. Any other guy would have jumped all over it. How refreshing.

She rummaged through her purse in search of her wallet, which always seemed to find the deepest corners in which to hide. By the time she located it, Christopher had paid for the items. "Hey, most of that stuff was mine. Now I owe you." She began tugging bills from her wallet.

Christopher put a warm hand over hers, stopping her. "You owe me nothing."

"But—"

"Let the man pay," the middle-aged, bleached-blonde clerk behind the register said. "It's rare to find a true gentleman these days." She winked at Ari.

They drove to her apartment in relative silence. Ari didn't like feeling indebted to a man. Most men she knew expected payment in some form. He'd paid for lunches all week, as well. Of course, most men weren't Christopher.

"Let's play in the kitchen." Ari was happy to put the round wooden table to use. She'd eaten most of her meals on the go or in front of the television. Although the small room barely fit the necessities, its cream-colored walls and floral curtains gave it a cozy atmosphere. She set the game up and passed out the letter tiles. Christopher made popcorn in the microwave and poured M&Ms in a bowl. After Ari gave a quick explanation of the rules, the game began. Ari had grown up playing Scrabble with her family and felt confident. Things went along quite well. Christopher picked the game up quickly. That is, until he played the word "dray."

"Ahem, that's not a word, Chris."

"Of course it is a word. Everyone knows what a dray is."

"Is that right? Then what is it?"

"It is a cart used for hauling. You know, with horses." He tilted his head and lowered his eyebrows as if to challenge her.

"You can only use words found in the English dictionary."

"You are telling an Englishman that the word 'dray' is not in the English dictionary?"

Ari hadn't considered that. "Well, let's just look it up." She pulled out her phone. There it was in black and white. *Dray: A low heavy horse cart without sides; used for haulage.* She blew out a breath. "Fine." She put her hands on her hips. "You got lucky that time."

The next word Christopher played earned him high points, having two Z's in it. "Mizzen? Now I know that's not a word."

"Are you certain you want to question my language skills again?" He gave her the eyebrow challenge once more and rocked back in his chair.

Sure enough, there it was in the dictionary—again. "You're killing me. I've never even heard of these words." She reached across the table and punched his shoulder.

He looked up, his eyes wide in surprise. He caught her hand as if he wished to pull her around the table, but let it go. Heat had spread through her body but cooled when contact was broken. She was disappointed, but pretended not to care.

After playing a few more words, he ruled the board.

"I don't believe you've never played this game before." She cocked her head and narrowed her eyes. "I think you're a ringer."

"A what?"

"Oh, don't play dumb with me. If you know all those words that sound made up, I'm sure you know what a ringer is."

"What, like someone who rings a bell?" His face creased in confusion.

Ari tried but couldn't smother a laugh. "Whatever, Christopher. I'm not buying your innocent act." He shrugged, looking completely clueless.

They both leaned over the table to pick up the pieces of the game at the same time. Christopher's hand landed on Ari's. Neither one moved. Ari's hand sparked with electricity beneath his. She finally raised her eyes. He was doing it again—giving her that look that said she was the most important person in the world. Warmth flooded her body. With his free hand, he ran his thumb along her jawline, then let it linger. His face was so close, she was breathing his cologne. Heart thumping wildly, she couldn't move. Perfect time for a kiss. He leaned forward, paused, as if he'd reconsidered, smiled, and gave her hand a squeeze. She so wanted him to pull her around the small table and into his arms, but he relinquished her hand and finished cleaning up the game. Ah! Would he never kiss her? Perhaps he was too much of a gentleman.

She helped, acting as if nothing had passed between them. Something had passed between them, though—a roomful of fireworks. Perhaps she was the only one to feel it. No, she'd seen that look before. It happens right before a kiss.

A few minutes later, before he tugged the door closed behind him, he poked his head back in. "Lunch tomorrow?"

Ari nodded. The door shut, but she remained standing for a moment.

I need Maggie.

She grabbed a blanket and sat in her comfy recliner to call her friend. The aroma of popcorn still lingered. She lifted her hand to her nose. She wanted to remember the musky smell of Christopher.

After telling Maggie all about her week of lunches with the handsome Brit, Maggie responded with, "Lunch every day, huh? Has he kissed you yet?"

"No. He nearly did tonight. There's definitely chemistry there. But maybe he just wants to be friends." She paused for a few seconds, then went on. "I don't know what it is, but something seems to be holding him back. Who knows? I'm really comfortable when I'm with him, and I'm more than ready for that first kiss." She let out a sigh.

"He's nuts if he lets you slip away. I'm sure things will progress. Ironic, isn't it?"

"What's ironic?" Ari pulled the blanket up to cover her arms.

"It's usually you keeping the boys at bay. I'm sure you just need more time together."

****

Arianna felt nervous excitement as she pulled into the parking lot at Abby's Diner on Friday. Christopher had asked if she wanted to try a different restaurant, but Abby's food made her mouth water just thinking about it.

She saw him through the window. He winked at her. A shiver ran down her spine. She mouthed, "Order me the meatloaf."

His forehead wrinkled. "Again?" he mouthed back.

She made her way through the sea of diners and scooted into the booth across from him. "Yes, again. It's the best meatloaf I've ever had."

The waitress snapped her gum and tapped her pen on her tablet. Christopher held up two fingers. "Make that two specials."

Arianna kicked him under the table. "You, too? Talk about the pot calling the kettle black."

"The pot calling the kettle black. That's an old English saying I've not heard in a while."

"Well"—she cleared her throat—"in America it means you can't make fun of me for ordering meatloaf when you've already ordered it."

"That's very specific. I will try to remember it." He smiled. She melted.

Those dang dimples were going to be the death of her. She ducked behind her menu to hide her huge grin.

She felt a tug and realized the waitress was talking. "I'll take that off your hands, unless you aren't finished ordering." Gum smacked as Ari reluctantly gave up the menu and no longer had a way to hide.

While they waited for their food to arrive, Ari began asking questions. She wanted to understand this man she was falling for. "Why did you leave London to move to Pueblo, Colorado?"

Fumbling with his napkin, he replied, "I actually moved from London to Denver four years ago to join the police force there."

"Were you a police officer in London?"

"Not exactly, but I was in the legal profession."

Arianna's curiosity was piqued and she pressed on with more questions until she realized that Christopher's demeanor had changed. The sparkle in his eyes had vanished and his answers became clipped and curt. She felt a wall being erected between them, and the comfortable feeling she had experienced throughout the week disappeared. She tried changing the subject, but it was too late. Before she knew it, Christopher looked at his watch and stood to leave.

Chapter Fifteen

Christopher suppressed the urge to phone Ari, though he sorely wished to. He couldn't undo the conversation—or rather, his *reaction* to their lunchtime conversation. Why must he always flee when things coasted out of control in his head? Because he'd been on his own for over four years now, not having to explain his situation to anyone, that was why.

Leather furniture emitted a comfortable smell in his apartment. He didn't have much, just a sofa and some chairs in the living areas, but he had what he needed. He paced the floor in his small kitchen, mentally kicking himself every few steps. He knew he'd been playing with fire when he'd invited Ari to lunch one day after another, but he couldn't get enough of her. Charming and beautiful in a refreshing way, she seemed so different from the other women he'd met in this century. The vision of her blue-green eyes, dancing cheerfully whenever she smiled, refused to loosen its grip on his consciousness. Electricity pulsed through him at the thought. Her fragrance—orange blossoms and sweet spices—so natural, so enticing. Not to mention her hair. He had no idea what kind of shampoo she used, but its tropical scent smelled fresh and clean, driving him crazy with desire.

He closed his eyes. How he'd wanted to kiss her Thursday night after they'd played that silly game. A longing sigh escaped him. He had nearly given in to temptation. Those full red lips were almost impossible to resist. Another current rushed through his body just imagining their warm softness and how he longed to kiss them.

He'd worked hard all week long to avoid broaching the subject of his history or anything else of a personal nature. He knew once the subject came up, he must lie or change the topic of conversation. Then it happened, a flame from the fire he'd been playing with reached out and singed his face. Ari had meant well. He knew that. She simply wanted to know him better, but that couldn't happen. He hadn't wished to hurt her feelings when she'd questioned him about his past, but he also didn't want to lie. Therefore, he'd had no choice but to flee. He'd never forget the sad confusion on her face when he'd summoned the waitress over to hurry the check along. He should have said something—anything about his past. He cringed, recalling the conversation—or lack of it.

I'm an idiot.

And things had been going so well. He'd not been this happy since arriving in Colorado. He sat at his table, head buried in his hands. He supposed they could never go as well as he'd like them to in the end. Still, she was different. She might believe him if he were to tell her the truth.

He would call her. Tell her everything. Lifting his phone, he scrolled until he found her number, then he let his finger hover over the screen. What if he did tell her everything, threw it all out there for her to accept or reject—and she reacted with the latter? Was he ready for that kind of devastation? His hand hovered for the longest time.

He set the phone on the table and walked away.

Chapter Sixteen

"All right already." Arianna pulled her feather pillow over her head to hide from the blinding morning rays that sliced through the shutters.

Monday came too soon. The birds chirped happily outside her open window. They must have had a better weekend than she did. She gave up the notion of sleeping a few more minutes, sat up and slammed the window shut. The sooner she got to work, the better.

After a quick shower, she grabbed a protein bar, climbed into her car and turned the key. The engine sputtered a few times, let out a puff of acrid smoke, then died. With a groan, she laid her head against the steering wheel.

Normally, she had plenty of work that could be done at home on her laptop, but today furniture was scheduled to be delivered. She must be onsite before it arrived.

She could call a tow truck to have her car taken to a shop, but then would need a ride to the Somers'. She bumped her head against the steering wheel a couple of times in frustration. She only knew one person in the whole city, and after his abrupt departure from Abby's on Friday, she wasn't sure he'd be receptive to a cry for help.

After pondering the situation for only a few more minutes, she rummaged through her purse and found the card Christopher had given her at their first meeting.

The phone rang once, twice, then his deep, British voice answered. "Hello."

Hearing him sent chills through her. She let out a breath and forced herself to remember their not-so-pleasant lunch. She explained the situation, apologizing profusely for any inconvenience, before he cut her off.

"Slow down, Arianna. Of course I will come get you. I'll be there in five minutes."

Relief spread through her entire body. Maybe he wasn't angry with her for—she frowned—she didn't know what; it just felt like he had been. She had to tamp down rising frustration.

As promised, Christopher arrived minutes later, dressed in his uniform and wearing a reassuring smile.

He seemed to be back to his old self again, or possibly his new one. She realized, despite all their time spent together, she didn't know Christopher very well, and it took a lot of energy to get him to open up— energy she realized she may not possess.

They had to wait for a tow truck to pick her car up before they could head to the Somers' house, so they took a seat on her sofa, facing a picture window. Her small apartment had the bare essentials, but being a decorator, she couldn't help but add a picture here, pillows there, and, of course, scented candles. The place needed some color and aroma. Ari justified that inspiration wouldn't happen in a basically beige room.

After some small talk and an awkward silence, she decided to take a timid step into his personal territory again. She wouldn't ask about England; that seemed to be a sensitive subject. She'd just ask about his family. She had nothing to lose. Things were already strange between them.

She pulled a pillow onto her lap. A form of security. "Tell me about your family, Christopher."

He blanched, clearly taken aback by the question, but quickly recovered. "Well, I have two siblings, a sister and a brother. Then, of course, there is my mother."

"What about your father?"

"He's been gone for a while now."

"Oh, I'm so sorry." Ari laid a gentle hand on his arm.

Christopher waved her apology away as if the statement didn't warrant her pity. She slid her hand back into her lap and clutched the pillow.

She needed to move on to a more pleasant subject, especially since further questions on the current topic would likely reopen her own healing wounds. "What do you like to do in your free time?"

Without hesitation, he answered, "Ride my horse, Maida Vale. I keep her stabled south of here."

"You have a horse?" Ari imagined Christopher's perfect form astride a black stallion. He looked stunning—in her mind, of course.

"Don't you?"

She turned to face him, wondering if he was serious. He quirked a grin and patted her on the leg. "Where do you ride?" she asked.

"Mostly on the outskirts of town. I've spent many a day riding in the area of your job. There are a lot of good trails out there. What about you, Arianna—what do you do for fun?"

She should have had an answer ready, but instead, had to think about it. "Well, I like to read. Um, and work—I guess that's not a hobby. I used to like shopping with my mom." Oops. She wished she could scoop those last words up and put them right back in her mouth.

"Used to? You no longer enjoy shopping with your mother, then?" He raised his eyebrows.

Ari paused for a moment before she responded. "Uh, what I mean, I guess"—she looked anywhere but at Christopher, whose intense gaze had now settled on her—"is, I used to like shopping with my mother." She swallowed. "She—and my father and brother—died in a car accident two and a half years ago." She couldn't act as nonchalant as he had. Tears burned in her eyes as she tried unsuccessfully to keep them from falling.

Christopher's mouth turned down and his forehead creased. He looked mortified and apologetic. Taking her hand into one of his, he wiped her tears away with the other. "Oh, Ari," he said in a low voice, "I am so sorry. I didn't know. I never would have—"

She cut him off and shook her head. "Of course you didn't know. I never meant to bring it up because of this." She motioned to her face with her free hand. "This is what happens when I do. Somehow, I know they're not gone forever. I feel it when I visit the cemetery each Saturday when I'm in Denver." The tears came faster, splashing onto her leg.

He found a box of tissues on the table next to the sofa and handed her one. After she wiped her eyes, he pulled her close, put his arm around her and stroked her hair as she lay against his shoulder. "I'm so sorry," he repeated.

Arianna realized she'd kept her memories so securely sequestered, the mere mention of her loss had unleashed years of pent-up emotion. While she didn't like allowing so many tears to escape, she felt relieved, at least a little.

Just as she began to get herself under control, the tow truck arrived.

She didn't want to leave the comfort of Christopher's arms. It had felt good to talk about the people missing from her life, but not forgotten—even if it had brought on the waterworks. She reluctantly stood, answered the door, gave the tow truck driver the keys and some instructions and sent him on his way.

Once it was just the two of them again, she faced him. "I don't know whether to apologize or thank you. I'm sorry your shoulder is all wet." She smiled through watery eyes. "But, thank you for listening."

He pulled her into a hug. Arianna breathed in his musky cologne and wished she could stay in his arms all day—it felt so right. "Don't worry about my shirt, and I am happy to listen any time you need to talk." He bent down and kissed the top of her head, giving her goosebumps.

She raised her head. The way he gazed at her made her heart thud in her chest. He moved his hand gently up her back and into her hair. Fireworks shot through her body. He bent his head toward hers and she closed her eyes, relishing in the moment and the thrill of anticipation. She could feel his breath on her face.

Chapter Seventeen

His phone rang, breaking the spell.

He loosened his grip on her and answered, "This is Officer Flemming. …Yes, I will be available for a meeting at that time." He hung up, disappointed, but knew it was for the best.

"Sorry about that. I guess I'd best drive you to work, so I can get to the station."

Ari peeked at her watch. "Yes, I'm expecting a furniture delivery in an hour."

Christopher let Ari do all the talking on the way to her jobsite. She didn't add much to her sad tale. When they arrived, he ignored her protests and walked her to the door. "I'll pick you up when you're finished here, since your car will still be in the shop."

"Thank you. I'm sorry to be such a pain. I guess I need to make more friends in Pueblo so I'm not completely reliant on you."

His heart pinched at the thought of Arianna calling anyone else for help. "I don't mind."

His work meeting was scheduled for after lunch, so he took the long way to the station, cranked up the air conditioner and aimed it at his soggy shoulder.

Grinding his teeth, he recalled how callously he'd mentioned losing his father. *At least I still have my family—out of reach, but living.*

He couldn't believe she had never said anything about losing her parents and brother before now. It had to have been devastating. Yet, she'd finished college and was doing well on her own. He shook his head. Only four years ago—yet, several lifetimes ago—any single female, without royal blood, in her situation, would have ended up as a servant or governess for an aristocrat's family—if they were lucky. Others would end up in a poorhouse, or worse, forced to work in a brothel. Times had sure changed in two hundred years. He pulled his squad car into the parking lot. One thing was certain—Arianna Miller was the most amazing woman he'd ever met. He glanced down at his phone, which, finally back in civilization, had sprung to life, and remembered the near kiss. "You, phone of mine, are not my friend right now. But, it's probably best to keep a safe distance, I suppose."

He looked up a local florist, dialed the number, and ordered a dozen yellow roses to be sent to Arianna's jobsite. He couldn't take away her pain, but he could try to cheer her.

"Sir, what do you want the card to say?" the voice on the other end of the phone asked.

Christopher thought for a moment. *Ari, your smile is like sunshine to my soul. I hope it returns soon.* That sounded nice. He opened his mouth to direct the florist to pen it, but he paused. Too intimate. "Just write, 'Ari, have a nice day. Yours, Christopher'."

Despite the emotional conversation at her apartment, all in all, his time with her today had been surprisingly positive. Perhaps she'd forgiven his abrupt exit at lunch last Friday. He hoped so. The more time he spent with her, the more he realized how much he craved her—craved any positive interaction with someone not wearing a police uniform. And it sure didn't hurt that she was pretty and smelled like happiness.

Since his transfer to Pueblo, until he'd met Ari, his thoughts had focused solely on his mother and siblings—how to protect them and remove them from his father's dominion. Obsessed. That's what he'd become. Then again, why wouldn't he be? He had little to do but work—which, with Pueblo's low crime rate, wasn't difficult—and worry for his family.

Living in Denver had been stressful in a whole different way. Work at the station had kept him absorbed in crime fighting, leaving less time to fixate on his family. But he'd been grateful to have a decent paying job—unlike the weeks immediately following his journey into the twenty-first century.

He'd spent the first week after being banished from his family in a daze. Thankfully, he'd stashed food, clothing, and a few other essential supplies in his satchel before being transported to this century, so he had sustenance until he could work things out. And his mother had slipped something in there, too. He'd fished around until his fingers snagged on a small leather pouch. When he opened it, details had become much clearer, at least about the crime his father had committed. His dear mother had somehow gotten her hands on a fistful of diamonds and slipped them into his satchel.

Using the diamonds to live on had been unthinkable. It was blood money. He'd rather die first. After he rescued his family from his father's clutches, his goal would be to somehow return the diamonds.

Residing on the streets had been surprisingly advantageous. There, in the underbelly of society, he'd been introduced to Denver's seedier residents. That homeless gang of riffraff—Stewart, Bags and the others—would never know what they had done for him. He smiled at the memories. From them he'd obtained an education as to how to create a new identity and acquire a Social Security number—essential to become employed in America. That's also when he decided to take his mother's maiden name, Flemming, as his surname.

He'd scrabbled around Denver until he'd found a group of men standing at a gas station. They'd seemed to be waiting for something. When he'd enquired about what it was they awaited, he was informed that trucks regularly stopped by to collect willing men to do yardwork. Though he'd never maintained a yard before, he'd been willing to give it a try and eagerly joined the group. However, for the most part, these were only weekend tasks—not paying enough to get him off the streets. He then added a job working at a carwash. While the work was regular, he still came up short financially. Finally, after he'd added a night job working at a fast-food restaurant, he'd been able to earn enough money to secure an apartment in lower downtown Denver. Not a prime location, but still better than east London had been.

He'd worked, saved, and observed life in the twenty-first century. Then, when he'd felt ready, entered the police academy.

Life over the last four years had not been boring. But through it all, he'd had one mission—tracking his father's movements to put him away and save his family. Arianna was a diversion. A beautifully sweet, and wonderfully welcome diversion. Just thinking about her made his pulse race like a horse competing in a steeplechase.

"Flemming," a crusty voice shook him from his musings.

"Chief?"

A pile of papers landed in front of Christopher. His workday had officially begun with his least favorite task—paperwork.

"There's been reports of a disturbance in this area." The police chief pointed to an address on the first page of the small pile. "Rumbling noises. One neighbor called it a sonic boom." He rolled his eyes.

Christopher perked up. "I'll look into it, Chief." He eagerly dug into the pages. Reports of this nature had come periodically in Denver and had often led to the same house—Benjamin Somers'. No one had answered the door when Christopher, or any other officer knocked. Unfortunately, irregular noise complaints didn't warrant the use of the police department's resources beyond the initial house call. He knew it was premature to go in, guns blazing, without a plan or evidence of a crime; he just wished to see his mother and siblings and know they were truly safe.

He was certain his father had been using his device to travel back in time, committing more crimes to increase his fortune. Criminals such as his father were never satisfied—the desire for money never fulfilled, the thirst for power never quenched and the urge to spill blood never quelled. Christopher didn't know how extreme his father's lust for power and fortune had become, but in his heart, he feared the worst.

His own memories of the machine were hazy, at best. He hadn't seen it, but he'd never forget the loud vibrations it had caused just before he'd slipped into complete darkness back in London. He'd been vaguely aware of them again as the device landed in twenty-first century Colorado.

He and his partner, Joe, drove to the address from the 911 call. His heart sank. This house, so near the city center, couldn't possibly have anything to do with his father. It was probably a complaint about noisy kids or something. No. Christopher was certain Father had built the mansion—his family's future home, Arianna's current worksite—outside of Pueblo, where no one would be bothered by such noises.

New fear for Ari's safety prickled his skin. What if the device was at the home already? What if she was there when Father decided to use it? What if he did something to Ari, then transported her to another time? Worry gnawed at him like razor-sharp teeth.

Chapter Eighteen

Ari couldn't believe she'd lost her composure in front of Christopher. Embarrassing. He'd acted so unfeeling about losing his own father. She wondered what kind of man he had been to warrant such a lack of emotion from his son? Perhaps he'd left his family or had been abusive. She really couldn't judge. Christopher was nothing like the images she'd conjured of his father. His comforting tenderness toward her had been surprisingly sweet. She wished she had *that* Christopher to talk to more often.

She set to work, preparing rooms for incoming furniture. After rolling out a spool of vinyl runner to protect the floors, she inhaled and smiled. "Why do I like that smell so much?"

Next, she opened her file to the bubble diagrams she'd created to know exactly where each piece of furniture should be placed. As she finished examining the papers, the doorbell rang. The furniture was here. She opened the door to usher in the workers. Her jaw dropped. Before her stood a delivery person holding, not furniture, but the most beautiful bouquet of yellow roses. She located her purse and dug out a tip, then took the bouquet and retreated to the kitchen to read the note.

The words from Christopher, short and sweet, set her off all over again. "Whatever he is doing to me, I'm not sure my heart can take it." She breathed in the wonderful fragrance of the long-stemmed roses and pictured his handsome face. A tingle ran down her spine.

****

Christopher arrived at six o'clock to pick her up from the Somers' house. She spotted his car through the window and motioned for him to come in.

"Thank you so much for the beautiful roses." She pointed to the table where they were displayed. "Yellow is my favorite color, and they are so fragrant, you can smell them from here." She closed her eyes and sniffed. "Ah."

Christopher's mouth quirked into a grin.

"Do you mind waiting for just a few more minutes while I finish measuring this room?"

"Not at all. Can I help?"

"As a matter of fact, you can." Ari handed him one end of a tape measure. "Hold this right—"

Just then there was a clang outside. They both jumped at the loud noise.

Before Ari knew what was happening, Christopher had pulled her behind him and stood in front, ready to protect her.

Ari tapped him on the back. "Christopher?" She stifled a laugh. "I think that was just the landscaper."

His shoulders relaxed, and he chuckled. "You can never be too careful around a man wielding a garden tool."

It was funny, but it also made her think. This guy was ready to protect and defend her against whatever evil forces he thought were lurking out there. She couldn't remember ever dating a man so concerned for her safety.

When they'd driven close enough to the city to receive cell phone service, Ari called the shop where her car had been towed. Optimistic it would be ready, she thought it would be easiest if Christopher just dropped her off there.

She was wrong, the car wasn't ready. And to make matters worse, it required an expensive part that had to be ordered and wouldn't arrive until the next week.

"Next week. I can't wait that long!" Her voice rose. "I'm going to Denver on Friday. I have to have my car."

"I'm sorry, ma'am. This is a small town and we don't keep many parts in stock. So, unless you've got a flat tire, or you need an oil change, chances are we'll need to order the part from Denver. It will take a few days to get here, then at least a day to install it in your car."

Disappointed, Ari hung up, then immediately dialed another number. "Maggie, my car's broken. I can't come to your baby shower. I'm so—"

Before she finished her sentence, Christopher tugged at her arm.

"Hold on, Mags." She looked at him and mouthed, "What is it?"

"I'll take you to Denver."

"No." That came out a little harsher than she meant it to. While she would love nothing more than to go to Denver with Christopher, she didn't think she could take it if she said the wrong thing again and his heart turned to stone, shattering hers. In those situations, he had disappeared immediately. She craved reliability. "I mean; I could never ask you to do that for me. You've already done so much. You drove me to and from work, sent me beautiful roses, and even let me mess up your shirt crying on your shoulder. I am becoming a burden to you. No. I'll just skip the shower; she'll understand."

He shook his head. "Ari, please don't refer to yourself as a burden." He pulled the phone out of her hand and put it to his ear. "Maggie, this is Ari's friend, Christopher. Please plan on her attendance at your shower." He ended the call.

"Thank you, Christopher. You didn't need to do that."

"But Arianna, I am more than happy to, so please allow me the honor."

She reached over and kissed him on the cheek. In return, Christopher gave her a sidelong glance and a crooked grin.

An uneasiness kept her from fully enjoying the moment. She twisted her fingers together nervously. She hoped she wouldn't regret allowing him to do yet another favor for her. She worried for her fragile heart, as well, as it insisted on constantly ignoring the warning signs. Was Christopher the man for her, or should she be running the other direction—away from him?

Chapter Nineteen

The work week seemed endless—or perhaps it was just Friday that stubbornly held on to daylight. Yes, Friday was definitely the culprit—the cause of Ari's complete exhaustion, and the reason she'd second-guessed her judgment in deciding to become an interior designer. She could thank Mr. Somers. He'd made Fridays—this Friday, in particular—nearly unbearable. Finally, as the afternoon ended, the dimming rays shining through the windows gave her hope.

Earlier that morning Mr. Somers had exploded at the painters, shouting curse words Ari had never before heard. Perhaps something had happened at his Denver residence to set him off, she didn't know, but she'd somehow found herself in the center of the storm. The greens weren't green enough, the creams not creamy enough. Even with Ari's expert eye, she couldn't see the difference between his samples and the paint on the wall. Henry, the lead painter, had stormed off the job. The other two had followed. With no cell phone service, Ari didn't have a way of calling to urge them back. There were other painters in the area, but she'd worked with this crew and knew why they'd been rated number one in the business. She needed them. There was no such thing as second best to Mr. Somers. Immature as it sounded, he threw fits to show who was in charge, leaving her to smooth ruffled feathers.

Thankfully, her morning jogs had made her a fast runner, and she didn't hesitate to chase their truck. She'd been able to catch up and flag the painters down, since they had been waylaid by putting away their equipment before driving off. It had taken some fast talking and hefty promises to get the men to come around, but she'd done it. Perhaps she should have become a lawyer.

By afternoon, Mr. Somers had found a scratch on his newly-delivered Mahogany desk. Okay, she'd admit it; scratches on furniture of such a high quality were not acceptable. However, she'd watched the furniture movers as they'd taken meticulous care in hauling in the desk. It had required some minor assembling, which she'd also examined. And now there was a scratch on the top left corner. It hadn't been there before Mr. Somers had gone in and begun unloading his belongings into the desk. While he'd blustered on and on about it, Ari spotted what she believed to be the culprit; an antique, ornate Victorian, brass footed oil lamp. It looked to have been moved from one corner of the desk to the other. Ari had slipped some felt pads from her pocket to apply them to the lamp, lest it do more damage.

"Get your hands of the lamp!" Mr. Somers had yelled. She thought he might burst a blood vessel when she'd touched his precious lamp.

"Fine," she'd said, handing the pads to him. "But I'm certain the lamp is what scratched the desk, as it wasn't scratched earlier." Ari hadn't known volcanoes existed in Pueblo, Colorado, but now she did. Mr. Somers had erupted like the worst kind of volcano, spewing profanities, and screaming about Ari's insolence—why wasn't she home tending to children where she belonged?—and on and on. Arianna left the felt pads on the desk and walked out of the room. Let the man sputter. There was no stopping him when his ego had been threatened.

His visits were generally short, but today he'd never left. Whenever possible, Ari had steered clear of him. She had received a smidgeon of satisfaction when she'd spied him through the open door, attempting to apply the adhesive felt pads to the lamp. Shaking her head, she'd watched while he'd fumbled with every part of the easy task. Why couldn't he just let her do it?

She looked at her watch, ready for a weekend away. Spending it with Maggie would be just the remedy she needed.

By the time Christopher pulled up to house to pick her up, Arianna stood outside waiting. She couldn't get out of there fast enough. She needed sleep, and she needed to put some distance between her and the Somers' home.

"Are you well, Arianna? You look a little pale and tired." Christopher opened the car door for her.

"I'll be fine as soon as we're out of here and on the road. It's been an exhausting day, that's all." She managed a weak smile. "This isn't your squad car. Did you steal it?" She attempted to lighten the mood she feared might follow her to Denver.

Christopher's dimples puckered. "No worries; I've not turned to a life of crime. This is my friend Joe's 1967 Chevy Impala. He calls it his baby." He ran his hand along the refurbished seat. "While the department doesn't mind me using my squad car in Pueblo, they do frown on taking it out on weekend getaways. Plus, I thought this would be a little more comfortable."

She gave him a grateful smile. The squad car he had used to shuttle her to and from work all week long had been a lifesaver, since her car still sat at Dave's Auto shop. But she hadn't looked forward to spending more than twenty minutes sitting on that stiff seat.

"You're right." She sank into the soft leather. "This is nice."

They drove to Arianna's apartment first so she could get her travel bag, then grabbed a bite to eat and headed north.

"Shall we listen to music? Joe said the radio is broken, but he installed a CD player. There are some pretty good CDs in the glove compartment." He reached across Arianna to open it.

With his head so close to her, Ari had to restrain herself from touching his dark, silky hair. One day she would just run her fingers right through it. She smiled at the thought.

"It seems to be stuck."

She turned her attention away from his gorgeous head of hair and added her efforts to open the compartment.

No luck.

Christopher gently pulled her arm away from the futile task. "I guess we'll just talk." He kept his hand gently clasped around her arm.

Electricity pulsed through her. She didn't want him to move it—ever—so she scooted closer to him, grateful for the car's vintage old-school bench seat.

He grinned at her and moved his hand down until it reached her hand and intertwined his fingers with hers.

She suppressed a huge smile that threatened to steal its way across her face.

They kept the conversation light, Ari having learned the hard way of which topics to steer clear. Christopher told her about his day, which hadn't amounted to much. Crime in Pueblo paled in comparison to Denver.

Ari told Christopher about the chaos at the Somers' house in general, and about Mr. Somers in particular.

"Mr. Somers was there today?" His happy countenance changed.

"Mr. Somers comes every Friday. He sometimes brings the rest of the family, too, although *he* does all the criticizing—I mean talking." Weariness crept back into her bones. "He must have locked the rest of the family away somewhere today. He seems to have them under some kind of spell."

Christopher appeared to be contemplating something before he spoke. "So, you have met the whole family?"

"Yes, but I could hardly tell you about any of them. They never speak—except when Sarah, their nineteen-year-old, asked me if I'd seen her journal. They seem sad all the time—maybe even frightened. And Mr. Somers rarely says anything kind to them."

Every frustration Ari had been feeling began to spill out. "And where on earth did they get so much money? I swear, Chris, the rug in the study alone is worth over eighty-thousand dollars!"

Was it her imagination, or had his hand holding hers turned cold and stiff?

Chapter Twenty

Arianna talked about her frustrations.

Christopher listened, trying not to let his intense emotions display themselves.

Finally, after a long pause, he realized she'd drifted off to sleep. He let out a breath of relief.

He didn't wonder where all that money had come from—he knew. Whatever had brought his family to the twenty-first century with a satchel full of diamonds was obviously still being utilized by his father. If Christopher could only locate and destroy the machine, then somehow bring his father to the justice he deserved, he could rescue his family. A tall order, to be sure. Four years of searching for it had yielded little results.

Arianna's words had driven a searing knife through his heart. It hadn't been her fault; she'd had no idea the effect they'd have on him. To her, Mr. Somers was just a frustrating client. Still, the picture she'd painted had confirmed all his fears. His father had not used his money and new environment to better himself—as a fresh start could. No, if it were possible, he'd become more of a knave.

Christopher clenched his teeth and tightened his hold on the steering wheel as thoughts of his mother and siblings dancing to their father's perverse tune of abuse cycled through his mind. The puppet master.

That's what his father was. And Mother, Sarah and Joshua were his puppets. He hit the dashboard with his fist, startling Arianna. Her eyes fluttered open.

"What happened? Is everything okay?"

"I'm sorry I woke you. Everything is fine. You should go back to sleep." He gathered Ari's hand into his again and gave it a squeeze. He realized her eyes had closed before he'd finished his sentence.

His thoughts returned to their conversation. Fear clutched his heart. Arianna had been with his father all day long. She was not safe there. He could only imagine what the man was capable of doing. The facts; what he did know about—the robbery and murder his father had committed before their sudden departure from nineteenth century London—were enough to make him worry for her life. A feeling of absolute helplessness overtook him. He gazed at the sleeping Arianna. He needed to protect her. He must protect her.

He was glad she'd fallen asleep—not only because of the painful conversation, but also because he could tell she'd sorely needed it. Except for her frustrations with his father, she hadn't complained, but he knew how hard she'd been working all week. This trip would be a welcome respite for her. He gently pulled her closer and laid her head on his shoulder. Watching her sleep so peacefully made him wish the ride would last longer. "You are so beautiful," he whispered. "I wish I could share my secrets with you."

Arianna stirred, then snuggled in closer.

As they entered the city, Christopher gently nudged her. "Arianna." He kept his voice low.

"Are we there?" She lifted her head from his shoulder and shook it. She looked adorable all sleepy-eyed.

"We're in Denver, and I need to know where to take you."

"I'm so sorry, Chris. Did I sleep the whole way?"

He squeezed her fingers. "Not the whole way. And if anybody needed a good nap, it was you." He lifted her hand to his mouth and kissed it. "Now, where should I take you?"

"Uh—take me to my apartment. Or, maybe to Maggie's house. I should have thought this through before now. Where are you staying? You said you have business in town tomorrow."

Before he could answer, Ari's finger shot up. "I've got an idea. If you don't have anywhere better, you can drop me off at Maggie's, and you can stay at my apartment."

The thought of it made his blood rush through his veins. Being surrounded by her scent alone nearly drove him mad with desire. "Are you sure? I'm certain it'll be nicer than the cheap hotel I'd planned to stay at."

"Of course. After all, I owe you a lot for driving me here. Not to mention letting me ramble on about the Somers, then sleeping on your shoulder. I'm afraid I haven't been very good company." She dug the key out of her purse and handed it to him.

After dropping her off at Maggie's house, Christopher let the GPS on his phone guide him to Arianna's place. Modern technology never ceased to amaze him.

When he stepped into the apartment, he sucked in a breath. "It is so," he paused to think of the right word, "Ari."

It wasn't large, but the décor was perfect. The colors were soft and the furniture delicate. Such a contrast to the dark colors and heavy furniture in the house she'd been decorating. Everything—her rugs, pictures, throw pillows and lamps—had been positioned in precisely the right place for a pleasing effect. So, this was how an apartment was supposed to look. It even smelled like her. Christopher didn't know if it was her shampoo, her perfume, or just her scent, but he loved it. Like orange blossoms. He took a deep breath.

One picture grabbed his attention almost instantly. He crossed the room to an end table and picked up a framed photo of a beautiful, smiling family. "And this is your family," he said aloud, almost reverently.

He frowned as he reflected back to just a few days before, when Arianna had told him of her loss. He traced an invisible line around her face. His heart ached for her, but also for his own helpless situation. "I guess we get through this life one day at a time, my dear." He kissed his finger and touched it to her picture.

Now, if he could get through the weekend without any missteps, all while guarding his heart, that would be an accomplishment. First things first, however; before he could think of the time he'd be spending with Arianna, he had to make contact with his family—without Father discovering him.

Chapter Twenty-One

"Ari." Maggie grabbed her by the arm and dragged her to the sofa. "Christopher is gorgeous! He's also polite and British, just like the men in those novels you love. What more could you ask for? He's perfect for you." Arianna had never seen Maggie's hazel eyes sparkle so vividly.

"You're right, Mags, he is perfect—or so he seems." She sighed.

"What are you talking about? I dare you to find anything wrong with that man. He drove you here, opened every door for you, even took your suitcase up to your room. He couldn't possibly be more gentlemanly—is that a word?" She tapped her chin. "I half expected him to bow."

Ari lifted a shoulder, then let it fall. "I agree, he's almost too good to be true."

Maggie tilted her head. "Almost?"

"I don't know. There's something that's just not right—like he's keeping something from me."

"Explain, girlfriend."

"Well, he is all those things you said, and more. It's like he walked right out of one of my books. I've never met anyone so courteous. I positively melt when he touches me. But he never talks about himself, and if I ask too many questions, he shuts down, changes the subject, or worse—he leaves. Then there's the house."

"House? What house?"

"The Somers' house—you know, the one I'm decorating. Every time he goes inside, he literally stiffens up. I can't explain it. There's just something about that house."

"Well, Ari, every relationship takes time, and you still have plenty of time in Pueblo to figure out Christopher's secrets."

"Relationship is the key word. I don't even know if we're in a relationship." She motioned air quotes with her fingers. "He hasn't kissed me, unless you count the time he kissed my hand."

Maggie's eyebrows raised.

"I know, I know. That sounds strange coming from me, your 'prudish' friend." Ari twirled hair through her fingers.

"You know I'm teasing when I call you that." Maggie gave her a gentle nudge.

"I know you are—kind of. I think most people think I'm prudish. Maybe they're right. I haven't always been that way; I did my fair share of kissing in school." She smiled, then sobered. "But my whole world changed when my family died. Relationships became more important and I don't want to waste my time kissing, you know, the wrong guys."

Maggie's eyes softened. "That makes so much sense."

Ari continued, "But Christopher and I see each other nearly every day, and, while there's definitely a physical attraction, at least on my part, he mostly keeps a safe distance. It's like he's afraid of something." She shrugged. "Maybe he's too much of a gentleman."

"Or he's gay." Maggie grinned wickedly.

Ari sighed. "Wouldn't that just be my luck?"

"I don't know, but it's obvious by the way he looks at you that he's got the hots for you. You two are made for each other. I guess time will tell." Maggie yawned.

"I think we'd better get some sleep so you'll be well-rested for your party tomorrow," said Ari.

Maggie gave her a hug. "I'm so glad you're here. I've missed you."

Ari climbed into bed, wondering what surprises tomorrow would bring—with Christopher, they could be wonderful, or heartbreaking.

Chapter Twenty-Two

It had been a snowy, winter day, colder than most. Flakes whistled through the air—not the light, fluffy, lazy variety that made Arianna smile. No, this was wet snow that turned to slush before it hit the ground, then froze on contact. The type that blew fiercely into your face until your cheeks became paralyzed from the cold as it clung to your eyelashes and hair.

Ari escaped the cold, ducked into the Art Design building and studiously listened to Professor Coulter drone on about the importance of balancing colors in a room. Her eyes occasionally drifted to the window as the snow splattered against the pane. She stretched her fingers to coax some circulation back into them. Without warning, a gust of freezing air slapped her in the face, and she found herself nose to nose with a Colorado State University counselor. His glasses made his eyes appear enormous as his mouth turned down in a frown.

"There has been a terrible accident..." The sentence oozed out of the counselor's mouth in slow motion. He spoke in low tones that threatened to break Arianna's eardrums. The rest of his words blurred together. In her mind, a piñata had just burst, and the rest of the world looked on as she frantically tried to scoop its contents back into the tattered remains. Futile.

She didn't want or need to hear about a terrible accident. Nothing made sense. She turned her back on the counselor and attempted to walk away, but every direction she faced, he was there spewing out nonsensical noise.

The next thing Arianna knew, she found herself in a morgue staring down at the faces of her beloved family. She began to tremble. The stiffness she'd felt in her fingers caused by the whipping snow had been nothing compared to the numbness that crept up her body while peering into the hollow faces of her mother, father and brother.

Icy roads, drunk driver, hit-and-run, no survivors. Icy roads, drunk driver, hit-and-run, no survivors. Icy roads... The words made an endless loop through her head. Try as she might, she couldn't quiet the police officer's voice. It burned and bubbled like acid. She wanted to retch.

"No, this can't be happening." She repeated it over and over, but nobody heard. There were people all around her, yet she seemed to be invisible. They weren't listening. She continued to explain that there had surely been a mistake, but her voice grew raspy and only pinged off earless, faceless people.

As she stood between her parents' slabs, her mother's eyes flew open and icy fingers latched onto Ari's arm. "Arianna." She heard her mother's voice, although her lips never moved. Ari stood motionless as if in a trance. Her mother's cold hand tightened around her arm. "Arianna!" The firm voice commanded Ari's attention.

"What, Mother?" Ari whimpered.

"Stay on your guard. Beware of—"

Her mother's warning was cut short as the door to the cold morgue banged open. Freezing snow blew in, stealing the breath from her lungs. She whirled around to see a pair of coal-black eyes drilling into her. The face belonging to those eyes materialized from behind the shadows.

"Mr. Somers? Why are you here?"

His glare never left Ari, but he remained mute.

She turned back to her family—surely they would help her. They were gone. In fact, she was no longer in the morgue. Instead, she looked down and recognized fine wood flooring. The flooring in Mr. Somers' house. But there was no sign of all the furnishings she'd spent weeks organizing. Anywhere. It was just a cold, cavernous house. Mr. Somers moved toward her, a menacing sneer pinching his face. She turned to run for the door when someone stepped into her path. Christopher. He pulled her into his arms, wiping away tears she hadn't realized she'd shed.

"Christopher!" she shrieked, grateful for his protective arms around her. "What's happening to me? Where did you come from? And why is Mr. Somers—"

"Ari. Arianna!" Awareness pulled her from Christopher's hold. Maggie's concerned face came into focus as she gently shook her.

"Mm…Maggie?"

"Wake up. You're having a nightmare." Maggie handed her a glass of water. "Drink this. Your voice is raspy."

"What happened? Where…?" Ari stopped trying to make sense of anything and willed herself into full consciousness.

"You were screaming Christopher's name. You looked positively terrified."

Ari caught her breath. She sat up and took a drink of the cold water and found a tissue to wipe the sweat from her forehead. She shivered and pulled the comforter up to her chin.

"What in the world were you dreaming about?"

"I"—she shook her head—"it was so strange." Ari stumbled over her words. Her thoughts clashed between wishing to explain and wanting to hide from the nightmare from which she'd just awakened.

"Start at the beginning. What do you remember?"

She hugged herself to ward off the chill in the air. The chill that still gripped her as images of icy snow, cold morgues, and cavernous mansions replayed in her mind. "What do I remember? I remember every detail. I don't think I'll ever forget." She began from the start. Memories of the horrifyingly unforgettable day when she had been informed of her family's accident morphed into a warning about something. "My mother was trying to warn me about something. She was adamant that I beware…beware… Ugh!"

"She didn't tell you what she was warning you about?"

"No, because Mr. Somers appeared. Oh, I don't know, Maggie. None of it makes any sense. I'm sure being here in Denver again has made memories of my family surface."

"So, why do you think you were screaming Christopher's name?"

Ari let out a breath and stared at the blanket in concentration. "He was there, too. When Mr. Somers was coming after me—"

"Mr. Somers was what? Is that man dangerous? What if this is some kind of warning for you to resign from this job?"

Shaking her head, Ari looked up at Maggie. "That's silly. It was just a dumb dream." A horrible nightmare that she hoped never to relive. She put her hands beneath the warm comforter so Maggie couldn't see them shake. "It's good I'm up. I need to shower and get ready for your big day."

"Are you sure you're okay? Your face is so pale."

"I'm fine. It's nothing a hot shower won't take care of." She forced a smile. "Thanks for waking me."

Maggie didn't seem convinced but must have picked up on the hint that Arianna didn't wish to dwell on her nightmare any longer. "That's what friends are for." She hugged Ari. "Jason's frying up some bacon and eggs, do you want to eat?"

"I thought I smelled something delicious cooking in the kitchen." Her stomach turned at the thought of eating. Maybe after her shower. She couldn't ruin this day for Maggie.

"Yeah, well, I'm always hungry, but never feel like cooking. Thank goodness for a husband with a bit of culinary talent. Go shower now; I'll keep a plate warm for you."

Ari faced the shower head and let hot water wash away the tears. They flowed freely now that she allowed the full impact of the nightmare to sink in. She wanted to believe it was nothing, that there was no symbolism there. "It was a dream. A dumb dream. It was a dumb dream!" She screamed out loud and yanked on the faucet until the water was unbearably hot. Her teeth still chattered.

"Ari?" Maggie knocked on the door. "Did you call me? I couldn't hear what you said."

"Sorry, Maggie," she shouted above the noise of the spraying water. "I'm fine…just talking to myself."

"More like yelling to yourself!" Maggie hollered back. "Glad you're okay."

Things weren't fine. Foreboding tingled up Arianna's spine.

When she stepped out of the shower, cool air hit hard. Goosebumps covered her skin.

Chapter Twenty-Three

While Ari was at the baby shower, Christopher took the opportunity to do some reconnaissance work at the Somers' Denver residence. Until he'd moved to Pueblo, he'd kept an eye on the home, but never saw anyone coming or going.

Four years. It had been four years since he'd seen his mother. Four years since he'd seen Sarah or Joshua. He hoped they hadn't forgotten him. That is, if he ever actually saw them again.

He squared his shoulders, determined that not seeing his family couldn't be an option, even if it was just through a window. If Father were around, there'd be no going in; he'd not risk their lives. But he had to know how they were faring—especially after the terrifying glimpse he'd gotten from Sarah's journal.

Keeping out of sight, he watched the house closely for any sign of life. When nothing came of that, he left his car parked down the road and crept around the house for a closer look.

He peered through the windows until finally spotting movement. He had to squint through bars crisscrossing the pane to finally see—Mother. She appeared to be alone in the room, folding laundry. Sudden tears stung his eyes.

Oh, how life had changed for her—for all of them. Images of his mother dangling clothes from a rope tied between two trees to dry, or in inclement weather, hung from the fireplace mantel in London, made him melancholy. On impulse, he lifted his sleeve to his nose, wishing to breathe in the smoky scent of their old home, but instead, the cloth smelled of flowery laundry detergent. He frowned and dropped his arm.

The urgency to make contact forced his thoughts back to the present. He gently tapped on the glass, careful not to alert the rest of the house, primarily his father, of his presence.

His mother startled, and her head jerked up, her eyes wild with fear. Then, as recognition set in, her features softened, and her eyes filled with tears. She dropped the shirt she'd been folding and sprinted to the window. "Christopher! You're here!" she said loudly.

"Shh, Mother, we do not want Father to hear."

"It's all right, son, your father went to Pueblo yesterday and isn't returning until tonight."

His tense shoulders dropped, and he breathed a sigh of relief. "Then may I come in?"

"Did you notice the bars on the doors? Your father doesn't trust us when he's away. We are locked in here."

Christopher felt the blood drain from his face. So, it was true—his family had been, and was still being held captive in their own home.

"Mother, I am a police officer. If I cannot get the door open, I know others who can."

The expression on her face didn't give him much confidence. She shrugged. "Do what you can, but we've tried every possible way to get out, and nothing has worked."

He wasted no time scuttling to the front of the house. The lock was obviously designed to keep the family in more than to keep strangers out. His jaw clenched and unclenched as he worked the lock free.

He pushed the door open, and his mother had her arms around him in seconds. Her grip suggested she might never let him go. Christopher felt the same. Finally, she took a step back and looked at her son. "I cannot believe you are here. Your father convinced us you were dead." She began to weep.

Christopher glanced around for a handkerchief. When one was handed to him, he looked over and his breath caught. "Sarah? You've gotten so tall—and beautiful." He pulled her into his arms. She, too, dissolved in tears.

Joshua, his gangly sixteen-year-old brother, also appeared and tugged on his arm. "Hi, Chris." He sniffed and averted his watery eyes. Christopher smiled at his brother's attempt to remain calm around the crying women.

The three of them managed a path to the living room, where Beatrice nudged him into a recliner. The family gathered on chairs and the floor around him. Although the modern home couldn't be more than a decade old, it smelled of candle wax.

He relished the reunion with his family. Beneath their smiles, however, he sensed an undercurrent of fear.

"I must get you all out of here."

"No, Christopher." His mother was adamant. "Where would we go? Your father has made sure that we have no way to survive without him. We would have no means of support, no home and, except for what we have seen on the television"—she motioned to the screen on the wall—"we know little of this modern age."

"I'd take care of you," Christopher said.

Mother shook her head. "Your father would find us and kill us all. You do not know what he is capable of, Chris."

"I think I do," he responded more to himself than his mother.

"We would be going from this"—she gestured to her surroundings—"to a, what is it you are living in?"

"A one-bedroom apartment," he said.

"Yes, to living as prisoners in a small apartment, never daring to step out of doors in fear of your father. It would only be a matter of time until he located us. Then we'd all face the consequences."

Christopher wondered what those consequences would be. He'd seen Father lift a hand to his siblings, but to Mother?

"A safe house, then. Father can't hurt you if he can't find you. There's no way I'm leaving without you. Sarah, Josh collect your belongings."

Mother shook her head and rose an arm to stop Sarah and Joshua. "We're trying to remain anonymous; keep hidden, Chris. None of us have identification. We are considered illegal aliens here."

"Mother, we'll work around that. I must insist!" He punched some numbers on his phone, then began a conversation with someone at the police station in Denver. "This is Officer Flemming." Since he'd worked as an officer in Denver, he knew several of the employees there.

After a brief conversation with the Denver police chief, he hung up the phone. "There's a statewide cocaine bust happening right now—a huge drug ring is coming down." He should have remembered that. It affected Pueblo, too. "The safehouses are bursting at the seams. With the proper papers, they could squeeze you in, but I'm afraid it's like you said, without identification…" He shrugged, exasperated. "I've got to get you out of here!"

"The house in Pueblo will be ready soon enough, son. Put your efforts into rescuing us from there. At least he leaves us alone—mostly." She touched her head, probably absentmindedly, but Christopher didn't miss it.

He left the recliner, walked to the chair his mother occupied and pushed her hair back, revealing an ugly gash. "What happened, Mother?" His eyebrows drew together, and a lump clogged his throat.

When she didn't speak, Sarah did. "Father threw her across the room. That's what happened. And check beneath her sleeves." Her tone bit through to Christopher's heart.

He gently lifted his mother's sleeves. Ugly welts in the shape of his father's beefy fingers rose and fell in hideous shades of greenish purple. He choked out a sob as he pulled his mother into his embrace. "I'm so sorry," he whispered. "I've spent the last four years puzzling out ways to protect you from that monster. I have failed."

Still clutching her son, she said, "The only person who has truly failed us is your father. You are lucky to be alive, son."

He cleared his throat and turned to Joshua. "Were you there when this happened?"

Joshua dropped his head and stared at his feet. "I—I was not in the room at the time. But I came as soon as I heard Mother cry. I helped clean her wound." Christopher's heart went out to Joshua, but he desperately needed to know someone would protect the family in his absence.

Sarah shook her head. Christopher read the disappointment written across her face. "Josh is good at hiding from Father."

Joshua stood up as if to challenge his sister. "If he hurts Mother again, I swear I'll kill him!" His face reddened as he pounded a fist to the wall.

Sarah rolled her eyes. "Those are big words coming from you, Josh."

Their mother stepped between them. "Stop this! Your brother is here with us now. Please do not waste this time squabbling." She sniffled, then directed her attention to Christopher. "We have been isolated so long, I fear we have lost some of our civility."

"No, no, I must apologize," Christopher said. "Joshua is sixteen, still just a boy." He pulled Josh in for a brief hug. "Sorry I barked at you." Then looked back at his mother. "What you have endured"—he motioned to the others—"what you *all* have endured is unimaginable. We must make a plan. How can we communicate?"

The room fell silent.

His mother wrung her hands. "I can think of nothing. Letters would surely be intercepted by your father."

"What about this: I'll give you my phone. You can use it when Father is away." Christopher shoved his cell phone into his mother's hands.

She dropped it as if it had scorched her, then shook her head. "If your father found it he would harm all of us, then hunt you down and kill you. Please, Chris, if you are living in Pueblo now, try to catch your father doing something illegal, and let the law do the rest. And whatever you do, don't let him discover you. It is best if he thinks you have perished, or at least forgotten about us."

Christopher let out a frustrated breath. He sorely wished to remove his family from their home but couldn't think of any arguments to change his mother's mind. "Well then, I guess we have a couple of hours to spend together before I must leave you to your prison." He nearly spat out the words. His expression softened when he saw the hurt on his mother's face. "I am truly sorry, Mother. Now I know why my efforts to communicate with—or even see you—have failed. Please understand, it was not for lack of trying."

His mother hugged him fiercely. "Son, after the way things ended between you and your father, I am just so happy that you are well."

"I promise I will set you free from that man, once you are in Pueblo—even if I have to die doing so." Anger flashed in Christopher's eyes. He felt his mother shudder in his arms. He took a calming breath. "Why is he there now, anyway? And where is the..." He couldn't find the right words because he had never seen the apparatus which transported his family from the early 1800s to the twenty-first century.

"Device?" his mother asked. "That is what we call it."

"Yes, then, the device. Where is it?"

"It is in the house in Pueblo. Your father uses it when he goes there without us."

Cold dread pulsed through Christopher's veins. Suppose Arianna found the device, looked too closely and began asking questions about it? Or if Father discovered Christopher's emotional attachment to Arianna and used that as leverage, and the device as a weapon. Or what if he used the device not knowing Arianna was on the premises? If she were discovered, he'd show no mercy. Christopher swallowed his fears for now and listened as his mother continued.

"He never tells me anything specific, but I'm certain he travels to different times and places, committing crimes that make him rich. Crimes for which he will never be held accountable. He has become a monster."

Christopher nodded. "I will stop him."

Chapter Twenty-Four

"Have you ever seen such cute sneakers? They're so tiny." Maggie dangled a pair of baby Nikes in front of Arianna.

"Ooh, and look at the adorable bath set, complete with a teensy robe and a rubber ducky." Ari squeezed the duck, which made a squeaky noise.

"You girls are having too much fun in there." Ari squelched a laugh as she heard Tasha bang a dish on the counter in the kitchen.

"Sorry, Tasha." She gave Maggie a guilty look. "I'm coming in to help you clean. I just can't get over the cuteness of all these baby gifts." She stood up at the same time Tasha rounded the corner.

"I'm coming to help, too." Maggie began to struggle out of the recliner.

"You'll do no such thing." Tasha stood in front of Maggie with her hands on her hips. "I'm the one who threw this shower, and it would have been in my home if we weren't in the middle of a remodel. Therefore, I will be the one to clean up."

"Natasha Tate, just because you order us around at work does not give you the right to boss me around in my home." Maggie tried to appear stern as she attempted once more to raise herself from the chair.

"Sit down, Maggie." Arianna gently nudged her back into the seat. "We've got this. You just relax and admire all the fun gifts you received today—especially that gift over there that your two best friends gave you." She winked.

"You mean that big ol' stroller? What am I ever going to do with something that clunky." A teasing grin spread across Maggie's face.

"Ahem"—Ari, hands on her hips, tapped her foot—"it's not just a stroller, it's a travel system—stroller, car seat, baby carrier—all in one. Your baby will be the envy of all the infants in the neighborhood." Ari lobbed a throw pillow at Maggie as she and Tasha left the room to clean the kitchen.

Ari picked up a dishtowel and began wiping the plates Tasha had just washed. It felt good to be with her friends again. Maggie was like a sister to her—sassy and fun. Then there was Tasha who filled the empty spot in Ari's heart left by her deceased mother. She thought how elegant and graceful she was, even while she washed dishes. Plus, Tasha's compassionate nature was exactly what Ari needed in a mother figure.

She adored Natasha—or Tasha to all who knew her. Her flawless dark skin, so different than the pallor of her husband, Reese Johnson. Ari often wondered how it was the two got together—first as business partners, then as husband and wife. Reese Johnson, a crusty, middle-aged architect with a massive amount of talent, had little charm, while Tasha—the very picture of fashion—brimmed with personality. Not a match made in heaven, but it seemed to work.

"How is your project going in Pueblo? I'm anxious to get out there and see what you've done." Tasha pulled Ari out of her musings.

Arianna gave her a thoughtful look as scenes from the nightmare she'd had the night before replayed in her mind.

"Ari, is something wrong?" Tasha put the last dish away, took off the apron she'd been wearing, and gave Arianna her full attention.

"Oh"—she shrugged—"no. I'm sorry. I don't know where my head was just now. The project's going well—I hope, that is. I don't get much feedback from the Somers. Mr. Somers is…" She let her voice trail off, not knowing how to describe the man. Should she tell Tasha about his volatile explosions?

"He's what, Ari? Is there something I need to know?"

Like the fact that he's an egomaniac who can't torture me enough with his outbursts at work, so he threatens me during my dreams?

"Ari?"

"No. He's just temperamental. That's all."

Tasha didn't look convinced. She narrowed her eyes. Then glanced at the clock. "Oh, dear. It's later than I realized." She wiped her hands and smoothed her skirt. "Ari, if you ever feel the need to be pulled off the job for any reason, don't hesitate to speak up. It's got to be tough working out there alone."

"It's not that bad. I'll be fine, but thanks."

"I'm sure with your talent, it is shaping up nicely." She patted Ari on the arm. "Thanks for the help with the shower. I wish I could stick around, but I've got to run." She gave Ari a quick peck on the cheek.

Arianna and Maggie put their feet up to relax, once everyone was gone.

"Finally. Now tell me how you're feeling. I've worried about you all day," Maggie said.

Alarmed, Ari sat straight up and looked at her. "I'm so sorry. Did I make your baby shower awkward? It really was a lovely party."

"Don't be ridiculous. You're the queen of hiding your feelings. The party was perfect. I just know that nightmare you had affected you. Ari, you were screaming in the shower!"

Heat spread through Ari's body. She ducked her head. "It's hard for me to not dwell on it, Maggie. Mr. Somers is crazy."

"Do you think he's capable of hurting you?"

"No. Well…I guess I don't know what he's capable of, but I don't plan on giving him a reason to bother me." She forced herself to smile at Maggie. She didn't want to talk about the madman she worked for any longer. She wished to forget work the rest of the day and anticipate an evening out with the handsome Christopher Flemming. "Can we talk about something else?"

Maggie squeezed her hand, obviously sensing her discomfort. "What are you wearing for our double-date tonight?"

Ari blew out a breath of relief. "I brought my red dress. The one you always say is your favorite."

"Perfect! You look fabulous in that dress—super sexy." Her eyes sparkled with mischief. "If that doesn't get Christopher's blood steaming, then he's simply not human." She pumped her brows as Ari's face heated.

****

Anticipation made Arianna nervous. She felt like she was getting ready for a ball. She examined herself in the mirror. Maggie was right—the dress accentuated her figure perfectly, and the color brought out the pink in her cheeks. She'd swept her hair up, leaving several loose tendrils to frame her face. "Well, here I go, ready or not."

Christopher arrived, and Arianna sucked in a breath. There he stood in a dark suit strikingly handsome. Ari didn't know what to say. Her heart skipped a beat. Well, at least *her* blood was steaming.

He seemed to be rooted in the doorway, his eyes making an appraisal of her. His lips parted in a silent "Ah."

Maggie beamed, as if she were a proud parent. "All right, you two, stand together. I want to take your picture—kind of like high school, when you went to the prom."

Christopher's head tilted in question.

"What? Didn't your mom make you do this before school dances?"

Ari intercepted the question, moving in near Christopher. "Things may have been different for him in England."

Christopher gave Ari a grateful smile and put his arm around her, pulling her intimately close. Currents of electricity collided in her chest. Oh boy, she was in trouble. She willed her heartbeat to slow down. Nope. It wouldn't listen—not with this handsome man leaning into her.

Maggie lifted her phone camera and snapped a few shots. "You both look amazing, but I guess we should get going if we want to make our reservation." She turned toward her bedroom and hollered, "Jason, it's time to go."

Christopher bent his head toward Ari's. "You're stunning," he whispered, tickling her ear and sending tingles to her toes all over again. He smelled spicy-fresh and Ari wished to close her eyes and relish in his scent.

The couples splurged on an expensive restaurant, The Palace Arms. "After all," Maggie said, "this will most likely be the last time Jason and I go out on the town without a baby in tow."

As they were being led to their table by the maître d', Ari noticed the romantic ambience of the restaurant. Soft music played in the background, and sparkling chandeliers cast low beams over the polished silverware, elegant, crystal glassware and hand-painted china expertly set upon crisp, white tablecloths. Delicate aromas of fresh-baked rolls and Middle Eastern spices wafted through the room. Patrons in formal evening dress sat on tufted burgundy chairs, and a murmur of subdued voices mingled with the romantic ballads which had enticed several couples onto the dance floor.

Arianna observed how Christopher fit in—as if he'd known Maggie and Jason all his life. Everyone seemed happy to be there. And the food tasted delicious—higher priced than what Ari cared to pay, but Christopher insisted this was a date and it would be rude for her to look at the prices. What a perfect evening. Arianna sighed contentedly.

As the dishes were cleared, Christopher stood and held his hand out to her. "May I have this dance, Arianna?"

She had taken a ballroom dance class in college and was a pretty good dancer, but she never expected Christopher—a police officer, no less—to want to dance. "I'd be delighted." She took his hand, which he tucked into the crook of his arm, and let him lead her onto the dance floor.

Ari was amazed at how ramrod straight Christopher stood, yet how gracefully he danced. "How is it that you are such a good dancer, Christopher? I really didn't picture you as the dancing type." She smiled up at his handsome face.

"Oh, I do believe there are many things you don't know about me." His eyes twinkled.

Electric currents pulsed through her. Dancing so close, she could smell his musky scent. She had to concentrate to get the steps right.

"Growing up in England, dancing was not optional. We all had to learn certain dances," he said.

"Let me guess, like the quadrille, uh, minuet and the reel?" She teasingly recited most of the dances she'd read about in her romance books. By the surprised expression on Christopher's face, she realized it was no joke.

"You know those dances?"

"As I said before, I read a lot of historical fiction." Should she mention the romance part? Nah. He didn't need to know that. "But surely you weren't required to learn such archaic dances as those, were you?"

He looked thoughtful before speaking. "Let us just say that I attended an old-fashioned school." He then cut the conversation short by dipping, then spinning her.

After dancing to a few songs and loving every minute in Christopher's arms, Ari glanced around to see they were the only couple still on the once-crowded dance floor. Everyone else had moved to the perimeter and all eyes were on them. The temperature in the room kicked up a few degrees—or was it just her? "Look around," she whispered to Christopher, nodding toward the crowd. His eyes widened, observing their growing audience. She thought he'd feel as embarrassed as she did, but he surprised her. When the dance ended, he stepped back and took Ari's hand and kissed her fingers, then bowed to the on-lookers who were applauding his chivalry. "Show off," she said as he gave her a sly wink and escorted her from the dance floor.

"I wonder if this is what it was like to dance at a ball in the nineteenth century." Ari nodded shyly as couples continued to clap.

"No. This is much better. It would have caused a scandal to dance so long with the same partner back then."

Ari arched her eyebrows, surprised.

"All part of British history," he quickly added.

"You two were stunning out there," Maggie said as they reclaimed their seats.

"Yeah, Christopher, you're making me look bad," said Jason. "I couldn't even attempt to do what you just did. And Ari, my wife would slap me if I told you how good you looked out there. You're a lucky man, Chris." Jason gave Maggie a sidelong glance. Maggie nudged his shoulder playfully.

Christopher squeezed Ari's hand, smiled, and accepted the praise graciously.

The conversation continued comfortably with all joining in. No one seemed to want to break the spell as they visited for hours around the restaurant table. Finally, Maggie yawned. "I guess I'm going to have to be the one who spoils the fun. I don't think I can keep my eyes open any longer."

"Come on, young lady," Jason teased. "Let's get you home." He helped his pregnant wife to her feet, and the rest followed behind.

When they arrived at the home of Maggie and Jason, Christopher said his goodbyes and turned as if to leave. Maggie grabbed his arm. "Jason and I are headed to bed, but you are welcome to stay if you'd like."

Arianna realized that, as often as she and Christopher had been together, until tonight it had never been in a "date" situation—unless she counted the picnic in the park. Her heartbeat quickened, and her nerves jangled. She doubted Christopher wanted to stay. She held her breath and tried unsuccessfully to make eye contact with Maggie.

But before anxiety completely took over, Christopher thanked Maggie for the offer, and she and Jason headed to bed. He took Ari by the arm, ushering her to the loveseat, where he sat close to her.

"If you are not too tired, Arianna, I would love to stay a while. After all, you've had Maggie to talk to all day, and I only have an apartment—a beautifully decorated apartment, I might add—to return to." He gave her one of his heart-stopping winks.

"Of course," she said, pretending to be nonchalant about the most gorgeous man in the world sitting so close to her. The smell of his spicy-fresh cologne awakened her senses, making it hard for her to think straight. He rested a hand on her leg, sending a heat wave through her body. Almost involuntarily she moved a little closer to breathe him in.

"I had nice time tonight." He pulled her hand into his. "You are an excellent dancer."

"Me? I think we can agree that you were the main attraction on the dance floor."

He shrugged. "You were the only one I was looking at." He moved his hand up her arm drawing little circles at the top. Heat followed his touch.

Her heart thudded erratically, making it difficult to converse. She focused on his tie, not wanting him to see the desire in her eyes.

He moved closer and ran feather-light fingers up her neck. "Arianna?" He gently lifted her face and gazed into her eyes. Tingles ran up and down her spine, warming her all over. His velvety-smooth voice gave her goosebumps.

She didn't respond, just looked into his intense, blue eyes.

"Arianna," he said again, in a near whisper. "You are so beautiful. How did I get so lucky to spend the evening with the prettiest girl in Colorado?" His gaze dropped to her lips.

He tilted her face gently toward his, and put an arm around her back, pulling her to him, lowering his head. His lips found hers and he gave her a slow kiss. Ari's stomach flipped in rapid somersaults. She'd waited so long for this, and it was everything she'd imagined. His warm kiss stole her breath. His musky scent was heady.

As he pulled away, she snaked an arm around his neck, inviting him back for more. He accepted the invitation, deepening the kiss this time. Passion took over where good sense once resided.

After several minutes, a clock chimed, breaking the spell. Christopher drew back and held her gaze for just another moment, caressing her cheek, before he released her.

There were no words. Arianna could think of nothing to say after that, even if she dared try to speak—which she didn't.

He stood and said in a husky voice, "I do believe I should take my leave now, before I am tempted to completely ravish you." Longing lingered in his eyes.

Arianna walked him to the door, gave him one more sweet kiss, then whispered goodbye. She closed the door behind him and sank to the floor. Her fingers absently touched her lips as her heart continued to thud in her chest.

She'd see him tomorrow. Would there be another kiss? *I think I'll die if there isn't.*

Chapter Twenty-Five

It was difficult to think straight with Ari's scent surrounding him. Christopher wished she was still with him, but that couldn't happen. He wouldn't risk ruining things with her—especially now that he knew with certainty where the device was hidden—somewhere at Ari's jobsite. He heaved a heavy sigh. Still, leaving her had been unimaginably difficult. He congratulated himself for the restraint he'd shown. Walking away from her before things heated out of control was the right thing to do, he told himself. Why did he feel so lonely?

He lay in the queen-size bed at her apartment—her bed, lost in thought. The day had been a roller coaster ride of emotions. First, he'd been elated to finally see his mother and siblings. He'd feared four years of absence might cause memories of him to fade—or worse, blacken, with Father brainwashing them. He'd been gratefully wrong, but also devastated to observe their situation. How did any father treat his family that way? Pent-up anger from earlier in the day began to creep back into his heart. Now the urgency and his determination to expose his father's crimes and have him put away—away from his family and away from society—grew even greater. He just couldn't work out how this could be done. He must find the device.

Then, seeing Arianna dressed for their dinner date—she had been a vision—served as an instant balm to his troubled heart. Even now, thoughts of her calmed his anger and soothed him once more. She was the most beautiful woman he had ever known. And those kisses. He blew out a breath. They were everything he'd imagined they would be and more. He'd wanted to kiss her for so long but had held back knowing once he started down that path it might end in heartache for both of them. But with Ari sitting so close and smelling so sweet, he'd no longer been able to restrain himself. If it was a mistake, it was a mistake he'd like to make again and again. He smiled as he drifted off to sleep.

The following morning, after many hugs and promises of a return visit as soon as Maggie's labor began, Christopher helped Ari into the car and they headed back to Pueblo.

He glanced over at her several times, worried she might feel awkward about the intimacy of the previous evening, but she seemed radiantly happy. He felt the same exuberance. Appraising her, he thought she was every bit as desirable in a T-shirt and jeans as she'd been in her dress.

She looked at him with a question in her eyes. He patted the seat closer to him. She snuggled in.

With his arm around her shoulders, he fingered her golden curls, set free of the hairdo from their enchanted evening. Her scent tickled his nose, tempting him to pull the car over and have a repeat of the night before. He resisted but lifted her hand to his mouth and pressed a kiss on her fingers. Her full pink lips curved into a smile that melted his heart.

They traveled along in a companionable silence, only making idle chit chat when it suited. She laid her head on his shoulder and intertwined her fingers with his. He silently pledged to stay near her—protect her. After all, her safety was at risk because of his father. Only Christopher knew the dangers threatening to befall her. The device was at her worksite. Knowing this only intensified his urgency to save her from harm. She needed him. He glanced at her face, bathed in sunlight from morning rays penetrating the window—beautiful. Or, perhaps it was he who needed her.

The stakes had ratcheted up. He'd have to play his cards with care in order to find the device and guard this beautiful woman next to him.

****

Torrential rains hit the windshield as Christopher made his way to Ari's apartment Monday morning. He pressed the gas a little harder. Ari couldn't be late. She'd mentioned the numerous deliveries scheduled to arrive today. He could only imagine the trouble she'd go to, ensuring the floors stayed clean and damage-free on a day like this. Her attitude wouldn't reflect it, though. The only time he'd seen her noticeably stressed about her work had been last Friday. And that was a direct result of his father's presence.

He shuddered thinking about Father being in the home with her. He knew it couldn't be prevented; she was his employee, at present. But without the exact knowledge of the machine's whereabouts…Christopher couldn't find it fast enough.

When Ari opened the door, he had an umbrella open wide to keep her dry. "You are the ultimate gentleman, sir." She tucked her arm through his. "I hope my car is fixed soon so I won't require a taxi—or, squad car—service much longer. Although I am developing a fondness for the devilishly handsome chauffeur." Her twinkling eyes met his gaze. His heart thudded. Beautiful.

He'd take her to work every day if she needed it. "You should know by now, my dear, that I enjoy driving you to work. Would you like me call Dave's to see if your car is repaired?"

She stared at him for a moment, as if contemplating. Her wide eyes, so trusting. He must protect her. She was fast becoming precious to him. "If you have time, that would be great. I didn't know how I would call without cell phone service at work. How'd I get so lucky?" She raised up on her toes and kissed him on the cheek as she ran a hand along the dark scruff of his jaw, sending a jolt of electricity through his body. He caught her hand and pulled her in for a kiss.

Yes, her kisses were delicious. He hadn't just dreamed it. The sparks igniting beneath her touch threatened to burn him. "We'd better get you to work, unless you'd rather do this all day," he said against her lips.

"I choose this." She kissed him once more. "Unfortunately, I have many men who want me today." She held up a folder marked "Deliveries." Her eyes sparkled. "And I'm sure you'd be missed, as well. Pueblo, Colorado, can't do without one of its finest."

When they arrived at the Somers' house, Ari ordered him to stay put. "I've got my running shoes on and will make it to the door in seconds. Besides, I can hear on the police scanner that you are needed, so get to work."

He squirmed. He'd heard the chatter on the radio as well, but sorely needed to search her worksite for a certain time-traveling machine. A machine, that if she found first, could get her into a lot of trouble. How could he leave when it meant she might be in danger?

Chapter Twenty-Six

"Wipe your feet!—please." All morning Ari had been telling men with wet, muddy boots to take care not to bring it into the house with them, but they either didn't listen, or didn't care. She gave up and scribbled a frustrated note to tape on the front door, adding the "please" as an afterthought. Most likely, they weren't intentionally messing up the floors. She sighed and ripped a piece of tape from the dispenser.

After attaching the note to the door, she hurried to readjust the plastic coverings on the floors before the next truck was due to arrive. Most of the floors were hardwood, or stone, but carpet lay here and there, and of course there was that expensive Persian rug in the study. The carpet would be difficult to clean; hardwood attracted sharp and jagged objects; and the stone, which had been polished to a brilliant shine, threatened to dull under the workmen's boots. The Persian rug—well, Ari hated the thought of it even being walked on, let alone muddied. Therefore, plastic runners covered every surface the workmen could possibly access.

A knock at the door after everything had finally quieted down brought Arianna to the realization that her busy day had come to an end, and Christopher had arrived to collect her. Before she made it across the room to let him in, he'd already entered. A sight for very tired and sore eyes.

"Oh, Christopher. Thank you again for coming." She walked into his open arms. "You are just what I need right now."

He held her back to look at her. "Rough day?"

She nodded. "There should be a 'no deliveries on rainy days' rule somewhere."

He chuckled and pulled her close again. She breathed in his musky cologne and sighed, relishing the moment. Being in his arms melted her cares away. He kissed her, and a few more muscle kinks smoothed out, leaving her relaxed but wanting more. She could get used to this.

Clearing her throat, she motioned to the open rooms behind her. "At least it has been productive. Do you want to see the progress we have made?"

"I would love to."

She took him by the hand and led him from room to room, giving a commentary on each piece of new furniture or accessory.

"How much longer until the project is done?" he asked. She noticed genuine curiosity and concern in his eyes.

"It's hard to say. I've only shown you four rooms, and they aren't complete yet, and there are so many more rooms to fill. I'd guess at least a couple of months still. Why? Are you ready to be rid of me?" she teased.

"Of course not. I just really don't like you working out here alone."

"Oh, that again. Well, if you'd been here earlier, you would have noticed that I am anything but alone. Or did you think I carried all this furniture in by myself?" She flexed her biceps.

The crease in Christopher's forehead flattened and his lips tugged into a smile. "I guess you're right. May I walk around and check out the rest of the house?"

"Sure. I'll start gathering my supplies while you wander."

When Ari had finished organizing her belongings, she went in search of him. She was surprised to see him going through the rooms so thoroughly. Most people would just take a peek into an empty room, but he was inspecting every nook and cranny. She didn't approach him, but rather observed him for some time before finally asking, "May I help you find something?"

Startled, he tried to act nonchalant, but still had a determined look in his eyes.

Something nagged at her. The house. It was this house again. It seemed to hold so many secrets for a home that had yet to be occupied. A chill made its way down her spine.

"Christopher." She said it loudly enough to demand his full attention. And she got it. "Come sit down for a bit."

He glanced back at the empty room as if he were reluctant to give up his self-guided tour but followed Arianna to the living room and sat next to her on one of the new, plastic-covered sofas.

Giving him an appraising look, she asked, "What is it about this house that interests you, and even seems to spook you so much?" She kept her voice gentle and earnest.

"What do you mean?"

"Every time you enter this house, you become a different person. I know the owners are a little odd, eccentric, and maybe even a bit crazy, but what's that to you? You appeared to be searching for something you'd lost just now—in a completely empty room." She realized her voice had begun to rise the more she spoke, so she stopped and waited for an answer.

He seemed to be weighing his thoughts before he finally broke the silence. "You are correct; this house holds a mystery I need to discover. It is—it's just—" He blew out a deep breath. "I just can't—"

"Can't what?"

"Ari, there are things you don't know about me. Things—" He shook his head. "There is too much at stake here." His expression turned stony.

She glanced around the room and narrowed her eyes. "Too much at stake here in this house? What is it you're not telling me?"

"I can't—"

"You can't or you won't?"

His brows furrowed. "Both. You wouldn't believe me even if I could explain." He stood.

Arianna didn't know whether to be more irritated or hurt by Christopher's confession. This house was her project, not his mystery. She couldn't let it go at that.

"What are you talking about? What is this secret?"

Christopher said nothing.

"I've been here all these weeks working my heart out to make this house into the castle some madman wants. It's a brand-new home, and I've seen every corner of it. If there's a mystery, I think I should know about it. So please, Chris, what is it?"

He turned toward the door, making it clear he did not wish to continue the conversation. But Ari didn't move. She had no intention of leaving it there. She needed to get to the bottom of his Jekyll-Hyde behavior. "So?" She stood but remained planted next to the sofa.

"There are things *you do not know*." He said each word with emphasis, then gave her a look that warned her to not press forward.

But press forward she did. "Then please— enlighten me." She took her voice down to a near whisper, biting back the frustration which had built to a near explosion in her heart—especially after the romantic weekend they'd just spent together in Denver.

Christopher paced, pain scribbled on his face. "We must leave now. There is nothing more that I wish to talk about." He marched toward the front door.

She followed. "That's it, then? No explanation?" She felt a mental slap to the face. It stung. "You could at least say the house is haunted, or something like that, except you know it's not. No one has occupied this house. What mystery could possibly reside here that drives you to distraction every time you walk through that door?" She jabbed her finger in the air.

He nudged her through the very door she had pointed to—clearly done with the argument. Ari stumbled over the sill. She looked back to see Christopher focused on his car. He said nothing.

She'd hit a nerve—what it was, she had no idea. She wanted to remind him of the wonderful time they'd had in Denver and how close she'd felt to him, but the door firmly closed on any further conversation when Christopher slammed it shut behind her. Tears welled in her eyes. This was not the man she was falling in love with. This man had secrets, and secrets hurt. "I can't do this, Christopher." She stopped to face him.

"I should have never let it go this far." His voice sounded flat—emotionless.

Arianna shook her head, incensed. "I'm sorry you feel that way. You don't have to worry about it going any farther." She hurried ahead and climbed into the car, wishing for any other way to get home.

She kept her head turned for the duration of the ride; she wouldn't give him the satisfaction of seeing her tears, but she couldn't quiet the sobs bubbling up from her throat.

Christopher gently laid a handkerchief on her lap, letting his hand linger for a moment. She wanted to both swat it away and cling to it for dear life. No. A life with Christopher was not an option. He'd made that painfully clear.

She watched her phone. The second they crossed into cell phone service range, she punched some buttons. "Stop the car."

"But we're still miles from your apartment."

"I've ordered an Uber—one service this small town *does* have!" She was out of the vehicle before it had fully stopped, then hustled across the street.

Christopher's car never moved. He watched, his face expressionless, until the Uber arrived.

As Ari pulled up to her apartment, the first thing she saw was her red Subaru parked out in front. What had Christopher done? The repair estimate had been over a thousand bucks. She'd have to somehow pay him back. But how? After the way he'd treated her this evening, she never wanted to see him again.

Chapter Twenty-Seven

Christopher closed the door to his own lonely apartment and collapsed on the sofa. He buried his head in his hands and groaned. "What have I done? What have I done?" The whispered question tortured him.

A folded paper tumbled from his pocket and landed on the floor between his feet. He'd found a new restaurant near the auto shop while picking up Arianna's car. Certain she would like the food there, he'd taken a menu to surprise and treat her to supper. Peering down at it, happy diners stared back at him. He gave the menu a swift kick.

Evening shadows dimmed the room, but he made no effort to turn on the lights. Darkness gave him cover—a false cover, yet a cover just the same. He could hide from so many things, such as the way he'd just treated Arianna. *Perhaps I am more like my father than I am willing to admit.* He scowled.

Thinking about his father ignited a fire in his soul. Anger mingled with despair as he rose and began to pace the room. What was he to do? He paused as if listening for an answer. He'd not only lost access to the house that he'd needed so desperately—he'd surely lost Arianna.

He'd tried but failed miserably to nudge away the feelings he'd known were growing for her, but he could deny them no more. He loved her. The hurt in her eyes had burned a hole in his heart. *And I could not explain any of it—she wouldn't have believed me if I'd tried. I should have tried.*

The room had fully darkened. He looked around with wild eyes until they fell on a candlestick. One of the few remaining items he'd brought in his satchel from two hundred years ago. He felt his way through the blackness for a match and lit the candle. The burning wax smelled of nineteenth century England. He placed it on the table and pulled his chair close. Suppertime had come and gone, but his appetite had vanished back at the Somers' house, along with Arianna's smile. Instead of eating, he spent the next hour watching the flame dance, transporting him to a happier time and place. Still, mocking shadows cast on the walls and ceiling—dark and foreboding—fought for space in his memories. Dark memories of the past fought against bright memories of his time with Ari.

Who was he kidding? He'd never been happier than when he'd held her in his arms. He angrily pinched the flame on the candle, snuffing out the light, and made his way to bed. "I need to make this right."

****

Tuesday morning rainclouds still hovered, fitting for Christopher's mood. He thought of all the work Arianna had gone to the day before to keep the floors from being damaged. The floors at his family's house; the floors at her work project; the floors he'd never be welcome to walk again.

He sat in his squad car a full hour earlier than necessary. He'd been transporting Arianna to and from work for over a week, but now he had time to spare.

The slight scent of her perfume still hung in the air. He breathed in deeply, wishing to cling to it.

His phone buzzed, signaling a text. He grabbed it, hopeful it would be from Ari.

The text read, *You have been entered into a drawing to win dinner for two*. His eyes jumped to the end. Ironic. It was from the restaurant he'd planned to take her last night before he messed everything up. He tossed the phone onto the seat beside him. He thought about picking it up again and texting her, but then he spied the handkerchief he'd given her to wipe her tears laying on the floor of the car. And he was the one who had put those tears there. Abandoning the idea, he drove to work early.

Christopher spent the rest of the week feeling helpless and hopeless. How could he possibly catch his father doing something illegal if he couldn't get into the house to uncover his secret? Break in? No. Having seen the alarm system arming the house, he knew he'd never get away with it. Not to mention, getting caught as a police officer would not only get him kicked off the force, he'd also face jail time.

Add to that his worry for Arianna. He hated the thought of her ever being exposed to such a vile person as his father—his critical eye appraising her careful work—the thought repulsed him. He didn't think Father would physically harm Ari, but now, knowing a little more about what Father was up to, he felt uneasy. She might stumble upon something she shouldn't. His blood ran cold at the possibility.

Chapter Twenty-Eight

Arianna went through the motions at the Somers' house. Immersing herself in her work had once been rewarding, but now, with nothing to look forward to at the end of each day—no ride home with Christopher—her life felt empty.

On several evenings, she had the urge to call him and apologize—to just be done with the hollow feeling in her heart. Then the realization that she had nothing to apologize for quieted the urge. Try as she might, she couldn't erase Christopher's angry face as he'd rushed her out the door of the house that had somehow come between them.

He'd been using her to get to the house—for whatever reason. He probably never cared for her at all. Doubts infected her. Then there were the kisses. Her heartbeat accelerated just thinking about his warm lips on hers. He'd kissed her with so much tender emotion. Of course, he had to be convincing. So many failed relationships marched through her mind. Hadn't she sworn off men like Christopher?

The weeks dragged on. Mr. Somers came alone again on Friday for the fourth week in a row. Sometimes he'd hole up in his office, saying little to her. Other weeks his glares and harsh criticisms created palpable tension. One misstep and she was sure he'd fire her. Why he disliked her so, she didn't know.

Worst of all was the dark cloud that followed him, as if surrounded by a crowd of demons. She wished the other family members had come so she might have an opportunity to speak with Sarah—if she could get her alone. Thoughts of the girl's journal still lingered in the back of her mind, and they were disturbing. She hadn't forgotten Mr. Somers' threat, but didn't care. She worried for Sarah and felt that somehow the journal connected Christopher to the Somers' house, although she couldn't figure out how that could be. The anguish on his face when he'd read it still haunted her.

****

"Tasha!" Ari's frown instantly turned into a huge grin as her boss arrived and pulled her into her arms for a warm hug.

"This looks amazing!" Tasha held Ari back and her gaze danced around the Somers' house. "Give me the tour."

After nearly three weeks of moping, Arianna was more than grateful for her boss's timely visit. She brought welcome encouragement, praise and advice, and Ari needed to see a friendly face now more than ever.

They slowly went from room to room while Arianna pointed out what had been done thus far. She also carried her notebook containing pictures of what hadn't yet arrived.

"I love these side chairs—so Victorian. Walnut, right?" Tasha ran her hand along the finely engraved wood.

"Yes, and the cushions are covered in chenille." Ari beamed.

"We just don't get to decorate in this style much anymore. I bet you're in heaven." Tasha's eyes sparkled. "I know how much you enjoy those old-fashioned British eras."

Ari nodded. "There is just so much history in it. But I won't bore you with all that."

Tasha let out a breath. "Thank you." She laughed. "I love designing, but history"—she shrugged—"not so much."

"How long can you stay? Please say you're staying all week."

Ari had anxiously anticipated Tasha's visit. It was her job to oversee the ongoing projects, which meant she traveled from site to site to check out progress, fix problems, and lend a hand. Ari didn't so much need the help as she did the company.

"I can stay for a few days, but I'll have to get back to Denver by the weekend."

"Only a few days? Well, okay, let's make the most of it." Arianna could hardly contain her excitement. She loved working with Tasha and revered her as one of the most talented designers she'd ever met. Even more important, at least to Ari, Tasha was kind. Exactly what the doctor ordered.

Ari hugged her again. "I've needed an extra pair of hands and someone with vision around here. The landscapers just ignore me when I ask about color schemes."

"Imagine that," Tasha said with a glint in her eyes.

The two put their heads together and studied Ari's notebook.

****

"Arianna," Tasha said, in her boss voice the next day, "you have gotten entirely too thin. Do you ever stop to eat?"

Ari blushed, realizing she rarely thought of food while she was on the job—especially in the dark frame of mind in which she'd been. "Well, as you can see, this part of town isn't exactly booming with restaurants. I should pack a lunch, but I'm always too tired at night to think about it and too rushed in the morning to do it." A guilty smile played on her lips. "I really should have been more considerate of your needs. I guess I just didn't think about it. I'm sorry."

Tasha didn't back down. "It's lunch time now, and I don't care if we have to drive a few miles to find some food. We've earned a break, and we're going to take one."

Arianna was happy that she finally had an ally. Since Christopher had disappeared from her life, she felt more alone than ever. He'd always reminded her to eat.

"Where do you recommend we go?" Tasha asked.

Only being familiar with a few restaurants in town, Ari suggested they go to Abby's Diner. "I've just been there a few times, but the food is delicious."

Nearly thirty minutes later, they were being ushered to a booth at Abby's. With her eyes on the hostess, Arianna didn't notice that, in some places, the black and white checkerboard flooring rose and fell unevenly. Her foot caught the corner of a protruding tile, knocking her off balance. She flung her arms out to right herself as someone reached out and steadied her. Her eyes flew to the diner she'd nearly hit to thank them. Christopher. She felt heat burn in her chest and rise to her face.

"Christopher." She regained her balance, but her mind remained muddled. "I—we—uh, this is my boss, Natasha Tate." She finally recovered enough to get out a coherent sentence.

"It is very nice to meet you, Ms. Tate," Christopher said in his perfect British accent. Ari's heart pounded so hard, she feared he could hear it. Traitorous heart.

"It's nice to meet you as well, Mr.—" Tasha arched her brows in question.

"Flemming," both Arianna and Christopher said in unison.

"I'm sorry." Arianna motioned to Christopher. "Tasha, this is my…uh"—she grimaced—"this is Christopher Flemming. And." She looked at the man sitting adjacent to Christopher, dressed in a similar uniform.

"Joe. You can just call me Joe." His face broke into a boyish grin.

"And you said you didn't have any friends here in Pueblo, Ari." Tasha's eyes twinkled.

Ari tried to will away tears she felt burning in the backs of her eyelids. She finally glanced at Christopher and saw a mirror of her own feelings in his eyes— feelings of sadness, loneliness, and longing. Then her gaze dropped to her arm, and she realized he still held it. He must have realized it, too, as he promptly released his grip.

"I'm back." A woman wearing thick make-up and tight clothing pushed her way onto the seat next to Christopher, forcing him to move over. "Oh, I'm sorry.

I didn't mean to interrupt." She draped a possessive hand over his.

Joe looked at Ari and cleared his throat. "Uh…this is Charlotte."

"Call me Char." The woman batted her lashes.

Ari's heart couldn't take any more abuse. She brushed at an errant tear, then promptly turned away. Without a word she tugged on Tasha's arm, motioning her to follow the hostess, who hadn't seemed to notice her customers had stopped. They took the offered menus and scooted into a booth.

"What was that about?" Tasha asked in a hushed voice. "It's obvious that he"—she pointed in Christopher's direction—"is more than a friend. And why the tears? Is it that horrid woman?"

Ari hadn't noticed the tears flowing freely now. Fighting to regain her composure, she struggled to find words to describe the relationship she had with Christopher—or at least, once had.

She usually saved these types of conversations for Maggie, but, for whatever reason, she'd not even told Maggie about what had happened between her and Christopher. She didn't have the heart. Or, perhaps she hadn't wished to relive something she honestly didn't understand. Things had been so perfect in Denver.

But here sat Tasha, looking directly into her swollen eyes, wanting to help. Arianna told her everything, from tripping the alarm to the hurtful conversation that seemed to end it all.

Tasha listened intently, as a mother would to her daughter. She placed her hand over Ari's. "The last thing you need is a man who keeps secrets. I'm glad you ended it before things got too complicated."

Arianna had no idea how much she needed the release from holding in the pain Christopher had caused her. It felt liberating to tell someone and, in return, have her feelings validated. But who was Charlotte? Christopher hadn't wasted any time moving on.

Chapter Twenty-Nine

Christopher shook his hand free of Charlotte's grasp. Of all times for her to show up. After she'd stormed off when they'd first met, he thought he'd never see her again. "Do you mind? We're having a private conversation here." He was in no mood to be nice. He could only guess what Ari was thinking about now.

Charlotte stood, looking affronted. "I was just making polite conversation." She huffed and walked away.

"Who was that girl you stopped from falling?" Joe asked. "Oh, wait, is she the decorator?"

Nodding, Christopher didn't trust himself to talk about Ari just yet. The unexpected encounter with her had his heart bruising all over again.

"You were right—she is hot!" He waggled his eyebrows.

Christopher grimaced. "Yeah, we're not exactly dating anymore."

"You're nuts, man. If I had a girl in my life anywhere near that good-looking, I wouldn't let her out of my sight."

Christopher bristled a little at Joe's comment. "She is pretty, but she is also talented, smart and kind. Looks aren't everything, Joe." Just then he realized he'd made a mistake—coming off as way too defensive. Not to mention, he'd snapped at his friend.

"Sorry, Flemming. I didn't mean anything by it." Joe popped a fry into his mouth. "If she is all those things you say she is, why is she sitting over there cryin' her eyes out, while you're over here reciting her every virtue?"

Christopher hadn't realized that from Joe's vantage point, he had a clear view of Ari and her boss. "She's crying?"

"Yeah, from the minute she sat down."

Christopher swallowed hard and dropped his gaze to the food on his plate, his appetite gone. More than anything, he wanted to take Arianna in his arms and kiss away every tear, but the way things were between them now prevented him from even carrying on a friendly conversation with her. He had hurt her too badly, and she'd made it clear things were over between them.

Jolted from his thoughts, he realized Joe was still talking. "What happened with you two? I thought you liked her. You seemed great after your trip to Denver together."

He couldn't exactly open up to Joe, or anyone, for that matter. He was destined to carry his burden alone. "I really don't want to talk about it right now, if that's okay."

Joe gave him a quick punch on the arm. "I'm here for you, man, if you ever do want to talk."

"Thanks. Any chance we could get out of here before she's finished eating? I don't wish to be the cause of more tears."

"Not a problem." Joe shoved his remaining fries into his mouth.

Seeing Arianna reminded Christopher of how close he'd been to finding the device. But then ruined any possibility by his behavior toward her. Now, not only was he worlds away from accessing the machine, but Ari was spending most of her time in the same place the devilish device was housed. The irony rankled, and the foreboding nearly choked him.

Chapter Thirty

Arianna managed to settle into a routine, with Christopher safely tucked into a dark corner of her heart. For a while she'd feared she would never fully recover. The ache in her chest began to dull, but still swelled when she allowed him entrance to her dreams. For now, she needed to focus on work. Days and weeks slowly passed as the Somers' house began to look more and more complete.

Decorating a house this size was a massive undertaking—especially for one person. When decisions were made, orders were then placed, and deliveries waited upon—some taking up to twelve weeks. *That's what happens when you must have the very best.* Ari let out a sigh. When everything came together in one room, there were still many more yet to finish. *It's good that I love my job,* she thought.

Another Friday arrived. It had a nasty habit of showing up on a weekly basis.

"Ugh—but I do hate Fridays." Arianna groaned as she stirred brown sugar into a bowl of oatmeal. "Friday—my killjoy, thanks to Mr. Somers and our weekly meetings."

Friday used to kick off the weekend—no work, all play. Now it meant a meeting with a task-master, not to mention the beginning of a lonely weekend without much to do—no Christopher.

She needed friends. The sad realization hit that any new friends she made at this point would be temporary, as she didn't plan to stay in Pueblo any longer than necessary.

It had been several weeks since anyone had accompanied Mr. Somers to Pueblo. Today, however, the whole Somers family arrived. Arianna watched each of them carefully, trying to discern if there had been something she hadn't noticed—a clue that would connect Christopher to them.

Besides their British accents, she didn't know what else it could be. Mrs. Somers, Sarah, and Josh all seemed sad and so standoffish, or maybe just shy, but Christopher was captivating and full of life. She reflected back to Denver and how he and Maggie's husband, Jason, had hit it off so easily. As if they'd known each other for years. Then, dancing at the Palace Arms, where Christopher had seemed to relish the attention they'd received. He hadn't been an attention seeker, but he'd never shied away from it as these people did. He was just so—

She had to cut herself off before she thought the word "perfect." He wasn't perfect or they'd still be together. She removed the scowl from her face and plastered on a smile.

Sarah carried a basket of bedroom supplies—robes, slippers, and an ancient-looking cardigan. Arianna followed her up the stairs to her room. The furniture had yet to arrive, but there would be plenty of space in the closet drawers to store her items.

Arianna decided if she were ever going to approach Sarah, it was now.

"Hello, Sarah." She kept her voice low so she wouldn't startle her. Sarah's lips tugged up into a timid smile. "Do you like your room?"

"Very much," Sarah said softly.

Relieved to hear her speak, Arianna kept the conversation going—casually, at first. "You will have plenty of room for your clothing in this huge closet." Ari opened the door to reveal an area as big as her own entire bedroom. "You have ample shelf space." She pointed to the neatly organized banks of shelving and drawers. "As well as plenty of hanger rods for your dresses and, well, everything. It's an incredible closet."

A shadow crossed Sarah's face as she scanned the empty storeroom. "I once had such beautiful gow—"

Arianna nodded at Sarah, encouraging her to go on. "You had beautiful gowns?"

Sarah's face drained to a chalky white. "I'm sorry. I do not know why I said that. The closet is very nice. I look forward to filling it." Her wobbly voice was barely a whisper.

Arianna didn't know what to make of it, but she left the area and motioned to a spot in the middle of the room. "And your bed will go here, with night stands on both sides. That's where you can keep things like your journal—but, of course, you already know that." She laughed, but it felt strained. She sucked in a nervous breath. It was time to fess up. "I'm glad you are here, actually. I have a bit of a confession to make." Sarah's gaze, which had been anywhere but on Ari, finally met hers with a questioning look. Her eyes were a startling blue Ari had never noticed before. Probably because she was always examining her feet.

"You see, before I knew the journal belonged to you, and when I was bored waiting for a delivery, I read some of the pages." She took a breath before letting the rest of the words tumble out. "I didn't mean to pry. I honestly thought it was a keepsake from years, or maybe decades ago." She wiped her sweaty palms on her pants.

Sarah's eyebrows drew together, and she clamped her teeth shut. She looked horrified. Or scared.

"I am really sorry. I know it was wrong." Arianna closed the gap between them and lowered her voice. "Sarah, some of the things you have written are frightening."

Sarah's expression didn't change.

Arianna plowed on. "Are you and your mother and brother in danger?" There, she'd said it.

Sarah's eyes grew misty, and her face relaxed a bit. "I wish you had not read my journal. It is meant to be personal."

"I know, and I am truly sorry. But I did it and I can't stop thinking about some of the passages. Does your father mistreat you?"

Sarah looked down. An awkward silence filled the space around them. Finally, she spoke. "I cannot…" she twisted her hands together. "This is really not your concern, Miss Miller."

"Sarah, please call me Ari. I just want to help you—if you are in any sort of danger. Can I alert the authorities for you?"

"No! Please do not tell anyone else what you have read. Swear to me. You cannot—you must not!" The urgency in Sarah's voice screamed at Arianna.

"Okay, I promise, but who will help you, then?"

"My brother has promised to help us, and I believe he will."

"Your brother is just a kid. What is he, fifteen or sixteen? How can he help you?"

Just then Sarah's eyes grew wide, and her face lost even more color as she looked beyond Arianna. "Hello, Father. Miss Miller was just showing me my bed chamber. It is quite lovely; do you not agree?"

Mr. Somers eyed Arianna with a suspicious glare, then curtly nodded his approval of the room.

Ari let out a silent breath and continued with the tour as if nothing had passed between them. Mr. Somers never left them alone again.

Hours later, exhausted from the long day she had put in, Arianna drove home, put on her sweats and grabbed a book. She wanted to relax, but thoughts of her conversation with Sarah nagged at her.

She'd promised not to tell the authorities, and she wouldn't. The fear in Sarah's eyes ensured that Ari would keep that promise. She didn't know what she'd say, anyway. She had no proof of abuse. None of them had ever appeared to be harmed physically—at least the few times she had seen them.

Thoughts like these, and the whole situation in general, badgered her throughout the evening and into the night. She finally dropped off to sleep in the wee hours, just before the sun came up.

Ari needed to clear her mind the next morning. The best way to accomplish that was a good run. She pulled on her Nikes, determined to shake off the worries of the day before. She enjoyed running and did it as often as her busy schedule permitted. It had been especially therapeutic in college, after her parents and brother had died.

Puffy, white clouds filled the sky as the sun slowly ascended. She breathed in the fragrance of summer blooms. It was a perfect morning to run. Her thoughts, however, returned to the same questions she'd fought with the previous evening—she still had no answers.

What would Christopher do, she wondered. After all, he was a police officer. Though he might think she had some kind of agenda if she asked him. He'd read the journal, too, so it wouldn't be as if she were divulging Sarah's secret to somebody new. An internal debate began.

She rounded the corner for the last mile of her run. Lost in thought, she barely noticed a car speeding toward her. What in the world? She leaped onto the grass beside her to keep from getting hit. Her insides jittered at the near miss. Was it a drunk driver? Squinting into the sun, she watched the car make a U-turn and drive toward her again, this time at a slower pace. She scrambled to the residence nearest her. The car slowed as it approached. Mr. Somers. She stood on wobbly legs and glared at him but kept a safe distance.

"Consider that your last warning," his deep voice rumbled out to her. A chill ran down her spine. She looked around for witnesses; anyone who saw his obvious attempt to kill, or at least, scare her. No one.

"Seriously? You just tried to hit me with your car!!" She stammered. "How did you even know where to find me?"

Mr. Somers waved her questions away as if they were flies needing swatting. "I asked you to stay away from Sarah. I'll not put up with your insubordination!"

"I'm calling the police!" She reached for her phone. Oh, no! Her running pants didn't have pockets. Until now, she'd never felt the need to bring her phone on a jog with her.

The jerk was still talking. "And tell them what, exactly? I simply swerved to spare the life of that dog over there." He pointed to a stray wandering down the road. "It will be my word against yours. And, Miss Miller, if I'd wanted to hit you, I would have."

Ari's heartbeat sped to double time. She had difficulty breathing.

"As I said, that was your final warning. So, go ahead, make your call. I'm certain the Pueblo police can be bought, just like any other."

He had her sitting between a boulder and brick wall. With no phone, she had no leverage. She thought of a few choice phrases to throw his way. He was a homicidal maniac! Instead, she turned and sprinted for home.

Had he tried to hit her, or not? Her foggy brain was having difficulty processing the whole situation. She should call the police and at least report it, shouldn't she? But if he had just been scaring her, would that be a criminal offense, or just a waste of time for the police? She at least needed to tell Tasha and Mr. Johnson. She needed out of this project and away from Mr. Somers.

Once home, she found her phone and began dialing. Wait. Did she really want to be pulled off this once-in-a-lifetime project because the owner scared her? She paused and deliberated. Shaking her head, she put her phone on the table. She'd endured a lot of things in her life. Mr. Somers and his enormous ego would not cow her.

If her mind had been unclear before she ran, it was completely muddled now. She took a shower. That didn't help. She wished Maggie or Tasha were with her. Then she could talk this whole situation out with someone. There was still Christopher. He was a cop, after all. She could ask his advice about Sarah and Mr. Somers' threat, but…

Chapter Thirty-One

Against her better judgment, she picked up her cell phone. She would just text him. That way, if he didn't want to see her, he could easily ignore it.

Christopher, it's Ari—not urgent, but I have some things I could use your advice on. Her finger shook as she pushed the send button.

She waited for a return text. Nothing. Well, she guessed that was her answer. Disappointment hung over her like a shroud. She shouldn't have texted him. Now she just felt foolish for reaching out. He was probably spending his day off with that wretched woman Charlotte. She flung herself onto the sofa and located her book. She'd lose herself in a pretend romance, where the hero and heroine always found true love.

An hour later her doorbell rang. "Christopher!" She didn't know why his presence on her doorstep surprised her so, his methods were anything but conventional.

"Ari." He shifted his weight from leg to leg, clearly anxious. "Are you all right? I was riding—just brushing down my horse at the stables when I saw your text. Sorry it took me so long to get here." He seemed out of breath.

"I didn't mean for you to drop what you were doing and come over. You could have just texted me back."

"I tried. Service is unreliable at the stables." He pushed his hand through his hair. "And, well, I was heading home anyway. I didn't know how long ago you'd sent it. I worried..." His eyes scanned over her again. "Are you well, then?"

"Yes, I'm fine." Now she was embarrassed he'd made the trip just to find her alive and in one piece.

His tense shoulders relaxed. "That's a relief. What do you need to talk about?"

Confusion nearly made her forget why she'd texted him in the first place. Having him in her apartment brought back a flurry of memories—mostly good. However, the last one—their argument at the Somers'—had cut deeply. An open wound, still bleeding.

She snapped to attention and invited him in. Sarah was more important than her aching heart, right now. "Have a seat. I need some advice, and you're the only one familiar with the situation." His forehead creased and his brows furrowed, but he did as she said, sitting on the sofa. Noting his confusion, she added, "Since you read that old journal way back when I first arrived. Remember?" She kept her voice cool—free of emotion. She could do this. She must—for Sarah.

He nodded, and she saw a mix of curiosity and wariness creep into his eyes.

She filled him in on the conversation she'd had with Sarah Somers the day before. "And the strangest part is that Sarah is depending on her brother, Josh, to help them. He's only a kid." Her voice rose as she spoke.

"Did she say that?" His head tilted, and he narrowed his eyes.

"Say what?"

"That she is depending on Josh for help."

"Yes, I believe she did. Well she just said 'her brother,' but she only has one. So, what would you suggest I do?"

He looked at her thoughtfully. "I don't think you should do anything about Sarah—at least not yet. You have no proof beyond a few entries from a journal—a journal you no longer possess. Reporting abuse will, most likely, cause more problems than it will help. Can you keep speaking with her and perhaps become her friend by earning her trust?"

She shook her head. "I don't think so. There's more." She shifted uncomfortably, then told him about Mr. Somers' visit that morning.

"Are you telling me he tried to hit you with his car?" Anger sparked in his eyes.

She shrugged, unsure. It had seemed like Mr. Somers had aimed for her, but thinking about it now, she couldn't be certain. "I think he was trying to scare me. I doubt he'd do anything to slow the progress of his house. Getting a new designer at this point would cause a huge delay."

He sprang off the couch and paced the room, moving like a caged animal needing to be let loose. She watched, wondering where his thoughts were taking him.

Finally, he sat down next to her. "Arianna, I know you are disappointed in me for how things have passed between us, and if I could, I would change that."

"You could." She said it so softly she didn't think he heard her.

He paused and shook his head, clearly not wanting to repeat the argument they'd had weeks before that had ended so badly. "But for now, please just trust me. Promise me you will keep your distance from that whole family. Do only what Mr. Somers asks of you at work, and if you ever see him in this neighborhood again, call me immediately."

She felt his blue eyes penetrating deep into her soul as he placed both hands on her shoulders and gave her a gentle shake. "Did you hear me, Ari? I do not want to frighten you, but I believe Mr. Somers is a dangerous man."

"Dangerous man? You know him?"

"Let's just say that Mr. Somers has a reputation, and if the rumors are true, he has committed numerous crimes in the past. Promise me, Ari."

She shuddered. The room began to spin. "Yes. Okay, I promise."

"You look pale. I have frightened you." Christopher's voice softened into concern. "I wish you would resign from this project."

She shook her head. "I can't. I'm too close to the end, and nobody else is available to take my place." Her voice wobbled.

"Just as I thought you would say. You're certainly no quitter." He patted her leg. "Have you eaten today?" Ari hadn't realized until he asked, that, no, she hadn't eaten. His lips curved into a lopsided grin as he brushed a thumb along her jawbone. "It is a wonder you have survived without me. I'll fix you some lunch."

She caught a whiff of his masculine scent and tamped down the flicker that threatened to burst into flame. "It should be me offering to feed you. Especially after you rushed over here to help."

Before the words were out of her mouth, Christopher had left her side and began rummaging through the kitchen. He set to work making sandwiches. "You don't have much in the way of, well, food. Your refrigerator is nearly bare. It looks like the choices are peanut butter and jelly, or whatever this is." He held up a bag of old sandwich meat.

"Um, that's a tough one, but I guess I'll take peanut butter."

"Good choice." His vibrant personality inched its way back, threatening to break through the wall she'd begun to build.

He brought the sandwiches over, along with a couple of glasses of milk, and sat down beside her again. "I hope it is all right if I stay for a bit. I don't feel comfortable with Mr. Somers roaming your neighborhood."

Relief washed over her. She was more than okay with him staying. She felt safe with him. It hadn't only been the magnetism between them she'd missed since they had ended things; she'd missed their friendship, as well. "Thank you. I don't think I'd realized how my encounter with that man affected me. He's really sort of creepy."

Once they'd polished off the last of the sandwiches, she began gathering the trash and glasses. "I've got it, Ari. You stay put." He winked as he extracted the items from her hands.

Wicked wink. She let out a sigh.

After cleaning up, he sat back down on the sofa. He looked over at Ari, whose eyes drooped from lack of sleep the night before. He tugged on her arm. "You look tired."

"I didn't really sleep last night. I've been worried about Sarah. Then Mr. Somers' impromptu"—she shrugged—"well, you know."

He shook his head. "Mr. Somers crossed the line. You could use a nap." He picked up a decorative pillow that had fallen onto the floor and handed it to her. She looked at him, wondering what she should do with the pillow—he took up a good portion of the sofa. She plunked it down on his lap and laid her head on top of it. He smiled down at her.

Supported by his muscular legs beneath her, she felt safe and secure as he draped a protective arm over her.

Chapter Thirty-Two

It seemed as if only seconds had passed before Christopher felt Arianna relax into the pillow on his lap. Her breathing slow and even now, he knew she'd fallen asleep. Good. She needed to rest. How ironic it was that his father could torture him through the treatment of his designer. Careful not to wake her, he wove his fingers through her hair, allowing himself to enjoy the sensation. She stirred. He let the tresses fall back into place.

Scanning the room, his eyes settled on a book within reach. As he picked it up and began to read, he chuckled softly to himself at the irony of the words. He examined the title. Sure enough, it was one of Arianna's romance novels from the 1800s—his era. After reading a couple of chapters, he turned the book around to see what year it had been published. It was certainly not Jane Austen. He wondered when his era became romantic. This was not the way he remembered it.

He continued reading about dukes and duchesses, forbidden love between classes of people, balls and duels.

Funny, it mentioned nothing about the extreme poverty much of England had been experiencing, nor the countless broken men returning from the never-ending wars. And the romance. He shook his head.

Hardly. Couples were united as business transactions. A man's fortune was matched to a woman's dowry. That is how it was. Plain and simple. No romance in that.

He reflected bitterly about a young girl he had been quite smitten with before he'd left for Cambridge University. He'd been certain he would marry Rachel Cartwright. Smart, pretty—and poor. But then he'd been given the talk about making a prudent match. "She is well below our station, son. You are the grandson of nobility." His father's words still sizzled in his ears.

How very low their station had fallen. And his dear father's station, Christopher scowled, would be among the prisoners at Newgate Prison, had they remained in London.

Still, he found it fascinating to read about the perception of how things had been through the eyes of an author living two hundred years later.

He guessed it was not entirely incorrect. After all, if Father's scientific inventions had been a success, instead of a failure, their lives might have turned out very different.

The thought took Christopher back to a happier time. His life centuries past—yet, in real time, less than a decade ago. His grandfather had been an earl, and his father, Benjamin Somerset, had been the third of his grandfather's sons, therefore not eligible to inherit the title. Grandfather was a kind and generous man. Christopher remembered him with tenderness.

While Grandfather Somerset could only pass his title to his eldest son, Robert, he had ensured the comfort of his other two by providing large estates for each. Christopher remembered the home and gardens with fondness. He'd spent many a day riding his horse, hunting and studying with his tutor.

He even remembered his parents being kind and loving. Their marriage had been arranged, just as others of his time, but Christopher had grown up believing his parents loved each other. Maybe that happened over time.

He had once adored his father. A brilliant scientist and inventor, who could do no wrong in Christopher's young eyes. And his mother, a paragon of patience, had indulged her spouse in his need to create.

Images of a happy childhood, interrupted briefly by the loss of two sisters—one at birth, another around the age of three—replayed in his mind. The deaths had taken a heavy toll on Mother, but the passage of time and the addition of two more healthy babies had helped her pick up the pieces and move on. It wasn't until Father's inventions had begun failing more often than not that he'd become a different man.

Christopher had overheard many arguments as his mother tried to reason with her husband. Her pleas had fallen on deaf ears. In the end, Father had turned his attention to the bottle and tuned his wife out. Still working on his inventions, he'd become something akin to a mad scientist. Christopher, his mother, and siblings had learned to stay out of his way to avoid his rages.

The reality of his family's situation jolted him, erasing any warm feelings he'd just experienced. Arianna shivered, as if reacting to his thoughts. Perhaps she was reliving her own encounter with his monster of a father. He tugged on the afghan draped over the arm of the sofa, and gently covered her.

The colors in the blanket reminded him of something from his youth. He closed his eyes to remember. An antique vase came to mind. He smiled at the memory of yellows, blues, and pinks, forming a floral design. As a young boy, he'd been captivated by it, and would stare until the design blurred into a kaleidoscope of color. "'Tis a Qing Dynasty vase, son," Mother had told him. "Very fragile. 'Twas a wedding gift from your grandfather."

The sweet memory soured as he envisioned the rare vase being ripped from Mother's fingers, boxed up and sent away to pay creditors. The first of many treasures his family lost before he'd left for Cambridge.

The eviction had happened while Christopher had been away at school. He'd received a missive from his uncle insisting he return home immediately. Confusion had given way to alarm when he'd arrived and witnessed Father's change of character. He had become a completely different person. Kicked out of their country estate and forced to live in a townhouse on London's east side, he'd spend his days in the bookroom, where no one else had been allowed; his evenings in public houses, drinking himself into a stupor—a frustrated, bitter man. When Christopher had tried speaking to him about the situation, it had only served to aggravate things further.

Then had come the final blow. Christopher's once loving father had planned something illegal. Christopher had become aware of the scheme because Father had needed his help. He shuddered at the memory of his father's contemptuous expression when Christopher had refused to help. It still haunted him. He realized he should have taken action then, but he'd doubted Father would truly go through with the deed. Now here he was, a nineteenth century man living in the twenty-first century, fighting to protect a family separated from him.

And sweet Sarah. She would have had her London debut and would likely be married by now. But instead of enjoying a coming out event; instead of donning a ball gown and hearing admiration whispered about; and instead of being sought after by gentlemen of the *ton*—London Society—Sarah had been locked away in a tawdry house as if she'd done something wrong.

Anger began to rise in Christopher's chest. He took a deep breath, then reprimanded himself. He must stop reliving the past. There was nothing he could do to change it. His focus must be on the future. He pulled himself out of his dark thoughts and returned his attention to the book. He continued to read, shaking his head in amusement.

Still asleep, Arianna turned over from her side to her back. Christopher looked down at her peaceful face in his lap. Her long lashes, perfect nose and full lips made his pulse quicken. "Arianna," he barely whispered, "I may never have you as my own, but you will always have my heart." He moved an errant lock of hair away from her eyes and continued to gaze at her. "This, my dear, would go against all propriety where I come from."

Chapter Thirty-Three

Arianna opened her eyes, peering up to see if Christopher had fallen asleep, too. She realized he had picked up the book she'd been reading earlier and seemed to be quite entertained by it.

"You're reading my book?" she asked in a sleepy voice.

He smiled down at her. "Indeed I am."

"What's so funny?" She pulled herself up.

He held the paperback up. "This book is funny." Mirth danced in his eyes.

"It's a historical romance, not a comedy." She feigned a pout.

"I am aware of that."

"Then what's so funny about it?"

Christopher put the book down and looked at her. His smile became lopsided, then flattened. "What is funny is the way this book describes the era, as if it were all rolling hills and romance. When, in reality, much of war-wearied England lived in poverty."

Arianna frowned. "Well, that wouldn't be very romantic to read."

"No, but much more realistic." His dimples puckered as his grin returned.

"You act like you were there. How do you know there hadn't been budding romances all over London?

With all the 'Coming Out' balls, and those beautiful gowns they wore, and—"

Christopher laughed out loud. "Do you truly believe those things to be romantic?"

"Why not? The books make them sound romantic." She shrugged. "If you're such an expert, why don't you tell me about the real London?"

"Well, for one thing, the women do not—rather, *did* not continuously smell of lavender," he said. "In fact, unless they were among the privileged royal, most went days and even weeks without bathing"—he cleared his throat—"back then, of course. So, you can only imagine what a lady smelled like. Add to that layers and layers of undergarments, and the gown. Then put her in a sweltering ballroom." He shook his head. "Those lacy fans they carried in their reticules weren't just for show. No, all the rosewater and lavender in the world couldn't make even the most delicate debutante smell pretty."

Ari narrowed her eyes. For not being a Regency Era fan, he sure knew a lot about the time.

Christopher continued, "Then there were the men. Most of them spent their days performing physical labor, or riding horses—if they were lucky—so they smelled even worse."

Arianna giggled as she pictured the ladies and gentlemen of her favorite era smelling bad. "Well, I like the way the book describes it better." She pulled it from his hands.

"Hey, I'm not finished reading." He grabbed it back.

"This book is for people with an appreciation of history." She reached for it again, but he held it away from her.

"Oh, I can assure you, my dear, I do appreciate history; however, this"—he held up the book—"is not history." She grabbed at it, but instead caught his arm. He held it higher and with his free arm captured hers. She wriggled and they both tumbled to the floor. She continued in vain to try to wrestle the book out of his hands. Finally, Christopher pinned her down, the book forgotten.

Only inches apart and staring into each other's eyes, Arianna felt his warm breath on her cheeks. She saw longing in his eyes and knew he saw the same mirrored in hers. Longing they had both tried so hard to suppress now held them captive.

Chapter Thirty-Four

Neither moved. Christopher's gaze dropped to her lips. It would be so easy to kiss her right now. Desire drew him in like a magnet. Perhaps ladies of his era smelled unpleasant, but not Ari. She smelled like tropical shampoo and orange blossoms. Irresistible.

She held perfectly still. His eyes left her lips and probed her eyes—her earnest, blue eyes. Had she forgiven him his poor behavior from weeks ago? Would kissing her now be taking advantage of her during a moment of vulnerability?

He released her from his grip. "I apologize; I seem to let my emotions get the better of me sometimes." He began to stand.

"It's not your fault. I wasn't exactly running away." Ari touched her face, probably an attempt to cover the blush which had bloomed. "I only wish things could be different between us," she added softly.

"As do I." Christopher extended his hand to help her up. "As do I."

Her phone buzzed. "I'd better get that." She moved to the table and answered.

"Hi Jason, what's up?" She paused. "Maggie's in labor? Now?" Glancing around the room, she walked out of sight, then came back to the table, notebook in hand. "I don't have any scheduled deliveries until

Wednesday, and I can bring my laptop so I can work from Denver. Tell Maggie I'll leave right away."

Overhearing the conversation, Christopher was relieved Arianna would be away for a while. He didn't trust his father and couldn't be around to protect her all the time.

"Bye, Jason. See you soon." She turned back to face Christopher. "Maggie's in labor." Her face split into a huge grin.

"I heard. You'd better pack some things. Sounds like you need to get on the road."

Ari seemed hesitant to leave him. Her smile faltered. "Christopher, thank you for coming today. I don't know what I would have done without you." She shivered, and he knew she was thinking about his father.

He closed the gap between them as he pulled her into his arms, inhaling her orange blossom sweetness. "It is never a problem." He didn't want to release her. She made no move to end the embrace, either. Finally, he talked himself into letting her go. Loosening his grip, he kissed her lightly on her forehead.

Her hand lingered in his. Longing shone in her eyes. "I should—"

"Don't worry, I'll see myself out."

As she disappeared into her bedroom to pack, Christopher headed for the door. Just then he caught sight of her keys. They sat in a glass dish on a table near the door. Checking to make sure she couldn't see him, he rummaged through the loose keys until he found one marked "Somers." He quietly slipped it into his pocket. He'd just borrow it to make a copy and return it later. He knew he could easily pick the lock to her apartment to replace it. The old building was woefully out of date where locks were concerned. The Somers' house, however, with its advanced alarm system required a key and a code to enter. Perhaps this sort of activity made him more like his father than he realized. The thought gave him pause. No. He needed to save innocent people from his father. If borrowing Ari's key to do it helped, so be it.

Leaving her apartment, he aimed his car south, toward his family's house, then realized it was too late to begin a search that night. He'd rather not turn lights on and arouse suspicion, should anyone happen by. Making a U-turn, he drove to the nearest hardware store to make a copy of the key. Once he was certain Ari had left for Denver, he picked her lock and replaced the original. Arianna had told Jason she would be in Denver until Wednesday. That gave him three days to scour the house from top to bottom searching for the device.

At first light he made his way to the Somers' home, armed with determination. Fate had dealt him a stroke of luck, to be sure. Before sliding the key into the lock, he punched numbers on the alarm pad. He'd seen Ari disarm it once and knew immediately why his father had chosen the numbers he had. "One, seven, five, nine," he said as he pushed each digit. Father's birth-year.

Upon entering the house, he was struck by how much Arianna had accomplished over the past few weeks. Amazing. His heart warmed at the thought of her. He hoped Father had been generous with his praise, although he doubted it. Father had always been stingy with compliments. "Well, I will say it aloud. Arianna, you are one talented designer. This house looks incredible." He hoped one day to tell her in person.

Christopher had no memory of what the device looked like, as he had been unconscious when he was, hmm, in it? On it? Under it? He had no idea. When he had finally come to, on that chilly night in April four years ago, he was in a bed. This made locating the device more of a challenge. He should have asked Mother for a detailed description. Too late now.

There was also the consideration that Father had designed more than one device, perhaps streamlining his idea with the aid of twenty-first century technology. He had to give the man credit; he was a gifted inventor.

Moving slowly from room to room, closet to closet, drawer to drawer, trying to think as his felonious father would, he analyzed, scrutinized, and examined every corner of the mansion. It took him longer than he had expected. A new appreciation for Arianna and the task she'd undertaken to decorate a home this size warmed him.

On Tuesday, after searching for three days, but coming up empty, he sat on one of the beautiful side chairs, discouraged. He'd looked everywhere. He closed his eyes and attempted to let the frustration dissipate so he could free his mind and puzzle out where he hadn't yet looked.

"What are you doing?" A man's voice startled him. Was it Father? Panicked, he felt for his gun. If it was his father, he'd finally get some answers. But not without protection. He was certain Father wouldn't hesitate to kill him. Ah! He'd left his gun in the cruiser.

"I said, what are you doing?" The voice hollered again. The man sounded irritated, but Christopher couldn't see anyone.

He flattened his body against a wall and moved in the direction of the voice.

"Stop!"

Christopher halted. Frozen in his tracks. Near the back door, he peeked through the glass to see—

"I said stop digging! You're in the wrong place. I just planted out there!"

The landscapers. Christopher let out a breath of relief. Keeping out of sight, he watched a man near the house continue to shout orders to another at the far end of the garden.

Heart beating furiously, Christopher avoided being seen through the windows and reclaimed his seat in the parlor, again channeling in on his task at hand.

In London, Father had built the machine and kept it hidden somewhere in the house. He replayed his last night there. The vision of Mother bringing his siblings, along with some belongings, past his room was still vivid. He thrummed his fingers against his leg while he called on every sense to recreate what had happened next. He sat up straight as memories came into view. He remembered now. He had been ready to take Father on, but he'd pulled him into the bookroom just before everything went dark.

He'd scoured the bookroom—or as they called it today, the study—several times before, but now he knew it had to be there. He'd rip the room apart, if he must.

He reentered the study. The décor in this room appeared to be finished—a perfect place to hide something. He'd not noticed that the first dozen times he'd scoured the house. A settee with a hand-carved frame nestled against the wall to his right, and a mahogany desk with several drawers sat to his left. He checked each one, more than a few of times. He did find a hidden compartment, but the only thing inside was a code of some kind. *This could be a combination.* Perhaps the device would fit into a safe.

He moved his search to the walls. He hadn't noticed before that there was more art on the walls in here than in any other room in the house. He began to carefully pull down each picture until he came to the largest one in the room. Aha! As he suspected, a safe. *It must be in here; it's big enough.*

Nervous anxiety made his hands clammy as he turned the knob on the safe to the appropriate numbers. "Click." It opened.

Christopher wasn't sure what to expect, but certainly not this. A glittering array of rich red rubies, green emeralds and sparkling diamonds came into view. His eyes roved over container after container of precious stones. He also discovered art he assumed to be valuable, several paintings and small sculptures. Searching further, he found rare coins. On and on it went. Of course, Father only collected items that would appreciate in value over the years. Christopher did find an envelope of U.S. currency, but he suspected it had been stored there from cashing in some of his stolen goods. "How much blood have you spilt to acquire this cache, Father? Was it worth it?" Bitterness infected his voice.

All this and no time-traveling device. He didn't know what his next move would be. Mother had assured him the device was in the Pueblo house, but there wasn't a square inch he hadn't explored. It simply wasn't there.

Making sure to leave no evidence of his presence, he closed the safe and rehung the large painting. Mentally and physically fatigued, he headed for the door, then realized the landscapers had moved to the front yard. Hopefully they'd not seen his motorcycle parked out of view on the side of the house. In order to lock up and set the alarm, he'd have to wait them out. He'd just find a sofa to rest on for now. Maybe take a nap.

Chapter Thirty-Five

Arianna spent a long night Saturday at the hospital with Maggie and Jason. Relieved the baby hadn't come before she'd arrived in Denver, she now wished the waiting would come to an end. Eventually it did. Ryder made his entrance into the world at 4:22 Sunday morning—a beautiful, healthy, eight-pound baby. His blue eyes sparkled, reminding her of Christopher's. His shock of dark hair curled in tiny circles around his ears. Baby Ryder definitely resembled his father, as his mother had auburn hair and hazel eyes.

Arianna couldn't get enough cuddles with the little cherub, and she realized, for the first time, how much she craved a family of her own. There was no rush, she reminded herself. She was only twenty-four, after all. She intentionally didn't consider her twenty-fifth birthday—a mere two weeks away. Maybe the yearning had to do with losing her parents and brother. She didn't know. It just felt wonderful to hold a baby.

She then enjoyed a short reunion with her coworkers on Monday. Even crusty Mr. Johnson seemed happy to see her. She shared pictures she'd taken, as the house had begun to shape into a home. Everyone's high praise warmed her heart. Perhaps this job would be worth the stress it had caused, after all.

Tasha Tate pulled Arianna aside. "I have dibs on lunch tomorrow. I need an update on your life."

Once again, Arianna felt an appreciation for the motherly tone Tasha exuded.

Over salads the next day, Ari explained her changing relationship with Christopher. It didn't take long, considering the only time she'd spent with him since Tasha's visit had been the previous Saturday afternoon.

Tasha perked up. "He seems to really care about you, Ari."

Arianna shrugged and frowned. "I know he cares, but I just can't be in a relationship with someone who keeps secrets."

"Did you ever consider the secrets he's keeping might have something to do with his job as a police officer? The man I met in the diner could hardly tear his eyes away from you. He seemed as if he were in as much, well, pain as you."

Arianna considered that. It didn't matter. To her, it just felt personal. And if he'd been using her to gain access to the Somers' house, she didn't know how to deal with that.

Tasha wanted to know more about the secrets that seemed to be multiplying at the jobsite.

Ari told her—holding back key information she'd promised Sarah she'd not disclose—about her frightening encounter with Mr. Somers, although, she may have toned it down a bit. It felt good to share the details of the house, the family, the journal, and especially the madman himself.

Tasha shook her head, clearly unhappy about what she was hearing. "Interior decorating is not supposed to be a dangerous occupation. We may need to pull you from the job, Ari. I know for a fact Reese won't like hearing about this."

"Oh, please, Tasha. I only have a few weeks' work left to do. You can't pull me away now." She leaned forward, pleading.

The crease on Tasha's forehead told Ari the argument was not yet settled, but Ari pressed until Tasha agreed to let her see it through. "At the first sign of trouble—even if Mr. Somers looks at you cross-eyed—you're coming home."

Ari relaxed back in her seat. "Mr. Somers won't do anything to slow down my progress. He's in too big a hurry to move into his mansion."

When the waiter cleared the last dish away, she said goodbye to Tasha and made her way to the hospital as Maggie was being released to go home. She cuddled baby Ryder for a few minutes, making silly baby noises and giggling over a whispered secret about his favorite Aunt Ari. Reluctantly, she handed the newborn back to his mother, who secured her bundle into the car seat.

"Love you, Ari. Maggie's arms closed around her friend. "I'll be so happy when you're home for good."

Ari blinked back tears threatening to fall. "Love you, too," she managed over the lump in her throat. She stepped away and turned to Jason. "Take good care of them."

He kissed her cheek. "Thanks for coming. I know it meant a lot to Maggie."

Ari waved as she located her own little red car.

Ever since Christopher had paid for and returned her car on that dark, gloomy Monday, guilty regret had poked at her. She had set up a car account to pay him back. She hoped to hand him a check soon.

She arrived at the Somers' residence early Wednesday morning, ready to prepare for more furniture deliveries. Raising her hand to enter the alarm code, she stopped short. The light indicating the home was armed wasn't blinking.

She never left the house without setting the alarm. Never.

Perhaps Mr. Somers had come a couple of days early. She stepped back, ready to bolt. Mentally, she wasn't prepared to see Mr. Somers…ever, but especially earlier than anticipated.

Before she had raced back to the safety of her car, however, the reason she'd come so early hit her like an electric jolt. Furniture deliveries. She had to stay.

Cautiously, she put the key in the lock and turned it. Wait! The door was already unlocked. Ari's hands trembled like an autumn leaf in a breeze. She clenched her chattering teeth and gently nudged the door open. She thought she heard rustling. Standing motionless in the foyer, she debated her next move. This house—the Victorian mansion she'd once so admired—officially creeped her out. She took two deep breaths and began a tour of the house. She'd been frightened here before, what was one more time?

Nothing seemed out of place, but something did strike her as odd—the smell. Christopher. She sniffed. It had to be her imagination. The spicy-freshness that was uniquely his hung in the air. She shook her head. *I must be losing my mind.*

By the time the furniture trucks began showing up, she'd nearly forgotten her earlier apprehension. Evidently, she *had* left the house without arming it. …Come to think of it, Mr. Somers had been the last one to leave that night. She scowled, wanting to punch something—preferably him—for causing her such anxiety.

By Friday, Ari had worked herself in and back out of a lather numerous times. She should say something to Mr. Somers about neglecting to lock and arm the house. No. He'd turn it on her, somehow. She'd leave it alone, and hopefully he'd leave her alone.

When the Somers did arrive—all of them, thank goodness—she was busy directing a delivery person to the sitting room. She took her time explaining exactly where end tables needed to be placed. Not only did she want the job done correctly; she also needed an excuse to be unavailable for as long as possible—determined to avoid the lot of them.

As the family set to work, bringing in dishes and small kitchen appliances, Arianna stayed in the living room, busying herself with her notebook. She felt someone watching her, but resisted the urge to look up, as it was probably the tyrant himself. She wished she could slip out the back door and disappear without ever speaking to him.

If it was Mr. Somers, he wasn't moving toward her. Puzzling. He liked nothing more than to make his intimidating presence known.

She finally raised her head to see who so quietly observed her. Sarah. When their eyes met, Sarah raised a finger to her lips, asking Arianna not to speak. Ari nodded her understanding, then cocked her head and raised her eyebrows in question. Sarah held up the journal she'd taken with her a month or so before. She said nothing but pointed to it. A flicker of understanding crossed between them. Sarah was telling her to read her journal. Her heart warmed. She didn't think Sarah had wanted anything to do with her, as she, no doubt, had gotten her into trouble by speaking to her the week before. But here she stood, giving her a message. Arianna smiled at Sarah and nodded her head. The shy girl slipped out of the room as quietly as she'd entered.

At the end of the day, after the Somers had gone back to Denver and the deliveries had all been made, Arianna made her way up to Sarah's room. Her heart thudded with anticipation.

The bedroom furniture had been delivered on Wednesday of that week. Arianna wondered for a moment where to look for the journal. Then she remembered having shown Sarah where her new nightstand would sit. Sure enough, when she opened the drawer, there it lay.

She thumbed through the pages until she found the last one with writing on it. Sarah's words looked like a normal journal entry. Ari guessed it was a precaution— just in case her father got his hands on it. She wouldn't put it past him.

Dear Journal,

It read in bold letters, just as all the other entries had begun. Then the font shrank considerably. "*A.*" Arianna assumed that meant her.

> *I wish to apologize for not being able to speak to you when we come to the house, as I fear my father will do harm to one or both of us if he finds we continue to communicate. After today, let us store my journal between the mattresses of my*

bed. I tremble to think of the consequences of Father finding it.

Ari shuddered. She wondered how badly this monster of a man treated his own daughter.

I thank you for wishing to help my family and me, as well as offering your friendship. I still desire that you not help us and fear any attempt on your part could put you in peril. I do wish for your friendship, however. I have gone several long years without the company of friends and have felt the impact of that loneliness. Sadly, our friendship must be kept secret and can only be through this type of correspondence, as I can think of no other way. But if you feel so inclined, I will very much welcome furthering our acquaintance. Yours, S.

Chills made Arianna's flesh prickle. She could hardly believe what she had just read. She reflected on her stay in Denver with her friends and realized just how lucky she was to have them. Poor Sarah. She had no one. If her father wouldn't even let her speak to Ari, she was sure he never let her out of his sight in Denver. Her eyes misted as she considered Sarah's situation. Of course she would be her friend.

She took her time in careful consideration of how to respond, then wrote.

Dear Journal.

She did her best to match Sarah's style of writing.

S, I understand your wish for me not to meddle in your family's situation. I won't, unless you change your mind at any time. I am very happy, however, about the possibility of becoming friends with you. I look forward to reading your journal after each of your visits. Please feel free to share any details of your life that you would like me to know. As for my story, it is very simple. I've lived in Colorado all my life. That must seem quite boring for someone like you. I have only read about living in such an elegant city as London. My family took a trip across the country when I was fourteen. That's as far as I have traveled. Do not feel the need to tell me more than you are comfortable sharing, but I do want to know you better. Sincerely, A.

With nervous excitement, Ari closed the book and placed it between Sarah's mattress and the box-spring.

Chapter Thirty-Six

Close call—too close. How could Christopher have fallen asleep at the Somers' house? He'd been fatigued enough for a nap, but the entire night? A tremor ran through his body imagining Arianna discovering him there. Thank the stars above he'd heard her fiddling with the lock and was able to exit through the back door before she'd entered.

Days passed. Christopher drove to Denver on Friday, hoping to get more information about the device from his mother. No luck. Father must have taken the family with him to Pueblo.

He'd exhausted every idea. Sleep had fled, along with his appetite. With Arianna back, he could no longer search the house, unless he was certain she wasn't there.

Sitting stiffly at his desk in the Pueblo Police Department, he contemplated his next move. If Father was hopping through time around the globe to commit his crimes, it would be impossible to catch him. He pounded a fist to his leg as desperation clutched his heart.

He had promised his family. They were looking to him for help, but he had nothing to offer—he couldn't even find the devilish device. Worthless—that's what he was; no good to the people who counted on him. Shuffling papers around his desk just to busy his trembling hands, he recognized he wasn't accomplishing anything at the office. Perhaps a week or two off from work would be wise.

At first light on Saturday morning, he headed to the stables south of town. He paid a farmer to board Maida Vale there. Riding his horse had helped him many times when he'd needed to work through frustrations. What he couldn't share with another human being, he could share with his horse. Even though he didn't voice his concerns aloud, his mare seemed to sense his every emotion.

He galloped hard and fast through a field that led to a rocky, desert terrain on the outskirts of town. He reluctantly slowed his horse to avoid a misstep into one of the many ruts on the path. Riding proved to be therapeutic. Although the horse provided no solution to his problem, he felt more relaxed as he returned to the stable and dismounted. Maybe this time off work would allow him to find the answer that had thus far eluded him. He must formulate a plan and act on it before tragedy struck the ones he loved—his family, and yes, Arianna. As much as he hated to admit it, Christopher worried for her more than anyone else. Mother, Sarah and Joshua had suffered under Father's cruel dominion, but he'd never inflict permanent damage on them— Christopher hoped. Ari, however, was expendable.

Chapter Thirty-Seven

"Over to your right. Higher. Yes, that's it." Arianna nodded to the man hanging the art, then stared down at her notebook to see where the next canvas should be placed. The graph paper she'd used to sketch her arrangements allowed her to calculate very precisely where each piece be hung.

Deliveries had been coming in at a rapid pace all week. After countless hours arranging artwork on paper, she'd finally be rewarded. Now the fun could begin—seeing her ideas come to life. She found it difficult, however, to maintain control when she could only be in one room at a time. There was a flourish of activity happening in several of the rooms, and every deliveryman, furniture assembler and art hanger pelted her with questions. "How high? How low? Which room? Which floor? How many? What color?" Her head began to spin.

I sure could use a partner, she thought for the tenth time today. She sighed.

Standing in the huge family room, still issuing directions, she admired the valances that had recently been hung atop the large picture window, which showed off the view from the back of the house. The landscapers had finished their work there. Beautiful. Gardens of flowers—asters, lavender, chrysanthemum, just to name a few—covered the grounds. Itching to get a closer look, as her work for the most part confined her to the indoors, she swung open one of the French doors. "I'll be right back," she hollered to Jack, one of the hired hands. "Feel free to take a break. You've earned it." And so had she.

She felt like a naughty child hiding from the babysitter, but she needed some fresh air, and the flowers beckoned her. The moment she opened the door, a cool breeze carrying an exquisite floral fragrance tickled her nose—aww, the light, innocent scent of primrose—what a paradox. She shook her head. Almost involuntarily, she started down the path that led around the garden. Her eyes danced from flower to flower. Then there were the trees and shrubbery: boxwoods, hydrangea, and dogwoods. She took her time smelling each variety of flower and admiring the carefully placed shrubs and trees. This really was an English garden. She'd been transported.

When she reached the farthest end of the garden, she looked back at the house, admiring the view from a different vantage point. Even from the back it was beautiful. She then turned to take in the contrast of the surrounding terrain. Her breath caught as she saw a man on horseback just up the ridge. *Is that*, she walked forward a few steps, *maybe...I think it's Christopher.* He'd mentioned he rode in the area, but it was the middle of the week. He should be working.

He moved at a slow canter, so Arianna called out to him. "Christopher, is that you?"

He jerked as if startled and squinted into the sun. "Arianna?" His voice sounded strained.

"Yes, it's me." She waved, happy to see him, as always. She began moving toward him. He seemed to hesitate before he nudged his horse to meet her halfway.

When they were finally close enough to have a conversation, she stopped short—her heart lurched. Christopher looked ill. Unshaven, he had the beginnings of a beard along his jaw-line, lending him a rugged, out-doorsy look. She didn't like how gaunt his face appeared and how dark circles framed his empty eyes—his intense blue irises had faded to gray.

"Are you feeling okay?" She tried not to sound alarmed.

He shrugged and looked past her. "I am well enough. And you? Have you had any further unwanted encounters with Mr. Somers? You're not here alone, are you?" A flicker of panic lit his eyes.

"Are you kidding? The place is crawling with people. That's why I'm out here." She gave him a guilty smile. "And don't worry; I'm doing what you said to do—staying out of Mr. Somers' way. What's going on? You don't seem yourself."

His lips pulled into a tight line. He fidgeted in the saddle but didn't say anything in response to her question.

"Do you have time to talk? I'm taking a little break from the craziness going on inside." She motioned to the house. He continued to stare off somewhere as if he were choosing the correct answer. "Come on, Christopher. You've always been there for me when I've needed you. Please let me return the favor."

He finally looked at her and gave her a single nod, then dismounted and tied the reins to a nearby tree.

Arianna sucked in a breath. The horse he'd been riding was magnificent—a rich chestnut color with a black mane and tail, white socks covering the bottoms of all four legs. And the size—it was huge. "Your horse is beautiful. What's its name?"

The question seemed to bring some life back into Christopher's eyes. He patted the horse. "Her name is Maida Vale."

"Maidabell?" She tilted her head in question.

"Maida Vale," he repeated. "I named her after a favorite area of mine in London. She reminds me of home."

They found a clump of grass under the tree he'd tethered Maida Vale to and sat down together.

Christopher didn't seem inclined to say anything, so Arianna began the conversation. "I don't know what it is you are going through, and I know you won't tell me, but isn't there someone who can help you? It hurts me to see you like this."

He began shaking his head before she finished her sentence. "There is no one who can help me, Arianna. I do not even know how to help myself. The problem is"—he shrugged—"complicated." His voice was just above a whisper.

She hated seeing him this way. There must be something she could do. After all he had done for her—driving her when she'd needed a ride, taking her to Denver, paying for her car repairs, sitting with her when she'd needed a friend after her run-in with Mr. Somers—she felt desperate to help him with this burden. She reached out to touch him, but he flinched.

"This was a mistake." Christopher began to rise. Ari tugged on his hand, bringing him back down beside her.

"I'm sorry. You don't have to tell me anything, or even talk at all. If it helps, can I just hold you?" She didn't know what else she could do, but she did know that the comfort of a loved one's touch had helped to heal her aching heart on many occasions. She moved closer and put her arms around him. He tensed, then relaxed a fraction and pulled her tighter into an embrace. She felt like he was holding on for dear life. Her heart hurt for him, but she was happy that he'd not pushed her away. She should be in the house doing her job, but right now Christopher mattered more.

He rested his head on top of hers. With her hand resting on his chest, she felt his heartbeat slow to a less frantic pace.

After several long minutes, he loosened his grip. Putting his hands on both sides of her face, he looked deep into her eyes. "Just being with you helps me, Arianna," he whispered. "Thank you." He lowered his face to hers and grazed her lips with his. She shivered and longed for more but knew what a mistake that would be.

Before she could reply, he stood and began to mount his horse. She helplessly observed him, feeling desperate once again.

She watched silently as he galloped away. He looked so natural on a horse, as if he'd ridden all his life. She turned back to the house—the house of secrets—made her way through the gardens and slipped in the back door.

Activity still buzzed all around her, but she barely noticed. Fighting off the heaviness she felt for Christopher, she returned to her lists and charts.

****

Images of Christopher haunted Arianna for the rest of the week, but she had a job to do, and he'd left her no choice but to put him in the far reaches of her heart and move on. She couldn't help him with something he was so unwilling to share with her. For the first time since this assignment had begun, she looked forward to Friday, anticipating more correspondence from Sarah.

Sarah didn't disappoint. While Ari nonchalantly went about her work, she spied the shy young woman making her way up the stairs to her bedroom, where Ari hoped she would read, then write, in her journal.

When all was quiet that evening, Ari once again crept into Sarah's room, pulled the journal from between the mattresses and began to read.

> *Dear Journal,*
>
> *A, thank you for reading and responding to my correspondence. I am so happy you are willing to become my friend. Your trip across the country sounds very pleasant. Can you tell me more about your family? My travels have not been as extensive as you might have imagined. I do miss England, though.*
>
> *You have met my family, and I daren't write too much about them, except to say that we were once happy, like you and your family. Someday, I wish to be happy once again. Perhaps then, you and I shall become best of friends.*
>
> *Yours, S.*

Arianna pondered each word Sarah had written. Her travels had to have been extensive, unless they'd flown from England straight to Colorado, only to have

Mr. Somers go berserk and hold them all prisoner. That didn't make sense. Nobody came to the United States from England without touring New York, Chicago, even California.

Then there was the part about being happy once. Arianna couldn't help but wonder what had changed to put an end to their happiness. Nor could she imagine being happy with Mr. Somers as her father—anywhere.

Wait a minute. Her pulse quickened. Christopher had said that Mr. Somers had once committed some kind of crime. Maybe they were trying to keep a low profile in Colorado.

She could wonder all she wanted, but she knew she should steer clear of too many questions. She would play it safe and describe her own family.

Just as she put pen to paper, a creak on the stairs startled her. She froze. More creaks. She closed the book and scanned the room for somewhere to stash it.

"Miss Miller?"

Too late.

Chapter Thirty-Eight

Arianna took a deep breath to calm her rapidly beating heart. She put the book to the side of her, hopefully out of sight, then turned her attention to the voice in the doorway. She cleared her throat, certain a frog had taken up occupancy in the last few seconds. "Yes?"

"We forgot the ottoman that goes with the chair in the master bedroom. The door was unlocked, so I told the guys I'd check to see if you were still here. Since you are, I'll just have them bring it on up."

A whoosh of air escaped her lungs. "Of course, Jack, go right ahead. I'll be here for a few more minutes." He nodded and left the room.

Once again, she picked up the pen, her hands clammy as she began to write.

Dear Journal,

S, I would be happy to tell you about my family. I had a very happy childhood. My father worked as an accountant and my mother, a nurse. I also had a younger brother, Seth. We'd probably be considered a typical American family. My father used to love the outdoors, so we spent many weekends hiking or camping. Those are my fondest memories. Sadly, nearly three years ago, while I was away at college, my family was involved in a fatal car accident. It was early December, and as you know, Colorado roads turn very icy. My parents and brother were heading home after attending a Christmas concert at Seth's school. As they entered an intersection, another car ran the red light, or maybe he couldn't have stopped because of the ice—it doesn't really matter now. He slammed into my family's car, spinning them out of control in the middle of the intersection. Oncoming traffic from both directions smashed into them. The car that ran the red light sped off. Witnesses at the scene told police the red Cadillac had come from a bar down the street.

Ari began to second-guess the wisdom of writing the whole sad account of her family's deaths to someone she barely knew, but something about it felt right. After all, Sarah's happy life had seemed to end just as abruptly as Arianna's had. This might help Sarah to trust her.

She continued.

It has been very difficult to adjust to a life without my family, but thankfully I have a good job and several friends who have helped me through it. I hope I can be that kind of friend to you. Sincerely, A.

Arianna realized that, for the first time since it had happened, she'd given a summary of the accident without becoming emotional. Perhaps, out of a deeper concern for Sarah, she had found a way to face her own grief.

****

"Who's texting me so early on a Saturday morning?" Ari moaned, reaching for her phone.

She scrubbed at her eyes to bring the small screen into focus. Christopher. Ever since their encounter on the rise behind the Somers' house, she'd worried about him. Whatever had bothered him back when they'd argued clearly had not been resolved.

She read the text. *Would you care to go riding with me today?* Hope sprang in her heart. Not a hope they would get back together, more a hope that he would allow her to help him. No matter how their relationship stood, she wanted Christopher to be happy. He deserved it. He was a good man. A true gentleman—when he wasn't pushing her out the door and out of his secret life.

It took her a minute to process what he meant. *Horseback riding*, she realized. She wrote back, *I'd love to, but I've never ridden a horse.*

Christopher replied, *You can ride with me on my horse, if you would like.*

Then yes, but only if you let me take you to lunch after. I think you've been starving yourself. There seemed to be an extra pause before his response came.

How soon can you be ready?

Ari breathed a sigh of relief. She'd thought he might have changed his mind. *Is thirty minutes okay?*

Perfect; see you then.

Ari jumped out of bed and frantically began rummaging through her closet. Her temporary resident *s*tatus meant she didn't have too many choices. She settled on some blue jeans and coral-colored, button-down shirt. Cotton, so she wouldn't get all sweaty in the summer heat.

She applied some make-up and heard the rumble of Christopher's squad car pulling up after she'd finished weaving her hair into a loose braid. She opened the door just as he began to knock.

She appraised him, hoping to see some improvement from earlier in the week. He still looked too thin, but his eyes flashed with a smidgeon of the old familiar sparkle she'd loved so much—a small comfort.

As they drove to the corral where he stabled his horse, Arianna kept the talk light. She didn't want him to change his mind.

He saddled the horse with a double seat saddle, something she'd never seen before, and gave her a brief explanation of how he would help her mount up; then, in one fluid motion, he wrapped his strong hands around her small waist and hoisted her atop the horse. Apparently, he hadn't lost any muscle. She tried to will away any shivers of excitement that accompanied his touch. Before she knew it, he was on the horse behind her.

"Just hold onto the pommel." He reached around her and touched the raised front of the saddle. "I will keep an arm around you so you needn't fear falling." He clicked his tongue and they were off.

At first they moved at a slow trot, then sped to a canter. The faster they rode, the more enlivening it felt. No wonder he liked to do this so often. Ari lifted her face to the sun and closed her eyes. She could get lost in this moment. She allowed her body to relax against Christopher's warm chest.

They rode along the ridge where Ari had spotted him just days before. "There are riding trails all along here." He moved his hand in an arc, directing her eyes to the many paths surrounding them. "I come here often."

She took in the view of the house from the horse trail. It was beautiful, but so out of place. "Do you ever wonder why the Somers chose to build such a pretty house out in the middle of nowhere?" She hoped she hadn't stepped into that imaginary pile of secrets of his.

Christopher sat silent just long enough for her to panic, then answered, "I am certain Mr. Somers has some very specific reasons for building his fortress away from the bulk of society."

A chill snaked down her spine as she recalled his admission of knowing something of Mr. Somers' depraved character. She wondered if it would be safe to tell him about her journal conversations with Sarah. She decided to give it a try. After all, in for a penny, in for a pound—or so they would say in nineteenth century England.

"I haven't spoken to Sarah since my encounter with Mr. Somers, but I have corresponded with her." She felt Christopher's arm stiffen around her waist. "Don't worry—it was Sarah's idea." She went on to explain what Sarah did to initiate their conversation and how grateful Ari was to be there for her.

"You are communicating through her journal?" His arm flinched, then hardened again.

"Yes. She really needs a friend, and we are careful and hide the journal between the mattresses, so no one will find it." She wished she could see his face. He'd become silent, and she wondered if it had been a bad idea to share anything about Sarah.

Finally, he spoke. "I trust you will keep the conversation light, just in case her father should find out."

"Of course. I care too deeply about Sarah to do otherwise." Not to mention what he might do to Ari.

"Do you want to gallop?" he asked.

She adjusted her position. "I guess. I've never—"

Before the words were out of her mouth, Christopher had flicked the reins and Maida Vale bolted into a sprint. She galloped as if she were being chased—furiously fast. Ari thought it would be bumpy riding at such a break-neck speed, especially sitting so close together on the saddle, but instead, found it smooth and exhilarating. She felt completely secure with Christopher's strong arm wrapped around her.

The wind whipped at her braid. She felt him move his arm from her waist to pull it back over her shoulder. She let go of the pommel with one hand to hold onto the braid so it wouldn't hit him in the face. Maida Vale chose that moment to leap over a small boulder. Ari began to lose her stability and found herself falling. Fear seized her heart, but before she could move into a full-on panic, Christopher hollered something to the horse and had both arms wrapped around her. Maida Vale slowed, then stopped while Christopher pulled her back onto the saddle. Her heart pounded wildly from the terror of almost being thrown. Christopher seemed to sense her fear. He gently rubbed her arms to calm her. She couldn't keep from shaking.

His breath tickled her ear when he whispered, "I'm sorry. Are you okay?"

Ari didn't trust her voice not to wobble, so she nodded.

He continued massaging his hands up and down her quivering arms. The horse made no movement. Ari kept her head down and concentrated on breathing.

"Arianna?" Christopher gently took hold of her chin and tilted her face toward his. "I am really sorry. Would you like to finish the ride—at a slower pace, of course? Or…" He looked around and saw what she had been seeing for the last hour: nothing but open space.

She shifted her body to talk to him more comfortably, then looked into his concern-filled eyes. "I'm sure I'm not the first person to almost fall off a horse." Her voice felt strained but became stronger with each word. "Other than walking—which would take hours—I don't see another way back."

His hand still held her chin. His thumb caressed her as it traveled up her jawline to her lips. This time the shivers that ran down her spine weren't from fear. She felt as if his eyes bored a hole into hers, searching. Yes, the answer was yes. He should kiss her. She knew it wasn't the right answer, but it was what she wanted all the same.

His breath hitched, and his hand dropped to his side, as if he'd come to his senses. "I'm glad you're all right. Let's get you home."

It's best this way, she repeated it in her head. But disappointment filled her heart.

Christopher guided Maida Vale back to the stable. Dismounting first, then lifting Ari down, he took the saddle off and brushed the horse for a few minutes. Ari couldn't help observing the tenderness in his eyes as he spoke in low tones to his mare.

"I can see why you love to ride so much. I feel the same way when I run—free from all my troubles for a while."

He turned his attention from the horse to Arianna. "I'm afraid, my dear, you may not love it so much tomorrow." He motioned to her backside.

She could already feel an ache in her muscles beginning. "So, this is what they mean by 'saddle sore'?"

His lips quirked into a grin—a heavenly sight. "It goes away after you've been riding a few times. Do you still want to force lunch down me, or are you too uncomfortable to sit?"

"Oh no, you're not getting out of lunch that easily—we had a deal."

They chose a restaurant neither of them had been to. Abby's seemed too raw just now.

Still leery about upsetting him with her questions, Arianna let him steer the conversation. She was happy to see some color tint his face, and his eyes appeared bluer. Riding did seem to suit him.

He didn't say much, and she watched as he pushed food around on his plate. Something was haunting him. She needed to know.

"If you don't eat, you won't have the strength to catch the bad guys," she teased.

He glanced up, startled, as if he hadn't noticed he'd been in another world.

"Look, Christopher," her voice gentle, "your problems won't be solved through starvation. Please eat for me. I can't bear to watch you go through this"—she waved her hand—"whatever it is." Her tone had risen in volume and tears stung her eyes. She had his full attention now.

"Arianna." He pulled her hand into his. She let it relax as her fingers unfolded. "I am truly sorry. If it is causing you pain to be with me, I shall not continue to bother you. It is just this—I did feel better after being with you, holding you—as if you somehow lessened my burden—when last we met. I suppose I just wished for something of the same balm today. It was selfish of me. Forgive me."

The tears flowed freely now as she listened to the man she cared for so much suffer from whatever demons haunted him.

He hailed the server and asked for the check as Ari attempted to regain her composure. "And a box for his food," she managed to rasp out to the waiter. The attendant nodded and walked away.

"You can't keep shutting me out. I care too much—"

"That is why I must. Because I care too much, as well." His hand tightened around hers. "I have never met a kinder person than you, Arianna. Please believe me when I say you deserve someone much better than I."

"But what if it's *you* I want?" she whispered back.

Chapter Thirty-Nine

Christopher's heart broke in half at Ari's admission. Making her angry had been painful; making her miserable, sheer torture.

Once he had delivered Ari to her apartment, he drove to the police station. He hadn't been called in; he just didn't wish to be home—alone. Busying himself until past dark, he worked through piles of paperwork. Finally, his desk offered no more diversions, so he headed to his empty apartment and aimed for his bed.

I just keep mucking up things. He could neither help, nor stop hurting the ones he loved the most. Locating a nearly guttered taper—finding solace in the precious few articles that still existed from his childhood—he lit the candle and breathed in the waxy, fragrant remains of a lost world.

Shadows danced on the ceiling as he lay in his bed. His crowded bed—congested with worry, fear, sorrow and hopelessness—no room for sleep.

He didn't desire sleep, anyway. He wanted only to remember the pink of Arianna's cheeks, so soft and flawless. The feel of her silky hair, woven into a braid that had pestered him when they rode. Her full lips he'd nearly kissed. The memories were tender. Her eyes—

He stopped himself there, wishing to remember everything but her eyes. They'd been too honest. He did not want to relive the hurt he had caused her—again.

I'm finished being a greedy fool—taking from Ari without giving back. *That's it. I'm going to tell her everything—the whole truth.* She'd likely not believe him. And if she did, she'd know he was the son of a thief and murderer. She would want nothing to do with him. ...Or perhaps he'd underestimated her and by telling her, they could conceivably share a future together. The possibility he'd been denying all along spread warmth to his heart.

Their relationship had suffered enough. It would either live or die with the truth.

He picked up his cell phone. The knots in his shoulders began to unravel. The truth, already setting him free, gave him resolve to make the call.

His text notification light blinked at him. Clicking it, he realized he'd missed a text from Ari. *Christopher, I made it clear where I wanted our relationship to go today. I realize you don't share my feelings. I'm done. I won't pursue more than a friendship with you. Maybe it's too soon for even that. Ari.*

His fingers moved quickly to punch in her number. He had no idea how long ago she'd sent the text, but he wouldn't let her believe she'd let him down. The phone rang, and then her voicemail answered. He dialed again with the same results.

His mood darkened once again.

He snuffed out the candle.

****

Christopher awoke Sunday morning to his phone ringing. He'd left it next to his bed just in case. Snatching it up, he was ready to tell Ari everything. Whether she believed him or not, she was going to hear it.

"Flemming, we need you at the station. Some things went down during the night. It may require a trip to Colorado Springs."

He ended the call from the police sergeant and his thoughts made a U-turn. He'd have to give Ari his implausible, yet true, life story another time.

Letting out a breath of disappointment, he readied himself for work.

Chapter Forty

"I refuse to cry one more tear for that man." Ari threw her soggy pillow onto the floor. She swung her legs over the side of her bed in an attempt to rise on Sunday morning. "Ouch!" She glowered as she remembered Christopher's prediction. He'd likely be happy she was sore.

After a sleepless night crying over a man she'd as good as handed her heart, only to have him reject it, she deserved a warm bath. Christopher hadn't even returned her text yesterday. After waiting an hour for something—a reply, an apology or at least confirmation he'd received it—she'd turned her phone off and put it in a drawer. When she'd turned it back on in the morning, the blank screen, though not surprising since she'd left it off, filled her with emptiness.

She hobbled to the bathtub and turned on the faucet, closed her eyes and let the warm water soothe her bruised muscles and broken heart.

So what if Christopher was everything she had ever wanted in a man. Kind and generous—she could never forget the number of times he'd come to her aid—and exceptionally handsome. She closed her eyes and pictured his face, his delicious dimple creasing when he'd smile. Great with kids—she recalled the Frisbee incident at the picnic—and most of all, he was a gentleman. He'd never pushed her to do anything she hadn't been ready for—but he'd pushed her away. She slapped the water, splashing white foam against the wall. He'd never have the chance to do it again. She was done. "Christopher Flemming, you are officially out of my life. You may have been the man I'd hoped to spend the rest of my days with, but it's obvious you don't feel the same. I came here to do a job." She blinked back a stubborn tear. "And that's that."

****

Monday morning shined bright and cheery—a complete contradiction to her mood—but still, Monday meant work and work meant a diversion from the slump she'd been experiencing.

At least she had plenty to do. She checked her watch, counting the minutes until the next truck was due to arrive. Deliveries were a daily event now. Everything had been ordered; it was a matter of awaiting their arrival, then seeing the pieces properly placed. Her heart hurt. Thankfully there was no one there to ask her about her foul mood. She didn't want to talk—just work.

As the week dragged on, Ari anxiously anticipated Friday—which still seemed an eternity away. She would have Sarah's journal to read; that was something to look forward to—unless Mr. Somers came alone.

Friday eventually made its way into Arianna's week. She brightened when all the Somers arrived with loads of personal items to put in their bedrooms. Sarah caught her eye and nearly smiled until Mr. Somers entered behind her. Her head immediately dropped, and Ari turned a page in her notebook, as if she hadn't noticed Sarah at all. She wanted so badly to hug her and converse with her like normal friends. She sighed. There was nothing normal about the Somers.

Now that their new furniture was in place, they could fill the closets and drawers. Ari noticed that Sarah spent an unusually long time alone in her bedroom. Of course, Sarah could be one of those slow, meticulous types who took more care than most in putting away her belongings. Arianna hoped that wasn't the case. She itched to find out if Sarah had written in her journal, fascinated by any glimpse into this mysterious family.

Mr. Somers seemed tired—or cross. Ari dreaded the conversation sure to happen before the family's departure. Every week he found something to grouse about—legitimate or not. Ninety-nine point nine percent not. She swore he got pleasure from other people's unhappiness. No sooner had she thought it than Mr. Somers entered the room wearing the scowl she'd come to realize was permanent.

"Miss Miller? Are you ready to review this week's progress?"

She was never ready to speak to him, but she saw no escape. Ironic—that was probably how Sarah felt. "Yes, Mr. Somers. I'm ready." She took a seat at the table across from the man who intimidated her, frightened her, threatened her, but unfortunately, also presently employed her.

His black eyes roved over the carefully prepared pages she'd set before him. Grunts and occasional twitches gave Ari no indication of what he thought. "Everything seems to be in order." He stood abruptly and barked at his family to stop their tarrying and head to the car.

Mr. Somers—the king of criticism—just said everything seemed to be in order, or maybe she was hallucinating. He always found something to complain about. She realized her mouth had fallen open, and promptly closed it. Maybe it was his birthday, or something. Whatever it was, she'd take it.

Peering through the blinds until the Somers' car disappeared, she bolted the door so there would be no surprise visitors, then headed up the grand staircase to Sarah's room. She retrieved the journal and thumbed through the pages until spying the one she sought.

Dear Journal,

Ari's heartbeat accelerated with nervous excitement as she began to read.

> *A, I am so sorry to read about the car accident and that you now find yourself without a family. I cannot comprehend the loss you must feel. Cars frighten me; they move so fast. My father drives them, but I do not. He drove a red car at one time, but for some reason traded it for the black one he drives now.*

A cold chill prickled Ari's skin. *No. No way. Too much of a coincidence.*

Rubbing her temples and releasing a few cleansing breaths, she read on.

> *I know I make complaints about my family's situation, but at least I still have them. Please accept my most heartfelt condolences. While my loss is not so dear as yours, I do so miss my homeland, as well as my own time.*

Sarah had written a lot more, then scribbled it out. Arianna could make out a few of the smeared letters, but not enough. She turned on the lamp that sat on the nightstand, then pulled off its shade. When she held the page close to the light, she could read Sarah's words.

> *I feel completely displaced here. In England, before my father slipped from his standing in society, I had a very happy family, too. Sadly, my father's bad decisions destroyed his once-fine character. He was not always a bad person. Now, however, I fear I will never be able to forgive the things he has done, and the pain he continually inflicts upon our family. Perhaps time will repair these feelings. I hope that has happened for you. Has time healed your wounds? Sometimes that is all we have on our side. Please know that I value our friendship. Yours, S.*

Ari's heart raced. Unable to organize the thoughts that jumped and rattled in her head, she put the journal down and wandered the halls of the empty house once more, just to make certain she was alone.

Phrases such as "before my father slipped from his standing in society" confused her. Surely modern-day England's social and political systems had evolved from the way her books depicted London two hundred years ago. She shivered. Perhaps not. And she wondered what Sarah meant about Mr. Somers' standing. "Please let Sarah be exaggerating," she whispered.

Then there was the line about Sarah missing her own time. There was so much she was not understanding about this mysterious family. So many secrets had been swept under the rug.

Arianna didn't know the most appropriate way to respond to Sarah, but she'd do her best. She had to be very careful not to mention anything about her father. Sarah clearly had second thoughts after she'd written it. Once again Ari had read something she shouldn't have. She just felt so desperate to help.

> *Dear Journal,*
>
> *S, thank you for your condolences. Time has helped in the healing process, and one day I am confident I will not miss my family as sorely as I do now. It does get better each day. I can understand missing your homeland, but what did you mean when you said you miss your own time? That puzzles me. I don't mean to pry; it's just that the more I learn about your family, the less I feel I know. Your secrets are safe with me, if you feel inclined to share them. On a happier note, next week on August 6th, it's my birthday. My friends are all in Denver, so I won't be doing anything special for it. How did you celebrate birthdays back in England? I treasure our friendship as well.*
>
> *Sincerely, A.*

Arianna did treasure her budding friendship with Sarah, especially after all she had been through with

Christopher. Sarah was perhaps her only friend in Pueblo.

As she stood to leave, her eye caught something new placed on Sarah's dresser. *Wow,* she thought, *this mirror, comb and brush set are positively vintage.* Ari knew a fair amount about antiques, having spent two semesters studying them in school. Gently fondling the brush, she wondered how something so obviously nineteenth century could look new. They definitely couldn't be found in stores today. And the set had been so well preserved. She snapped some pictures to send Maggie. *She won't appreciate them as I do, but I've got to show someone.*

After putting the articles back where they belonged, she began her routine tour of the house. Ari loved looking around and observing the improvements of the day, adjusting anything that was not precisely in its place, as well as soaking in the beauty of the house. A perfectionist, she always left everything in order. Tonight was more rewarding than most, as the Somers had brought with them several interesting items. Arianna went from room to room searching for more antiques, and she wasn't disappointed. There weren't many, but some of the things she spotted—antique candelabras, picture frames and even some furniture pieces—absolutely fascinated her. They were in mint condition. She needed to find the antique store where the Somers shopped. It had to be in Denver, unless they'd brought them from England, a more likely scenario.

There were candles—lots of them, as if they still used them for light. The Somers seemed to be even more intrigued by the nineteenth century than she was.

She held up a taper, puzzled. Flipping the light switch on and off, she chuckled, wondering if she should let them in on a little secret.

One of her favorite rooms to walk through each evening was Joshua's. He reminded her of her brother, Seth. She hadn't been given specific instructions as to how Josh would like his room furnished, so she'd taken some liberties and decorated it the way Seth would have liked, adding a basketball-hoop hamper and shadow boxes filled with helmets, nets, and balls of every kind. Horizontal, broad-striped bedding gave it just the right touch. It appeared much more modern than the other rooms, but Arianna felt certain Joshua would like a sports-themed space, as opposed to a floral Victorian room. Judging by the expression on his face when he'd seen it with all its furnishings today, she'd made the right call.

That night, she sat in the room and spoke to Seth as if he were with her. She missed her brother. "You would like this room, Seth." She tossed a baseball from hand to hand. "Wish you were here, little brother." She tossed the ball once more. As if an invisible hand held it, the ball hung, suspended in the air, as the nightmare she'd had in Denver revisited her memory. Shivers of fear clutched her chest and she could hardly breathe.

"Run, Ari, run!" She swore it was Seth's voice she heard.

The ball dropped to the ground.

Chapter Forty-One

Christopher spent a frustrating few days in Colorado Springs. A murder suspect had stolen a car Saturday night in Pueblo and had been apprehended by the police in the Springs. Christopher, having worked on the homicide case in Denver before he'd been transferred, was assigned to connect the dots that led the suspect to Pueblo then Colorado Springs, collecting enough evidence to get him off the streets for good.

He'd tried calling Ari a few times, but between the lack of cell phone service at her jobsite, and his demanding work situation, he never made a connection. Maybe it was better that way. By the time he'd headed back to Pueblo on Friday, he'd convinced himself to stop trying and focus on his family.

However, he couldn't quit thinking about Ari's and Sarah's journal conversations. There had to be a way for him to communicate with Sarah. If he could, she might be able to lead him to Father's device.

He still had the key to the house he'd copied. Fingering it in his pocket, he decided he would investigate the possibility of finding and using his sister's journal.

On Saturday, when he figured nobody would be working there, he disarmed the alarm to his family's home and let himself in.

Making his way through the house, he checked each room until he was certain he'd found Sarah's. Dropping to his knees, he felt between the mattresses until his fingers bumped into the leather book. He pulled out the journal. This could somehow be the answer that had evaded him for so long.

Opening it, he immersed himself in the conversation between Ari and Sarah. Arianna seemed to be a balm for Sarah, just as she had been for him. He closed his eyes as thoughts of Ari tumbled through his head. His heart lurched. The heavy sadness made him physically ache. He quickly began reading again, before reflections of her completely drowned him.

Glancing down the page, an illegible paragraph caught his attention and he skipped ahead a few entries, curious to decipher the words. They appeared to have been scribbled out. He held the page up to the light streaming through the window. His heart immediately began pounding harder and faster. No, no, Sarah was divulging too much. Perhaps Arianna hadn't read this, but what if she had? Any reaction on Ari's part could land her in serious trouble. He so badly wished to write in the book and admonish his sister to take more care in what she wrote. He feared for both Sarah and Arianna, should the journal be discovered by Father.

Looking around, he realized the room had been fully furnished and would soon be ready for its occupants. They would be moving in any day. The idea struck him. Maybe he could leave a note for Sarah in her bedding. She might not find it right away, but she would have to go to bed in this house at some point and would find it then.

He tore a page from the back of the journal, took a pen from Sarah's desk and began to compose a letter.

My Dearest Sarah,

Do not wonder how I am able to come into this home, but I have found a way to do it. I need to communicate with you. Please write on the back of this paper and leave it where you've found it. We can have a conversation. I need your help if I am ever to find the device—I am certain you know of what I speak. Sarah, do you know where it is? I have searched this house from top to bottom and cannot find it. I do so need your help. But, as always, be careful, let no one know what you are about.

Yours, C.

With hopeful anticipation, he placed the letter just beneath the covers, out of sight, then left the house.

Chapter Forty-Two

Convinced her imagination had gotten the better of her Friday night, Ari refused to let the frightening incident in Joshua's room bother her. She must remain focused.

Today, butterflies fluttered in her stomach as anxiety pulsed through her veins. She always felt this way when a project entered its final weeks. But never having worked solo, she felt the stress of it all more keenly. She bore the full weight of its success or failure. Activity moved at a fever pitch. The next few weeks were critical. During this time every loose end must be tied and every detail addressed.

She tried to smile at her reflection in the mirror as she brushed through her blonde tresses. "I think I can get to the finish line." She touched two fingers to her wrist, noting the reckless rhythm. She frowned. "That is, if I don't have a nervous breakdown first."

Monday and Tuesday flew by with constant commotion in the house—deliveries, installations—as usual, but times a thousand. Ari loved seeing the final touches applied, but also found it exhausting. Wednesday was no different. When she had a second to eat a sandwich she'd packed, she scooted up to the table to scan her notes. The date at the top of her planner popped, catching her attention. *Today's my birthday.*

Strange I didn't think of it 'til just now. She shrugged and continued perusing her notes.

By day's end, she was too tired to care what the calendar said. She flopped onto a sofa and the protective cover crinkled beneath her. *I can't wait to remove it.* She poked a small hole in the plastic. For now, she just wanted to drag herself to her car, pick up some fast-food—something terribly bad for her, but sinfully delicious—go home, and veg out in front of the TV. She let out a huge sigh. And she'd do just that as soon as she had the strength to move off the couch. She almost closed her eyes but decided that celebrating her birthday would be far better in her apartment than asleep on the Somers' sofa.

As soon as she entered cell phone service range, her phone buzzed with a text message from Maggie. She waited until the next stoplight to read it. *Wishing you a super happy birthday. Call me!* Ari smiled, amazed at how one little line brightened her day.

Things were going according to plan. An aroma of hot fries wafted through the car, making her mouth water. Arms laden with food, along with her purse and work-supply bag, she plodded through the complex parking lot and headed for her apartment but stopped short when she saw a dark shadow next to her door. She edged around the building until she was out of sight, then peeked over to see who it could be. The figure moved, and she sucked in a breath. She bit down on her lip to minimize escaping noises. It had to be Mr. Somers. No one else was bold enough to just wait to torment her. Panic rippled through her body.

After several long moments, her legs wobbled, and her arms began to tire from holding everything. She'd had enough. If he wouldn't move, she'd face him head-on. Heart thudding wildly, she took a few steps, closing in on the intruder. If only it weren't so dark.

A breeze whispered by and the figure lurched toward her.

"Wha—" She nearly dropped the food.

She burst into a nervous giggle. "A balloon!" Make that several balloons in a bouquet sat next to her apartment. Her hand still trembled as she opened the door and turned on a switch, shedding light on the offender. Propped next to the balloon bouquet was a birthday card.

Somehow she managed to lug it all to her table, then collapsed on a chair and took a long, calming breath.

She tore open the envelope and pulled out the card. It had a simple generic birthday greeting on the outside. When she opened it, her eyes dropped directly to the bottom. Christopher. She wondered how he knew it was her birthday. She didn't remember telling anyone in Pueblo. Her emotions teetered between excitement and anxiety.

She returned to the beginning of the note.

Arianna, I could not bear the thought of you spending this special day alone. For now, however, this is the best I can do.

Typical Christopher. Even when they weren't speaking, he couldn't let her birthday go by without doing something thoughtful. She wanted to smile, but her heart smarted from the dull ache of loneliness. She missed everything about him. Everything except for the thing that mattered most—he didn't trust her with his secrets.

Temptation beckoned her to sit down and have a good cry. She resisted. She knew him well enough to know he did this to cheer her, not to make her cry. He'd never hurt her intentionally. She paused to think about the irony of that statement. Almost never. She decided to enjoy the party atmosphere the balloons created rather than allow herself to grieve losing Christopher all over again.

****

On Friday, Mr. Somers showed up alone, much to Arianna's dismay.

She was too busy to worry about it for long, however, as the last of the draperies and other window coverings were being installed. "This pulls the whole décor plan together," she said to a nearby worker. He nodded. She appraised the beautiful colors popping from every room of the house. Mr. Somers even acted the tiniest bit pleased with the effect.

He still sat at his mahogany desk studying some papers when Ari had finished her work and prepared to leave. He was probably looking over her contract, trying to figure out a way he could still fire her. She would have smiled at her joke, but, knowing Mr. Somers better now, it wasn't funny. She craned her neck to covertly peer at what he scrutinized so intently. A newspaper, and unless he could read upside-down, he was just waiting for her to leave. She was all too happy to oblige. Mr. Somers—such an odd, odd man. She pulled her bag over her shoulder. It was his house, and he could do whatever he wanted. Taking a quick glance around, she exited, grateful to have made it through another Friday. Yay for her. She let out a big sigh of relief.

After eating dinner, Ari snuggled up on the couch and turned on the television to unwind. Clicking the remote, she looked for a comedy, something to get her mind off work. Commercials seemed to be playing on every single station.

"Arianna!"

She jerked to attention, her heart in her throat. Who was that? It'd sounded like her father, but that was impossible. Perhaps it had been the TV, or maybe she'd dosed off for a moment.

"Pay attention!" the man's voice said with great urgency. She must be hallucinating.

"Attention to what?"

Was it her imagination, or had the volume on the television increased? She peered closely at the ad still playing. A car commercial. She switched stations. The same ad played. Blood pulsed through her veins so fast, she thought she'd faint. *What is it about this ad that's so important?*

A red Cadillac cruised across the screen. Ari's heart stopped. The driver, who looked eerily like Mr. Somers, paused long enough to sneer at her, then drove away laughing.

Her entire body shook. Had she been dreaming? No. Her father had been trying to tell her something. Warmth enveloped her as if to confirm she was on the right track. Mr. Somers. What if he'd been the drunk driver who'd killed her family? And if so, how could she ever prove it? Nobody would believe her. They'd think she was nutty. Maybe she was.

She spent a long, tortuous night coming up with no answers.

The next day, as she prepared to work out the last details in her notebook, she realized she must have left the book at the Somers' house. Just what she wished to do—go back to work on a Saturday, especially after the fright she'd experienced the previous evening. She climbed into her little red car and headed south.

She let herself in and absorbed the full beauty of her work for a moment. It had rarely been calm enough in the house lately to do that. She didn't think she would ever see anything so pretty as long as she lived. A wistful sigh escaped her as she scanned the rooms for her notebook.

The ground jolted. "What the heck was that?" Another one soon followed. "Could it be an earthquake? Doubtful." She looked outside and saw nothing but quiet, deserted landscape. A hum began and grew into a rumbling vibration. Still searching for her notebook, her pulse quickened exponentially. Where was it? She needed to leave. Now! When she walked into the study, she noticed the Persian rug wasn't lying flat. The perfectionist in her knew she hadn't left the house with the rug pulled up like that. As she crossed the room to straighten it, the ground shook violently, and she lurched forward. She steadied her legs, but the vibrations came even stronger and louder. She had the end of the rug in her hand, ready to pull it back into place, when she spied what looked like a trapdoor. A cold chill swept over her like a frigid Arctic blast. A thousand questions assaulted her as she stared at it. Whatever was shaking this room was down there. She jumped back, as if suddenly stung by the rug. Notebook or not, she was getting out of there.

She sprinted out of the room and the house, only turning back long enough to set the alarm. Her hands shook so hard she had difficulty sliding her key into the car door. She couldn't get away fast enough.

Mr. Somers had to be down there. She shivered. He'd been parking in the garage lately, so she hadn't seen his black Cadillac. Thoughts of Christopher nagged at her. No. She would not run to him.

Not this time.

Not anymore.

Chapter Forty-Three

Christopher galloped hard and fast. Maida Vale loved speed, and so did he. The warm wind whipping against his face helped calm the nervous anxiety roiling in his stomach.

Riding along the ridge behind his family's home, he wondered if he should go in to see if Sarah had found his note. A thunderous rumble pulled his gaze to the house. Peculiar. He cantered in a bit closer and began to dismount, then looked down at his muddy boots. Not yet. He'd clean up and return. He wouldn't want anyone—especially Ari—to know he'd been there.

Once he'd gone home and showered, he drove back toward the Somers' residence. Perplexed about the rumbling noises he'd heard from the ridge, he racked his brain, mentally searching for the source, certain he'd heard it before. Déjà vu perhaps. A sudden realization had him pressing hard on the gas, lights on, sirens blaring. The Device. Father must be on the premises using it. This was it! He'd finally catch his father red-handed doing, he shook his head, he didn't know what, but Christopher would find something to nail on him.

The silent house gave no clues of his father's whereabouts. That didn't stop Christopher from storming in, gun drawn, prepared for a fight. He began a search. The smell of sandalwood hung in the air, a sure sign his father had been there. It was especially strong near the study, but he didn't bother entering the room. A quick look through the glass doors told him Father wasn't there. He scanned each room, taking a few extra minutes in Sarah's bedroom to check for the note. He found it still nestled in her sheets, undisturbed. Disappointed, he finished examining the home in search of his father, but soon realized he must have just missed him.

He wanted to kick himself for not entering the house earlier—muddy boots or not. He'd lost at least an hour and a half finishing his ride, showering, then driving back. He ground his teeth, frustrated.

Defeated, he left the house. As he approached his squad car, he noticed a large paper twirling in the soft breeze near the drive. He plucked it up and began to read.

Travelogue: Date August 9
Destination: Paris, France—Louvre Palace
Year: 1867

Christopher's heart nearly stopped. His hands twitched as he realized what he held. Father kept a log of his nefarious travels, and somehow today's entry had gotten away from him.

He took the paper to his apartment to read, needing to analyze every word. Surely, he'd find evidence of a crime—something exposing his father.

After pulling a chair up to his table, he spread the paper out. The writing, although not from the quill pen he'd been accustomed to, brought back a flood of memories. The unique lettering confirmed to him the author's identity. Father, no doubt at all. Now for the crime.

The log read as if it were a journal. Christopher wondered why his father would include so many details.

> *It was a bumpy start, but a smooth ride into Paris, France. Arriving at the Louvre Palace, I could not escape the wretched smell of the nineteenth century. That world is dead to me. Now it is my servant, and I its master. Instead of the rejection once heaped upon me from that century and those people, I am feared and esteemed by all I encounter. Powerful beyond measure, wealthier than the Almighty Himself. I am Benjamin Somerset, earl of nothing, but ruler of all. For one day, all shall bow to me and do my bidding.*

Christopher smirked. Delusional! Father had lost all bearings on reality. He continued reading.

> *No modern alarm systems alerted guards of my arrival, of course. I stowed my traveling device and began my search for art and artifacts—décor for my mansion. Just a few more to round out the collection. The Louvre brimmed with priceless possessions. I had no plans of stealing anything as ostentatious as the Mona Lisa—much too showy. I kept to the more obscure, yet invaluable, pieces.*

Dismantling art that hangs from iron pegs is a bit difficult, but with twenty-first century tools, such as battery-operated drills, the challenge is more of a game—a game I always win.

Two guards must have heard the noise. They rounded the corner just as I had freed the third of three paintings from its iron fasteners. They spoke French, but I understood them. One asked the other about my intense candle. I nearly laughed aloud. They'd seen nothing like it, I'm sure. I shined my flashlight directly in their eyes. They ducked from the powerful beam that blinded them. I heard muffled voices, then shuffling toward me. I feigned fear of being discovered. One man hollered something to me I couldn't understand. I readied my weapon. Shuffling and more muffled whispers followed. I adjusted my position. A man dressed in a uniform stepped from behind a display. Aiming a pistol at me, he told me to stand down. I brandished my semi-automatic, taking pleasure in his astonishment. The knick-knack he held looked like a toy in his quivering fingers. The other guard appeared, gun in hand. He began to approach, but the first man held an arm out, stopping him. I told them I'd had hopes of someone making this lift a bit of a challenge. For a moment, the stunned guards seemed rooted to the ground, but finally one fired on me, the bullet grazing my arm—nothing a bandage can't fix. I fired back, leveling both. Oh, how I like to see the bodies tumble.

Christopher's stomach churned. No longer amusing, Father's narration had turned deadly. How many lives had been taken at Benjamin Somerset's hands? The thought soured in his stomach like curdled cream. Equally alarming to his father's blatant disregard for human life was his thirst for blood. It was as if he relished in his crimes. Why else would he write it all down? And in such morbid detail.

He pushed the page away, needing a break from Father's madness. Flipping through the channels on the television, he searched for a distraction, but found no solace. His mind constantly returned to the words on the ledger. Eventually curiosity summoned him back to the table.

A whistle sounded. I considered waiting for the reinforcements—two bodies were not enough. But greed is not characteristic of a gentleman—or so I was taught. I located my traveling device before more guards arrived and loaded the bin with my newly acquired treasures. Once again, the padded compartment I'd built specifically for art worked out splendidly. The new pieces will fit well in the parlor. Beatrice will thank me.

Note: along with tightening the time-travel parameters, I really must fix the loud vibrations this machine generates upon departure—it does cause such a ruckus.

Blood rushed through Christopher's veins. This was the proof he needed; his father's confession to his most recent crime. And if he went back to the house, he'd certainly find the purloined art in the safe he'd discovered earlier.

Keys in hand, he headed out the door, but common sense stopped him before he reached his car. He had the ledger, he could get the art, but the crime took place one hundred fifty years ago. Who, in their right mind, would believe his father had traveled back in time to commit the crime?

As he turned the narration over and over in his mind, any possibility of nailing his father for his crimes faded. Without more evidence, this paper was nothing but fiction. He *must* find the device.

Chapter Forty-Four

As she arrived at her apartment, Arianna's heart still thudded rapidly, threatening to crack her ribs. She pulled her laptop onto her trembling legs and began a Google search. If Christopher wouldn't tell her what Mr. Somers had done, maybe she could find it online. Entering key words: *Denver, Benjamin Somers and Criminal*, she pushed the search button. Nothing.

She changed the location to England. Many sites popped up, but none looked as if it could be what she searched for. His name was just too common.

As she stared at her computer screen, pondering what to do next, her phone rang. "Hi, Ari, I haven't talked to you in a while. How are you?"

"Maggie. It's so good to hear your voice. I have so much to tell you." She pushed her laptop aside, along with thoughts of Mr. Somers. Maggie's voice helped calm her.

"Can't wait to hear." A baby cooed in the background.

"Ooh, is that Ryder? He sounds adorable." Ari could hear Maggie jabbering baby talk.

"Yes, I have you on speaker so I can dual-task. I'm getting good at that nowadays."

"I love the pictures you've texted me. I can't believe how much he's changed already."

After chatting about Ryder, and motherhood in general, Ari glanced at her computer. An idea sprang to mind. "Maggie, you know how you are always digging into your roots, or, you know, doing ancestry stuff?"

"Yeah, why?"

Arianna went on to explain the unusual happenings at the Somers' house and Christopher's suspicions. "I've looked Mr. Somers up on the Internet but haven't found anything."

"You're looking under the name Somers?" Maggie asked.

"Uh-huh, why?"

"Somers might be too common, and if he really is a criminal, I'm sure he's using an alias. What you need to do is an image search."

"How do I do that?" She ripped a piece of paper from her spare notepad to take notes.

"Well, first you need a picture of him. Can you get one?"

Ari frowned as her excitement ebbed. "No way. I don't know how I could possibly get a picture of him. The camera on my phone works at the house, but can you imagine what he'd do if he ever caught me taking his picture?" Just the thought of it made her shiver. She paused. "Oh, wait, there's a portrait of him and his family in their home. It's old and more of an artist's rendering. Do you think that will work?"

"It won't hurt to try. And Ari, it sounds like this guy is dangerous. Maybe you should call the police."

"Christopher is the police." She huffed. "He said there wasn't enough evidence to convict him of anything and that his crimes were only rumors that may or may not be real." She waited while Maggie seemed to process it all.

"Well, promise me you'll be careful. And call me if you find anything."

Maggie proceeded to give detailed instructions on doing an image search if Ari could obtain a picture. Ari took careful notes.

After they said their goodbyes, Arianna found a book to read for a distraction. Helpless. Until she could get her hands on that portrait, she was helpless. Her shoulders slumped.

****

On Monday morning she took a calming breath before unlocking the door to the Somers' residence. *Just act as if it's any other day*, she repeated to still her jittery nerves. At least she had lots of deliveries and installations scheduled today, so she wouldn't be alone. The first item of business, however, had to be locating her notebook. It didn't take long. It innocently sat on the kitchen counter, right where she'd left it on Friday. She snatched it up.

The formal rooms gradually filled with Victorian furniture. She ran her hand over an antique, carved, cameo-tufted sofa. She wouldn't dare sit on something so decadently cream colored, for fear of smudging it. The side chairs complemented the sofa perfectly, with matching rosewood frames. A soft floral design woven into the fabric of the chairs added a subtle hint of color. She let go of a wistful sigh.

The last of the deliveries had arrived by four o'clock. Arianna watched as two men carefully tightened bolts on the legs of a walnut table. As anxious as she was for them to be finished and gone, she also felt protective of each meticulously selected piece. The workmen seemed to be extra precise when she watched them work. She had to give them credit; no one had been careless with the expensive furniture. Furnishings of this quality begged for reverence.

"We're finished, ma'am. If you'd sign here, we'll be on our way." A workman handed her a clipboard and a pen. She signed, and the men gathered their tools and left the premises. She locked the door behind them.

Finally, she could look for the picture. She knew where it had been when the Somers first brought the crate over, but they'd since emptied the boxes.

She searched all the logical places—fireplace mantels and tables—and even peeked into the study—but no portrait. Maybe in a bedroom. She ascended the stairs and continued her exploration. This felt invasive now that so many of their personal items were there. She shook off the feeling and reminded herself of her determination to solve the mystery that was Mr. Somers.

Entering Joshua's room was difficult, she'd avoided it all day. She rubbed the goosebumps on her arms and took a deep breath. There the small portrait sat on his nightstand. Interesting. That's pretty much the last place she'd expected it to be. She snapped a picture of it, then made sure nothing looked disturbed before she left.

Hurrying through her nightly inspection so she could be on her way, she paused in the doorway of the study. She had the fleeting thought to peek through the trapdoor to see what lurked down there, then decided she'd rather get a head start on the image search. This room officially spooked her after her experience on

Saturday. She turned to leave when a streak of red caught her eye. Apprehensive to enter, she switched on the light, hoping to see it was nothing to worry about. The scarlet color brightened beneath the beam. Her legs felt wooden—frozen in place. Forcing herself in, she examined the wall. It was only a smudge, perhaps paint. She peered closer. Or maybe, her pulse quickened, blood. Her flesh prickled as her eyes traveled down to the floor. Sure enough, there were droplets of the same crimson red that stained the wall. The hair on her arms stood on end. She needed to call the police. She reached for her phone, then remembered the lack of cellular service in the area.

Her imagination ran wild about what went on below her. It could involve torture or maybe a drug deal gone bad. If Mr. Somers were a drug lord, that would explain why he'd had the house built so far from civilization. There could even be a dead body down there. She hopped backward. The thought sent a shiver to her toes.

Between the blood and everything Christopher had shared with her, she sensed a terrible secret loomed beneath that trap door, and she needed to get out. She sprinted to her car and stepped on the gas.

****

"9-1-1. What's your emergency?"

Ari realized she hadn't thought it through before dialing. "Uh, I'm calling about a possible crime scene. There's a bloodstain on the wall of a house I'm decorating."

"Is it an emergency?"

"I—I don't know. There could be a body, or something." She sounded ridiculous.

"There are many reasons for blood that don't involve a dead body." The operator said.

"Can you just check it out? I have to work there, and I'm more than a little freaked out right now."

The operator clearly heard the urgency in Ari's voice. "Okay, ma'am, I'll send someone over. Are you there now?"

"No way! If you saw blood on the wall, would you hang around?" Her voice hit a fever pitch. "And I'm not going back there tonight. Can't you get in without me?"

"Only if you feel someone's life is in immediate danger. Will you be there tomorrow?"

Ari swallowed down her fear. She never wanted to return to that house, but she had to. "Yes." Her voice cracked.

"I'll send an officer out first thing."

Ari hung up the phone and let out a breath. "She'd be scared, too, if she worked for Mr. Somers."

The microwave beeped, sending Ari several inches off the ground. She had to calm down. She retrieved her scanty meal and grabbed a soda from the fridge. With her TV dinner next to her laptop, she forced herself to eat a few bites, then signed onto the computer. She'd waited all day for this. Her nerves jangled out of excitement—or fear—she didn't know which. Probably both. Then followed Maggie's careful instructions to search for an image.

"And enter." No hits. She frowned. Then, a passage Sarah had written in one of her journal entries replayed in her mind—something about wanting to go back to her own time. *What if I'm looking for him in the wrong era?* She shook her head, thinking it sounded crazy, but decided she had nothing to lose by trying. She might at least find a relative.

She broadened her search to include the last decade. Nothing. Two decades, five decades, then a century. *This is just getting silly, but I'll go back to Adam and Eve if I must.* Two centuries, then another decade—bingo. Just as she calculated how much time she'd wasted on something that couldn't possibly be, there it was on the screen—a drawing of Mr. Somers staring back at her. Oh my, this couldn't be true.

She read the name under the picture, Benjamin Somerset. Somerset, *that's him!* Her heartbeat accelerated until reality set in. It couldn't possibly be him, it would make him over two hundred and fifty years old. She continued scrutinizing the picture. If it wasn't him, it had to be an ancestor. They could be twins.

Ari decided to Google him again, armed with this new information. She entered: *Notorious crimes of the nineteenth century, London,* and *Benjamin Somerset.* It paid off. Several articles popped up about a jewelry heist in London in the year 1814.

Although it was nearing ten o'clock, Ari had an adrenaline rush that kept her reading for hours.

As far as she could tell, no one had been arrested after the heist, but there were a lot of suspicions about who'd done it. Every clue pointed to a man named Benjamin Somerset, son of the notable Earl William Edwin Somerset. "Whoa!" she nearly yelped. "He's the son of an earl?" That must have caused a scandal.

Bold headlines read "Suspect in the London Diamond Emporium Jewelry heist, Benjamin Somerset, disappears without a trace." And "Somerset name ruined as son of the Earl of Hemington, Lord William Edwin Somerset, is suspected of killing one man and injuring two guards in jewelry heist, then fleeing with his family."

Arianna rubbed her eyes and read each article again. This would make sense if it'd happened recently, instead of hundreds of years ago. There was just no way; it couldn't be him—unless, she swallowed, she had to see what was under the trapdoor in the study. Maybe that was the missing piece.

Tuesday morning Ari entered the house. Although the summer sun shined through the windows, the house took on a surreal, eerie look. The beautiful furnishings, although new, seemed soiled. A knock at the door startled her.

"I'm Officer Wright. I'm here about a possible crime scene."

"Oh yes." Ari stifled a frown. Deep down she'd hoped Christopher would respond to the call. "This way." She led Officer Wright to the study. "It's right over—" The stain was gone. She dropped to her knees and examined the floor. No blood.

Officer Wright peered at the wall, then back to Ari.

He must have thought she was crazy. She scowled. Maybe she was. She pointed. "It was there on the wall, and on the floor."

"It looks like someone cleaned it up."

"That's just it. No one lives here yet, and I was the last one to leave last night."

"You're the decorator, right?"

Ari nodded.

"I assume the owners come and go as they please." He tapped his foot and arched his brows.

Ari felt like a kindergartener listening to the officer explain common sense to her. Before she could think of an appropriate response, Officer Wright disappeared. "He didn't even take my statement. And who cleaned up the blood?" She shivered and closed the door to the study. It had to be Mr. Somers, but she had no idea when or how. The eyes of every portrait in the home seemed to follow her. She shook her head. Ridiculous. Now she was imagining things.

****

For the rest of the week Ari couldn't get the blood or what she'd read on the Internet out of her mind. Her thoughts continually warred with each other. All logic told her everything she'd learned had just been a coincidence—there was no such thing as time travel, which this certainly would have been—that, or reincarnation, which was equally unbelievable. But then, if, by some highly implausible chance the Somers *had* traveled through time, everything she'd discovered made sense—especially Sarah's journal entry. Then there was the blood. She couldn't think about that without spooking herself.

It was distracting her from her work. She needed to focus. And she had to find an opportunity to look through that trapdoor, although every particle of her being screamed at her to stay away from it. Her skin broke into serious goosebumps each time she passed the study.

She did her best to ignore thoughts of the Somers, or Somersets—whoever they were—and put her energy into the last few rooms. There weren't many, but they needed her undivided attention.

The week crept on at a turtle's pace.

Tossing and turning Thursday night, sleep eluded Ari. Her apartment had no air conditioner, so she had to keep the windows open to allow a breeze to pass through. Noises from outside spooked her. She knew it was because she'd have to see the Somers tomorrow—more specifically, Mr. Somers—that caused her anxiety, but she needed to sleep.

The one time she did manage to doze off, she dreamt of Mr. Somers breaking down her door and storming into her room, an evil smirk on his face. Beady eyes bored into her while blood dripped from his hands.

She startled herself awake. Cold sweat moistened her pillow. How could she face him in the morning and act as if nothing was wrong? She just couldn't make sense of it. Turning her pillow over, she gave it a punch.

Mustering all her courage Friday morning, she headed to work. Despite her fears, she wanted to discover the mysteries of the house, and she ached to help Sarah.

She nearly cried tears of joy when the whole Somers family arrived, instead of just Mr. Somers—the devil himself. They went straight to work unloading and locating places for the boxes of items they'd brought with them.

Having them all there, especially Sarah, helped Ari relax and focus on her job.

At the end of the day, she crept upstairs to Sarah's room. Retrieving the journal, she sat down on her bed to read the latest entry. Something crinkled beneath her. Odd. This was the softest bedding ever. She stood and pulled the beautiful Barclay Butera bedding back. *I wish I could afford even one pillowcase from this designer*. She caressed the comforter.

Under the plush spread lay a note to Sarah. Arianna knew that reading it would be an invasion of the girl's privacy, but, she shrugged, when had that stopped her before? She scowled at the thought of what this project, this house, this family and even Christopher had transformed her into. No one had ever accused her of being a paranoid busy-body before, but that's what she'd become.

She spread out the paper. Perhaps Sarah had an admirer. Maybe one of the workers. She brightened at the thought.

She began to read.

My Dearest Sarah.

Definitely a love-letter or at least a like-letter. Continuing, she read to the end. Different phrases darted out, raising a platoon of red flags. "I need your help if I am ever to find the device. I have searched this house from top to bottom." And, "Never let anyone know what you are about. Yours, C."

Ari's hands shook, and a dull ache grew in her chest. She thought back to the birthday card left on her doorstep the previous week. The unusually elegant script—script no longer used by anyone she knew—caught her attention. Nowadays no one, especially men, wrote like that. This note was from Christopher.

A deluge of questions bubbled up and threatened to drown her. The ache in her chest spasmed into pain.

Then there was the matter of the device. She was sure this was the secret Christopher had been keeping from her, along with his involvement with Sarah. She thought she'd be sick.

Her emotions sparked and sizzled. They ran amok, bouncing from confusion, to jealousy, to anger, and then to fear. This explained so much. Christopher could never commit to her because he already had a girlfriend. Why he couldn't tell her that, she didn't know. Unless it was because of Mr. Somers. A forbidden love, then. The pieces of the puzzle began to squeeze together. But how did the device fit in?

She turned the letter over, checking for a reply. Sarah hadn't seen this yet.

Her eyes began to burn. Taking deep breaths to calm herself, she carefully replaced the note under the covers, then turned her attention to the journal.

Dear Journal,

A, first of all, I hope you had a pleasant birthday, even though you were away from your loved ones. In England, we celebrated birthdays much like you do here in America, I imagine. Our current circumstances have not allowed me the opportunity to learn much about your American culture. As to your other question, I would like to tell you more about what I meant when I said I miss my own time, but I fear you would not believe what I say. I am still struggling to believe it myself. I have been forbidden to ever speak of what brought my family here. My father frightens me and I daren't divulge his secrets, lest we should somehow be discovered. I will say, however, that I fear for your safety more than for my own, only because

*death would be a welcome escape from
my imprisonment. That is all I feel I can
say for now. Yours, S.*

No. Surely she couldn't mean it. Ari read the
passage again, horrified for Sarah. And if the Somers
were somehow transported through time, the fragments
of information would begin to fall in place. She had to
know more without jeopardizing Sarah's safety.
Rubbing her aching head, she closed her eyes and blew
out a breath.

After taking several minutes to ponder, Ari wrote.

Dear Journal,

*S, you cannot imagine how much your
situation disturbs and frightens me. I
will believe anything you choose to tell
me. I was here last Saturday and
something strange happened. A loud
hum and vibrations shook the house. It
was terrifying. Have you ever
experienced that? Do you know what it
was?*

Arianna needed to know what, if anything, Sarah
knew about her father's machine.

She went on.

*And have you ever gone by a different
surname?*

She knew she was taking a huge risk.

*Please don't tell me anything that would
put you in danger. I couldn't live with
myself if anything happened to you. I am
sorry your circumstances are so bad that
you would welcome death. That breaks*

*my heart, and I so wish you would allow
me to help you.*

Ari couldn't think of a polite segue into asking about Christopher, so she just plowed ahead.

Don't worry about my safety. I met a police officer named Christopher who was very interested in your house. He is kind enough to check in on me now and then as I'm working. Yours, A.

She felt her heart bruise, as if she'd been punched in the chest. Thinking of Christopher often caused a twinge of sadness and regret. Thinking of him with someone else was unbearable.

Chapter Forty-Five

Forgoing his weekly horseback ride in favor of driving into the desert on the off-chance Sarah had found his note, Christopher made his way to his family's house—a madman's estate in the wilderness. The thought left a bitter taste in his mouth.

Every time he turned his key to enter, he felt a pinch of guilt for borrowing Arianna's key to make a copy—it echoed deceit—but finding the device was his top priority now. Once his family took up residency in the home, it would be impossible for him to continue his search. Before long, he expected bars to go up on the doors, transforming the house into a prison, like the family's residence in Denver.

He hiked the stairs to Sarah's room, taking them two at a time. Anxiety tugged at him—as it had each time he'd entered the house—but he ignored it and forged ahead. Pulling back the bedding, he retrieved the note. He let out a breath of frustration, disappointed to see there was no reply written on the back. He frowned. Maybe next week.

At least there was the journal. He reached between the mattresses to retrieve it.

Diving into Sarah's entry quickened his pulse. "She is saying too much." When he read Ari's reply, his blood ran cold. "Arianna was here when my father was using the device." He groaned. She might have been discovered. The thought put him into sheer panic. He could never let that happen.

It crossed his mind that Father could be on the premises at that moment. Perhaps he could find him and end this whole wild goose chase. He stood for a split-second, ready to search the house again. Then logic brought him back to his senses.

No, he was certain Father came to Pueblo *alone* when he planned to time-travel. He held up the journal. At least Sarah had accompanied him this week. He allowed his tense nerves to relax a fraction. He was certain no one else knew the exact location of the device. Unless—it struck him like a bolt of lightning—Arianna. If she'd been there when Father used the machine, she possibly knew where it was. He shoved the journal between the mattresses and paced the room.

Unsure of what his next move should be, he concluded that he only had one option—scour the house again.

By the end of the day his eyes burned—exhausted from another futile search.

Though body and spirit were fatigued, his mind continued to torture him on his drive home. He needed to ask Ari if she knew about the machine and its location. His heart wrenched with guilty memories from their last meeting. Asking her would reveal he'd read the correspondence between her and Sarah. That would open an entirely new dialogue he'd rather not have with her. Worse still, he'd have to explain his relationship with her employers. He let out an exasperated sigh.

And Sarah. Tears stung his weary eyes. His father had made her life so unbearable, she'd wished to end it. He shuddered at the thought.

Arianna had written she would believe anything Sarah shared with her. He could only hope that she would give him the same consideration.

Perhaps the time for questions had come to an end. He was there solely to protect his family any way he could.

Chapter Forty-Six

The letter Arianna had found in Sarah's comforter left her unsettled. Saturday morning's run would help. She pulled on her sneakers, studied them a moment, then kicked them off. Memories of her last run sucked the desire right out of her. She fell back on her bed and let out a frustrated groan. Perhaps a shower would help. It didn't. She tried to read but found focusing on the words impossible. Finally giving the book up altogether, she spread out on the sofa, and let her mind roam free.

The letter had to be from Christopher. She winced. He couldn't possibly just be a police officer watching out for a rumored criminal. No police she knew hid letters in women's bedding. She pondered for a minute. But if Christopher knew Sarah, she wondered for how long. They could have met in Denver or even London.

She sucked in a breath and sat motionless while reality sunk in. Ari had been Christopher's ticket into the Somers' house. He'd never cared for her no matter how much she'd thought he had. She felt queasy and the room began to spin. The most painful part of all was she loved him. She had thought she'd been in love once or twice before in her life, but this had been so much more real—until it wasn't. The ache in her heart intensified.

Being used hurt in a whole new way. She could dissolve in tears, as she'd done many times before, or put her wounded feelings aside and focus on Sarah. She took a deep breath.

"I choose Sarah."

Christopher, I believe we have a mutual friend in need. Ari's finger shook as she aimed it at the send button on her phone. She let her hand drop. While stepping up to help Sarah was the right thing to do, she couldn't reach out to Christopher. Not yet.

She dragged herself off the couch and to the bathroom. Staring at her reflection, she noted how pale her once-rosy cheeks had become. She wouldn't let him hurt her over and over, she thought as she splashed cool water on her face.

Something, besides Christopher, still nagged at her.

Mr. Somers.

She dried her face and reclaimed the sofa.

Could it be possible he'd been the hit-and-run driver responsible for the accident that killed her family? The Denver Police Department had only come up with the color and make of the driver's car. Christopher had transferred to Pueblo from Denver. Perhaps she should ask him to look into it. What was she thinking? Her resolve to protect her heart and take the high road for Sarah's sake didn't mean she ran to that man with her problems. She took a drink of ginger ale to calm her stomach and lay back on the pillow.

Within a minute she sat bolt upright. *Mr. Somers must be engaging in criminal activity here in Pueblo, which gives me an idea.* She located her laptop on the end table. She had minored in world history, and while she hadn't known how to do an image search, she definitely knew something about researching crimes from the past.

She began to type. If the picture she'd found online was Mr. Somers, that meant he had some kind of time machine. She shook her head and let out a breath. It sounded completely ridiculous. Nothing about this made sense, but she must think outside of logic.

If it were true, and if he had the ability to go anywhere he wanted to, whenever he wanted to; the possibilities were endless. He could rob, plunder, murder across the globe and never be held accountable. She shivered. The idea sent a chill down her spine as she remembered Christopher saying something very similar about the man.

If he moved backward in time, it would make sense that he'd steal only items that increased in value over the years. And forward, she shrugged, she didn't know what he'd steal moving forward. She'd start with the past—especially since she couldn't look up the future. It felt good to do something productive. With renewed energy and a now settled stomach, she downed her ginger ale and ate a protein bar.

It was a tedious thing to do, going back through the corridors of time in search of unsolved, mysterious heists, but she found some success. She took a break to dash to the store and purchase a world map and some small sticky notes, wanting to date and label each location she suspected Mr. Somers had visited.

****

After devoting an entire weekend to researching criminal activity from the past, Arianna experienced an exhilarating exhaustion. She proudly looked down at a map peppered with colorful notes. It surprised her that so many crimes had remained unsolved over the years. She knew they weren't all committed by Mr. Somers, but if her theory was correct, several of them could have been. Too bad this kind of evidence wouldn't hold up in court. She sighed. She needed to prove there was an actual machine.

With that, she decided she had earned a long bath and a good night's rest. She packed up her computer and headed to her room.

By the next morning Arianna felt invigorated. She got up early enough to go running. Surely Mr. Somers wouldn't be skulking around on a Monday.

He wasn't, and she was happy that some of her emotional kinks were relieved by a good run.

Later, at work, when she perused the orders scheduled to arrive throughout the week, she realized how few remained. One and a half, two weeks at the most, and this project would be history. She'd be relieved to never set foot in that house again, but wondered what would become of Sarah.

At the end of the day, she performed her nightly ritual—an examination of each room to make sure everything was in perfect order. Moving through the house, she picked up packaging left by the deliverymen, pushed chairs up to tables, straightened pictures, and such. She always left the house looking like a model home. She loved this part of the day. It also served as a measure of how much she had accomplished.

As she went from bedroom to bedroom, everything seemed to be in place—until she got to Joshua's room. The nightstand drawer sat ajar, and she could see some items peeking out.

As she crossed the room, her eyes settled on the picture resting on the offending nightstand. The Somers family appeared normal. Not happy—nobody looked happy in those old portraits. They never smiled, but they did look normal. As she reached over to close the drawer, something else caught her eye. She slid it open wider to get a better view. Tucked neatly to one side was a strip of paper with a picture on it. She peered closer. "Christopher?" she whispered. It had to be him. He was dressed in old-fashioned clothing and had longer hair, but that face belonged to Christopher. She analyzed the paper it had been drawn on and realized it'd been cut or torn on one edge. Her eyes shot up to the portrait of the Somers family. Careful not to rip it, she removed the backing and took out the portrait. She placed the jagged strip she'd discovered next to the larger picture. The two fit together as if they were pieces of a puzzle.

She gasped and her hand flew to her mouth. She could hardly believe what she was seeing. Touching each face gently, she said, "Mr. Somers, Mrs. Somers, Sarah, Joshua and Christopher Flemming. Who are you, Christopher? I don't think I know you at all."

Hands shaking, she carefully reassembled the original picture and decided to borrow the clipped-off portion of Christopher's image—just for a day or two. She entered Sarah's room and reached under the comforter, retrieving the note from Christopher, as well. She shook her head, "Siblings, not lovers."

She tucked the items into her bag. He may not want to, but he was going to give her some answers.

Chapter Forty-Seven

By the time Arianna arrived home, she realized it was too late to confront Christopher. Besides, if she caught him at work, maybe he wouldn't shut her down so readily—or, on the other hand, it might backfire and have the exact opposite effect.

She opened her notebook to check her calendar for deliveries. There were none scheduled for Tuesday. Perfect. Then he could take his sweet time explaining his way out of this—whatever it was. She held up the picture and letter.

If she thought sleeping on it would make her lose her nerve, she was wrong. Her need for answers only intensified as she tossed and turned through the night.

Adjusting the rearview mirror in her car the next morning, she caught a glimpse of the resolve in her eyes.

She wasn't sure where the police station was located, but her GPS led her there with no problem. Taking several deep breaths, she squared her shoulders and marched through the double doors. Nerves made her insides jumpy, but determination kept her moving. She glanced around the room, which buzzed with activity, and suddenly felt small. Glancing back at the doors, she had a momentary impulse to abandon the whole idea and leave. Before she could act on it, though, someone wearing a police uniform stopped her. "Ma'am, may I help you with something?"

She took a calming breath. "Uh, yes. I'm looking for Christopher Flemming. Is he here today?" It was then she realized there was a good chance he'd be out on patrol.

"Flemming's over there." He pointed to the far end of the room. So far away.

"Thank you." She weighed her options. The man who'd pointed her to Christopher watched, clearly waiting for her to make her move. She swallowed her anxiety and walked around the perimeter of the room, hoping not to attract attention.

He sat hunched over a desk studying paperwork. Ari silently approached and stood in front of him, waiting for him to realize she was there. It felt like an eternity, but, in reality, only seconds passed before he looked up. His eyes widened as shock registered on his face. "Arianna? Why are—" He stopped when she began pulling papers from her bag.

Laying down first the letter, then the picture, she said, "It's time you gave me some answers." Once she laid the proof she'd sought in front of him, she was too intent on her purpose to feel nervous anymore.

His face drained its color. Glancing around the room, he said in a low voice, "Not here."

She narrowed her eyes and didn't budge. He rose to his feet and told the officer nearest him he'd be out for a while. Before she knew it, he had taken her by the elbow and was escorting her from the building. She thought he might push her through the door, then go back to his desk, but he remained close behind her.

"Where are we going?" she asked, unsure now they'd left the bustling station.

"Anywhere but here." His hand pressed firmly on her back.

He took her to his squad car, opened the door and motioned for her to slide in. She did what he wanted, wondering how it was he seemed to be the one in control now.

They remained silent as he drove to the park where they'd had their picnic all those months before. It felt like a lifetime ago. She found it hard to swallow over the lump of memories growing in her throat. He parked the car and scanned the empty grounds for some shade, then motioned her to follow. They sat on a bench under a large oak tree. The park was empty, and Ari felt miserably alone.

She still clutched the picture and letter. She thrust both items on the bench between them. "Well? Are you going to explain? And don't dismiss me as you're so fond of doing."

Christopher's intense blue eyes appraised her as if discerning how much he should say.

"From the beginning, Christopher. I want to hear it all. I need to hear it all." Her voice cracked. He still seemed unsure. Ari put on her best "we're-not-going-anywhere-until-you-spill" look. "I've got all day." She'd regained her composure and was now speaking in a low voice.

He let out a resigned breath. "First of all, let me tell you how truly sorry I am for all the pain I have caused you. I don't know why the Somers had to have their house decorated in the first place. It is not as if they are going to be throwing balls or galas there."

"You call them the Somers as if they're strangers to you. You can stop the act now."

"They practically are strangers, Ari. Up until our trip to Denver, I had not seen them in four years."

"Our trip to Denver? You saw them there?" This just got better and better. Bitterness infected her glare.

"Please let me start from the beginning. But understand that what I am about to tell you will be hard to accept as truth, and that is why I felt I could never share it."

"Christopher, I am so beyond the 'hard-to-believe' stage it's ridiculous. I dare you to shock me!" Anger rose in her voice.

He put his fingers on hers, clearly hoping to calm her, but she yanked her hand away as if his touch repelled her. He held his hands palms up. "Okay. You win."

He picked up the picture of himself torn away from his family portrait. "Ironic, is it not?" Arianna realized he meant he'd been severed from his family, just as he had been in the picture. She allowed her glare to soften, but not disappear. "Where did you find this?"

"In Joshua's room. I was cleaning up and his drawer was open. But that's not important."

Christopher's eyes misted. "Joshua struggled when I left home for Cambridge. It makes sense he kept my picture this whole time. I had become the closest thing he had to a father—after our real father, the notorious Mr. Somers, as you know him, went mad. Mother said he cried for weeks after I'd gone." His voice, wistfully sad, yanked at Ari's heartstrings, but she had to know everything.

"The beginning, Christopher."

"Very well. I suppose I've nothing left to lose in reciting my history." He didn't wait for a reply, but looked down at the picture and letter and began telling about childhood memories in his once happy home. He told her about attending Cambridge only to be summoned back because of lack of funds due to his father's botched inventions. "I would have forgiven him that. What I couldn't forgive was the man he'd become because of his failures."

He shifted uncomfortably, clearly agitated by the memories.

"Mr. Somers—I mean your father—he's an inventor?"

"A scientist who dabbled in inventions—certain he would create something spectacular, making us wealthy. Hmm, perhaps one would say he'd succeeded. But that's beside the point. When I returned from school, I found he had truly transformed. He'd been a loving father when I was young. But at some point, he must have snapped due to so many dreams shattering about him. His demeanor had markedly darkened. He cared for nothing and no one, and he spent his evenings in pubs, returning home besotted and violent. Then he approached me to help him execute a jewelry heist. That is when I realized just how low he'd descended."

Ari's eyes widened. "How did you get here?"

"Here?" He looked confused.

"Yes, here. In the twenty-first century. In Colorado. U.S.A. Did you come on a magic carpet? Did an evil witch cast a spell sending you here? How did you get here!" She knew he didn't deserve the sarcasm, but her frustration had picked a hole through her patience.

He raised both hands as if to say, I get your meaning. "That I cannot answer. Ironically, Father invented something that worked—a sort of device that catapulted us two hundred years forward through time. Four years later, I still don't understand it. Nor can I find the device."

Ari shivered as each of her suspicions was validated, one by one. She pressed him with narrowed eyes. "How could you forget a machine transporting you through time? Could there be any other explanation? It's just too hard to believe." Her voice rose.

"And this is precisely why I did not wish to tell you." Christopher looked into the distance, as if he wanted to escape.

She cleared her throat and lowered her tone. "I'm sorry. You're right. I've vowed to myself to be open-minded. Please, go on."

His eyes met hers once more, then dropped to the picture. He expelled a breath. "I was twenty-five years old and taller than my father when it happened—strong enough to overtake him if necessary. Sadly, I did not get the opportunity." He explained the events of his final night in London. "My own father attacked me, knocking me unconscious. When I awoke, I was in a bed in Denver, two hundred years in the future. I confronted him then, only to have him pull a handgun on me, sending me on my way to battle it out on the streets of Denver. I'm certain he thought I would perish. I might have, save for the group of indigents who took me under their tattered wings." He paused and brushed a finger over the picture before continuing. "I believe my father thought being in a foreign time and place would make me cower into submission to him—even perhaps entice me to participate in his crimes. Otherwise, why would he have gone to such lengths to include me in the transport? He could have left me in London, and even allowed me to take the blame for the heist."

Arianna listened intently, taking in every detail. She could tell he needed to puzzle the events out in his own mind, just as she had in hers, even though he had the clear advantage of having been there. Her emotions ping-ponged. One moment she hurt with Christopher; the next, frustration made her want to slap him and walk away. If her heart hadn't become involved, this would be much easier. She gave herself a mental shake.

"Ari," his voice sounded strangled. "I've tried to help my mother and siblings, but before Father kicked me out of the house in Denver, he forbade me to see any of them." He swallowed hard. "Once I was able to negotiate the twenty-first century in a foreign land, I focused on watching out for them. However, I encountered a problem—I never saw anyone other than my father exit or enter the house. It was not until our trip to Denver—when Father came here—that I was able to break in and actually see and speak with my family."

He paused, looking directly at her as if to see if there was doubt in her eyes.

"Please, go on," she whispered.

"I had been working as a police officer in Denver and was granted a transfer to Pueblo. You see, by following Father's movements, I knew he'd been building a house here and I needed to stay close by. I'd anticipated them moving here in May, not September, and I was ready. Of course, that is where you came in."

"And I was your avenue into the house." Arianna narrowed her eyes at him. Anger, which had cooled to a simmer, bubbled to the surface again.

He blanched. His mouth turned down and his forehead creased. "Is that what you believe?"

Ari sat motionless. She didn't want to believe it, but after mentally boiling down the facts, that was all she had left. Forgiving his behavior might be possible someday. However, allowing her heart to be trampled—again and again—was just plain foolish.

"You think I am so unfeeling and deceitful that I would pretend feelings for you only to use you?" His eyes flashed with anger. "My feelings for you are genuine. I have never been dishonest with you—not in that way."

Ari tilted her head, keeping a pessimistic expression on her face. Not willing to concede, she continued to push. "What I believe is our whole relationship has been a lie. You did what you needed to do to help your family." She wanted to hide from the hurt in his eyes.

He threw his hands in the air. "Is there nothing I can say to change your mind?"

Giving a slight shake of her head, she swallowed back her rising emotion.

"If that's how you see it, I won't try to convince you otherwise." His face turned stony. "How can I blame you?"

She wanted to believe she was wrong but could tell he'd reached his limit and would not beg her to see things his way. Disappointment settled in her heart.

She pressed on. "And what about this 'device' you've been searching for? What will you do if you find it?"

"I need to destroy it. My father must be stopped. He has ruined enough lives."

"And if you destroy it, how will that prevent him from creating a new one? The machine is not the problem, Christopher. Your father is the problem."

His face contorted, as if he'd never thought of that possibility. "What else can I do? It is impossible to catch him in the act when he commits his crimes in an entirely different dimension." His voice was steeped in bitterness. "Besides killing the man myself, and believe me when I say I have contemplated such a thing, I don't know how to stop him. I promised them. I promised my family I would stop him. They are depending on me."

Ari dropped her gaze and studied the bench between them, then let out a breath. "My family was murdered," she whispered.

"As you have said." He sounded confused.

Ari raised her eyes to meet his. "I know it's a long shot, but the drunk that killed my parents and brother drove a red Cadillac. Sarah mentioned that your dad once owned a car like that. Their murders have gone unsolved."

Christopher blanched. "You think—"

She shook her head. "I don't know, but it's worth a try. That is, if you have time to investigate it. If he is found guilty, it might be enough to lock him away from your family." She shrugged.

His brows arched.

"Don't overthink it, Christopher. Like I said, it's a long shot."

"That you're giving me a shot at all—something I can work on in this century—is a step in the right direction."

His phone buzzed. "Officer Flemming." He stood and turned his back to take the call.

Ari let a puff of air escape her lungs. She hoped she'd done the right thing. Overcoming the tower of trust issues she'd erected between them would be a challenge. Potential justice for her family came at a price but would be worth it.

"I need to get back to the station." Christopher extended a hand to Ari.

She looked at it for a moment, swallowed, then allowed him to help her to her feet. She watched his tense shoulders relax a fraction.

"Oh. I nearly forgot." Ari pulled an envelope from her purse and handed it to him. "It's half of what I owe you for my car repairs. You'll get the rest when I get my next paycheck."

"That isn't necessary."

"For me it is."

He tilted his head to meet her gaze. "Arianna, forgive me for the secrets. I never meant to hurt you. I tried unsuccessfully to call you and tell you the truth. I should have tried harder."

Ari flinched, then dipped her head, unable to face the intense honesty in his eyes.

Chapter Forty-Eight

So many thoughts and emotions left Ari frustrated. Her grip on the steering wheel tightened as she drove. Christopher wasn't the criminal—his father was. His father was Mr. Somers. She trembled, but continued driving south to the exquisite, terrible mansion.

When she let herself in, without the flurry of activity which had become commonplace, she was once again struck by the beauty and peacefulness of the home. The colors and furnishings were soothing, yet subtly striking. The mood was short-lived, however, and bitterness replaced the serenity when she thought of all the secrets, mysteries and lies the house now held.

One more week to help Sarah. One more week; then she'd never have to come to this haunted house again.

With no deliveries expected, she decided, if she could summon enough courage, she would venture through the trapdoor and see this "device," as Christopher referred to it, for herself. She wondered why he hadn't asked her if she knew where it was hidden. She was convinced he'd been reading the journal correspondence she shared with Sarah.

She entered the study. One thing was certain— She'd take pictures. This was something nobody would ever believe. After digging out her phone, she slung her purse over her shoulder and cautiously pulled up the

Persian rug, exposing the trapdoor. It creaked as she lifted it open. Lowering herself down the ladder, she found the rungs ended before she reached the floor. She jumped the last few feet. Immediately, a heavy chemical smell assaulted her, making her want to gag. She covered her nose with one hand and activated the flashlight app on her cell phone with the other.

There had to be a light-switch somewhere. Within seconds, with the aid of her phone, she spotted the switch, made her way over to the wall and flipped it on, illuminating the room.

"Wow. Just wow." She scanned the room, realizing it was much bigger than she had imagined. Next to the wall opposite where she stood sat a very large, disc-shaped plate made from some sort of metal alloy. In the center of the plate was a wooden podium-type device. On it rested what looked like vials. A wire was attached to each vial and snaked down the wood meeting the metal disc at the bottom. The apparatus looked positively rustic, fashioned from wood and crude steel. There were two knobs next to the vials. Creeping in for a closer view, she thought this must be the original machine. It was large enough for a family of five to stand or sit, or in Christopher's case, lie down.

Her curiosity piqued. How in the world could a device that traveled through time be invented in the 1800s? If she were going to guess, she'd probably say that Mr. Somers mixed chemicals for the vials, then used the wires to conduct extreme power to move through time. And those two knobs—she peered closer, observing the hash marks on them—they must represent years, or rather centuries, as there were only three marks with numbers and arrows on them. One knob for forward, one knob for back. But what about location? There wasn't a knob for that. Maybe that was how they ended up in Denver, Colorado. Mr. Somers didn't know how to get to a specific location, just a time. She exhaled, proud of her deductions.

The phone in her hand reminded her she hadn't taken any pictures yet. She started snapping, being as thorough as possible. As she moved to her right, she discovered another machine.

Here was the modern version of the original. This device looked similar in its disc-like shape and came complete with a podium, but much smaller. However, it still appeared large enough to carry items such as art and small sculptures. In fact, it had some sort of bin filled with foam padding to contain the valuables while being transported, she guessed.

I'm sure it isn't the smoothest ride through time, she mused, recalling the vibrations she'd felt while standing just above the machine. This device had the same basic equipment attached, except the knobs were different. They looked very modern, of tempered steel and aluminum. There were three. The first two, she guessed, were for the time. It looked as if he'd broadened his time-travel to enable moving forward or backward in increments all the way down to one year. *I think that means he can travel in real time—go somewhere and return—or he must travel by the year. Hmm. I guess I'm relieved to know he can't pop into my life a week ago and threaten me.*

She continued perusing the device. The third knob on this vastly advanced machine had specific locations: major cities around the world, such as London, Tokyo, New York City, Beijing, and Moscow, just to name a few. "I guess the twenty-first century has served you well, Mr. Somers." She snapped more pictures.

Turning away from disc number two, she smacked into a steel rack. It wobbled, making a clanking noise. Her heart skipped a beat. She knew she was alone in the house, but still. A shiver ran down her spine. From the rack hung a large vest made from the same metal alloy—much finer in weight and more pliable—with oversized pockets covering its entirety. One pocket contained a miniature version of the second podium—but very modern. She was certain the other pockets served as storage for stolen goods, and perhaps weapons. She took more pictures, trying not to miss any details.

Next, she came upon a huge cabinet. She opened the doors, surprised they weren't locked. It contained an arsenal. There were weapons of every kind—guns of various sizes and calibers, a crossbow, knives, and even grenades. Her pulse quickened. She could only imagine what blood had been shed from their use. Her eyes scanned each piece, landing on one far different than the rest. It had to be from the nineteenth century. She picked up the antique pistol to study it, then replaced it next to a small container of gunpowder. She never figured Mr. Somers to be the sentimental type, hanging onto his old gun. *I guess he likes to measure his progress.* She took more pictures, then carefully closed the cabinet.

Coming full circle, she strode toward a desk with a huge bookshelf abutting it. The chemical odor intensified. She coughed down the gagging reflex. Labeled beakers filled with colorful fluids sat in neat slots on the left side of the desk, writing tablets and tools on the right. Atop the shelves stood volumes of both ancient and modern science as well as chemistry books. There was one which had been written in similar elegant script to what she'd read in Sarah's journal—and in Christopher's letter. She picked it up and thumbed through it. It was as if she were reading a foreign language. Page after page of numbers and ingredients were followed by instructions for their use.

What a waste of such an intelligent mind. She frowned. "I guess it has been anything but a waste for Mr. Somers." After taking one more look around, she decided she'd covered it all.

Crossing the room to turn off the light, she heard the floor above her creak. She froze, and her heart thudded. She switched off the light, but didn't dare make any big movements, for fear of knocking into one of the devices. Silently shuffling backward, she moved until her elbow found the wall, then slid down to the floor. She waited and listened. The ceiling above her continued to creak. Someone was up there. Her heart pounded so hard, she feared it could be heard through the walls. She groped in the direction of the desk to the side of her and crept beneath it. If Mr. Somers found her, he'd probably kill her and bury her body behind the house. Her whole being shook, but she remained curled up as tightly as possible, listening to the noises above.

Ari mentally walked through her movements before coming down the ladder, squeezing her eyes shut to picture the room. She was sure she'd closed the trapdoor, but she couldn't know if the rug came down with it.

Straining to listen, she heard a soft thud, silence, then the bang of a door—maybe a drawer or a safe. It sounded like metal. Silence again, then more creaking. A sliver of light pierced the darkness as the trapdoor opened. She put her hand against her mouth to quiet her chattering teeth. Her flesh crawled with a prickling sensation. The light grew, then just as quickly disappeared as the door closed. Ari let out a huge breath.

Her phone shook in her hand as she held it up to check the time. 8:13. She swallowed a gulp of air. Had she really been there so long? Her car was outside. Mr. Somers had to know she was still there. And if he wanted to use his device…

She practically held her breath for the next half-hour, until the sounds upstairs stopped. And even then, didn't dare venture up the ladder.

It was midnight before she finally made her way out of the basement.

Carefully opening the trapdoor, she maneuvered herself from under the rug, then sat for a few minutes—just to make sure. Moonlight spilled through the window into the study. There, its gleam rested on something sparkling to the side of her. She reached over and picked up a jewel. A diamond?

"Mr. Somers, it looks like you dropped some of your hard-earned income." Placing a hand over her mouth, she glanced around. Once her nerves had calmed, she held the diamond up to the moonbeam. An array of colors sprinkled through the room. Beautiful. Not knowing what to do with it, she put the jewel back on the ground where one of the installers or cleaners might find it. It would make their day.

Gathering her belongings, she left the premises feeling colder than usual. The house no longer spoke of beauty, peace, and a replicated bygone era. No, it hissed of secrets, crime, and blood money. A dark foreboding followed her home.

Relief washed over her when she finally entered the safety of her apartment. A shudder ran through her body as she thought about the possibility of Mr. Somers finding her down in his dungeon.

Too jittery to sleep, she opened her phone and began analyzing each picture. Christopher needed to know. She worried about what he'd do with the information. He'd been so desperate to find the machine, she feared he might do something that would get him hurt, or killed. She snapped one more picture. He should also see the map where his notorious, yet anonymous father had been committing his crimes.

She then texted him the pictures with a caption of what she believed each one to be.

Chapter Forty-Nine

It was late for someone to be texting. Christopher forced his eyes open to look at the clock radio. The neon green numbers read 1:04. Certain there had been something go down at the precinct, he picked up his phone to read the text. Arianna. He rubbed his eyes to bring them into focus. Picture files began popping up, one after another.

When he opened the first one, his heart skidded to a halt. *This cannot be.* Fully alert now, he began going through them more quickly, taking in the detail of each photo. His hands trembled at the realization of how these pictures had to have been obtained. He attempted to text Ari back, but his shaking fingers kept hitting the wrong letters. He gave up and called her.

"H—how did you"—he swallowed—"why did—" He couldn't think of the right words. Finally, he collected his wits and formed a sentence. "What were you thinking, Ari? If my father had found you, he would have killed you!"

"It's all right. He didn't. I only thought you could use some of this information as evidence against him."

"And the map—was that there, too?" He'd begun dressing, ready to leave immediately to confront the reality of the dreaded device.

"No, I came up with that myself. I've spent a lot of time trying to figure out what Mr. Somers was up to." Her voice sounded flat.

"I'm coming over."

Silence. "Okay." The line went dead.

Christopher thought about turning on his siren and lights so he'd have an excuse to speed through red lights between his place and Ari's, but there wasn't a point; the streets were deserted so late.

When Ari opened the door to him, he was struck by her pallor. White as a ghost. "Are you well?"

"I just spent hours in your father's den of iniquity while he wandered around in the room above me. That I got out alive—"

"Father was there?" His breaths came out hard and fast. He pulled Ari into his arms. "No, Ari. You cannot take risks like that." Her body trembled in his embrace.

They remained in the doorway until she calmed. She motioned him in and pointed to the couch, where they both took a seat. "You didn't need to come. I sent you everything I have."

"I had to know—to see for myself that you're okay. Can we figure out a plan? Something that keeps you out of harm's way but allows me to catch my father and help my family."

Ari's nod looked feeble. She needed sleep, not this. "I'm sorry." He reached a hand up and caressed her cheek.

She turned bloodshot eyes on him and pulled his hand away from her face. "I will help you, but after the way you used me, I can't—"

"Trust me?" Christopher shook his head and exhaled. He willed his heartbeat to decelerate. "I won't waste valuable time trying to convince you otherwise, but I wish you could see what's in my heart." By the way things had ended—make that began and ended—at their last meeting, he was grateful she'd even shared this information with him. He'd not ask for more. This, after all, had been his goal for over four years. "May I see the map?"

"It's on the table. While you're looking it over, I'll transfer the pictures to my laptop. That way we can study the details."

He scooted a chair up to the table. Amazing. If Father had committed even a fraction of the crimes she'd tagged, he'd done so much more than Christopher had imagined. He jotted some notes. He'd seen some of the purloined goods in his father's safe. A little research could back up Ari's theory.

Chapter Fifty

Bleary-eyed, Ari studied the pictures on her laptop. With Christopher there, exhaustion replaced the jitters. His protective presence calmed her.

"May I join you?" He sat down beside her to look at the screen. His musky scent smelled good.

She nodded and angled the computer so he could view it. He moved closer.

"The details are much clearer on your laptop." He began taking notes.

"What's the plan?" Ari yawned.

Christopher was much too awake for such a late hour. She realized that this information had invigorated him. She, however, drained of all her energy, wished to sleep.

His gaze met hers. He narrowed his azure-blue eyes and tilted his head. "I believe the plan is for me to leave so you can sleep. I will take what I've learned and work on it." He wrote something else on the paper and tucked it in his pocket.

"I would argue, but I'm too tired." She managed a half-smile "Christopher, if I tell you where the machines are, what will you do?"

He sat back and rubbed the stubble on his chin. "If I'd found them before today, I would have attempted to destroy them, but someone helped me realize that the machines are not the problem."

"So you won't do anything stupid if I tell you that there's a trapdoor in the study?"

"A what?" He jerked forward.

"Promise me, Christopher."

He patted her leg. "Don't worry. I have plenty to do with crimes in the present."

She became alert. "What? Did you discover something about the hit-and-run?"

"Don't get your hopes up, but I found a salvage yard in Denver that has a car fitting the description you gave me. I plan to drive up and check it out. I'll likely not uncover anything new, but it's worth a try."

A thrill of excitement sparked through Arianna. She set her laptop on the floor and pulled Christopher in for a hug. "Thank you."

He stiffened, then relaxed. She knew her attitude toward him had him on edge. It still irked her to think he'd used her to get to the house, but the gratitude she felt was overwhelming. Happy tears filled her eyes. She released him and swiped at her eyes.

"I should go now," he said.

"To your apartment?"

Christopher flinched.

Aha! She'd read his mind. Her nerves couldn't handle it. If he went back to the Somers' house tonight, she'd have a complete melt-down. Why, she didn't know. Total exhaustion, no doubt. "Promise me you aren't driving out to the Somers' home right now."

Chapter Fifty-One

If Tuesday had been calm, as far as deliveries went, Wednesday and Thursday were anything but. Arianna rushed everyone to get remaining art hung, furniture arranged, and last-minute details attended to. She welcomed the chaos. No longer did she wish to be alone in the house.

She had less than a week to help Christopher. Less than a week to help Sarah. It was at the same time too long and too short. Armed with fresh determination, she plodded on.

****

Early Thursday morning her phone chirped, signaling a text. Christopher. *I believe I have located the car and registration. Police records missing. Have suspicions why. If I get what I need, the local officers can arrest Father here in Denver.*

Ari's heart raced and tears filled her eyes. The mystery of the hit-and-run might finally come to an end. She wiped her eyes and focused on her phone. *Fingers crossed things will come together there. If not, your family will be here tomorrow. They will occupy the house on Tuesday. Thanks for the update…and for doing this.*

On the long drive to her jobsite, her thoughts turned to Sarah. She had to help her. Do something—

anything. Friday would be the last time they could share information using the journal.

Distractions of every kind stole her attention. One last delivery, touch-up painters and installers all kept her busy.

"Have a good evening, Jack." She waved.

Jack nodded and closed the door behind him. She dead-bolted it and let her shoulders sag. The long day had ended for the workers, but not her. She headed to Sarah's room and tugged out the journal. After making a large X through her previous entry, she wrote.

> *Dear Journal,*
>
> *S, I know everything—where you're from and how you got here. Christopher and I are working on a plan to stop your father. I wish we had more time. Check your bedding. Christopher has been trying to communicate with you, as well. Even after I'm gone, he will continue to fight for you. Trust him.*
>
> *Yours, A*

Those last two words hit her like a wrecking ball. Strange advice, coming from her.

****

Friday roared in, hot and humid. Arianna was especially glad to have the house abuzz, in preparation for the impending arrival of the Somers. If things had worked out for Christopher, they wouldn't be arriving at all. Mr. Somers would be occupying a jail cell in Denver. Christopher hadn't sent further updates, however, so she didn't know what, if anything, had happened.

She watched through the front room window as the black Escalade slowly ascended the drive. Her heart sank. Hand in a fist, she lifted her fingers one at a time. There was the rest of today, Monday, and finally Tuesday—sign-off day. A meeting had been scheduled for Ari, Natasha Tate, and the Somers to go over every detail of the job, and, if everything was in order, sign off on the project.

Sarah entered behind the other three. Ari fell in step beside her. "Sarah," she whispered.

Sarah flinched, but her eyes remained fixed ahead.

"I need to talk to you."

Mr. Somers stopped, turned around and narrowed his eyes at Ari.

She cleared her throat and spoke up. "You look nice today, Sarah. Blue is your color."

"Thank you." Sarah ducked her head and quickened her pace to match the others.

Ari let out a frustrated breath. What she'd written in Sarah's journal wouldn't save her but would perhaps give her some hope.

At the end of the day, without any incidents with Mr. Somers, Ari began making her rounds, pulling everything back in to "model-home" appearance. When she reached Sarah's room, she claimed the journal for the last time.

Sitting on Sarah's bed, the crunch of paper reminded her of Christopher's note. She'd replaced it after their confrontation. She tugged the bedding back and smiled. Sarah had written to her brother. Without reading it, Ari folded and put it in her bag to deliver to Christopher. There might be time yet.

Opening the journal, she read.

Dear Journal,

A, I apologize for my behavior this morning. I fear Father distrusts both of us. I must avoid the very appearance of friendship, though I long to do the opposite. Thank you for your words of optimism. I will depend on Christopher to come to our rescue. He is a valiant brother. I am saddened to discontinue our correspondence. Perhaps, after he is able to help us, we can renew our friendship. Yours, S.

Sorrow stabbed at Ari. Her heart ached for Sarah. Living even one more day under the same roof as Mr. Somers was too long. She didn't know what she could say to encourage her, but it would be her last opportunity to say anything. She tapped the pen to her head in concentration.

Dear Journal,

S, please don't worry about today's events. I understand your predicament. I hope my failed attempt to speak to you didn't make matters worse between you and your father. I just wanted to reassure you about Christopher's fierce determination to help you. Remain positive.

Your friend always, A

Short and to the point, yet she had nothing concrete to offer. She'd probably failed Sarah, but she wouldn't fail Christopher.

Chapter Fifty-Two

Christopher had resisted the urge to drive to his family's home immediately following his visit with Ari. He didn't know why it mattered to her, perhaps the anxiety she'd experienced there had been worse than she'd let on—although, she'd seemed pretty shaken. He worried about her making it through the next few days. Honoring her wish was a small price to pay for what she'd provided him. Not to mention, now he had something concrete to work on.

Ari's hunch had been correct; the red Cadillac had been registered to Benjamin Somers. Locating the car and registration had been simple. Locating the hard copy of the file, not so much. He'd called the station to inquire about it, but the file had somehow vanished. He'd have to start from square one and investigate it himself.

As he drove to his old precinct on Evans Street—District 4—memories flooded back. It had been less than a year since he'd last been there, but it seemed a lifetime ago. He'd developed a good working relationship with the men and women at the 4th, so when he'd asked, they'd had no qualms about helping him.

Nothing but a few faces had changed at the precinct. The office was noisy with police chatter—

much busier than Pueblo. He was directed to an unoccupied desk to conduct his business.

Digging into the information provided on the computer, he recognized the name of the officer first on the scene. His skin crawled. Officer Cratchen. One of the dirtiest men in blue Christopher had ever encountered. If Father had gotten to him, the missing file was no mystery at all. "Cratchen would throw his own mother under a bus for a dollar," he whispered.

"What's that?" Officer Hunt, the man nearest Christopher, asked.

"Oh. I just wondered, is Cratchen still around?"

The officer pulled a sour face. Apparently, he shared Christopher's opinion. "Transferred last month. What do you need?"

Christopher explained the cold case to Officer Hunt. "There is silver paint on the Cadillac. I need to run a paint analysis to see if it matches the victim's vehicle."

"And Cratchen investigated?"

Christopher shrugged. "He was first on the scene. The file is missing now."

Officer Hunt shook his head. "Doesn't surprise me. If you can talk Captain Murphy into reopening the case, we can get the analysis done."

Christopher knew how long these processes took. He didn't have much time. Aiding his family had already taken four years longer than he'd hoped. They needed him to come through. Arianna needed him to come through. The chance that the paint didn't match, loomed in his subconscious. He could easily disappoint them all.

"Did I hear my name?" Captain Murphy stalled in his path through the maze of desks.

Hope surged in Christopher's soul. "Yes. Do you have a minute?"

Captain glanced at his watch. "Only just." He motioned to his office.

Once Christopher obtained permission to reopen the case, the wheels began turning at a snail's pace. At least they were turning.

"I can phone you with the results of the analysis, if you want to head back to Pueblo." Officer Hunt scooted a chair up to the desk next to Christopher's borrowed workspace.

Christopher sat with his elbows on the desk, his fingers steepled. He only took a moment to realize he'd done all he could in Denver. He nodded his thanks to Officer Hunt and left the station.

Everything hinged on those results.

Chapter Fifty-Three

Chris, are you back from Denver? I have a letter from Sarah. Ari pushed the send button on her phone. There had been enough secrets between her and Christopher. That stopped now.

Just got in. I'll head over.

She paced the length of her living room, not only anxious to deliver the letter, but also to find out what Christopher had discovered in Denver.

She jumped when someone knocked. "Breathe," she told her herself as she opened the door to Christopher.

"Well?" She motioned him in.

He chuckled. "I am fine, and you?"

"Sorry. I've just been thinking about this all day. And without a way to call you"—she shook her head—"it's just been hard." Lowering herself onto the sofa, she patted the seat next to her.

Spicy freshness filled her senses, and she immediately regretted the seating arrangement. She needed to focus, not get heady over Christopher's scent.

"I found the cars and took some paint samples in for analysis." Christopher's deep voice brought her back on task.

"And?"

"They'll call me with the results."

She frowned. "How long will that take?"

He shrugged and shook his head. "Hopefully not too long."

"What about the missing file?"

Christopher explained his theory about Officer Cratchen and the mysterious missing file.

"So, you're saying you think your father found Officer Cratchen and paid him to lose the file?"

"Precisely."

Ari let go of a breath. That would explain why the detectives had run into so many dead-ends in their investigation. Cratchen stood between her and the truth. And the truth, if she and Christopher were correct, was terrifying. The very man she'd spent months working for might be responsible for her family's deaths. A sharp pain shot through her heart. She'd help Christopher any way she could.

"You said you have a note from Sarah?" Christopher's eyebrows arched.

"Oh, yes." She tugged it from her purse and handed it to him. She thought he'd take it into another room to read, instead he flattened the small note and held it up for her to see, too. Christopher must be done with secrets, as well.

> *My Dear Brother,*
>
> *Arianna has assured me you are doing everything within your power to help us. I thank you with all my heart. You give me hope, and hope is what I need. I fear I would find an escape from this existence without it. I love you, dear brother.*
>
> *Yours, Sarah*

Christopher stared at the paper as if he were reading and rereading it. Finally, he dipped his head.

Ari, helpless to know what to do, gently took the note from his hand and intertwined her fingers with his. "It's going to be okay. If the hit-and-run conviction falls through, you'll figure out something else."

He tilted his head to face her. Her eyes burned, looking into the blue pools of his gaze. "I—" His voice hitched. He dropped his head again and lifted his hand linked to hers and pressed a kiss on her fingers. He cleared his throat. "I should go."

"No. Christopher, please stay." She tightened her grip on his hand.

He narrowed his eyes in question.

"With my trust issues toward you, I know I've sent you mixed signals, but I have never doubted your sincerity to help your family. In fact, I admire you for it."

Christopher's eyes widened.

"Please allow me to help you. I don't know how, but with all the demands from me and your family, you must feel hollow by now."

He released her hand and dropped his head, as if defeated.

"You need someone in your corner." She scooted closer and put an arm around his shoulders. "Let that be me," she whispered.

He turned his head toward her.

She caressed his cheek. "I'm here for you, Chris." She leaned forward and gave him a tentative kiss, then searched his eyes.

He pulled her into an embrace. "Thank you, Ari." He ran his fingers through her hair, sending sparks shimmering through her body. She peered up and locked eyes with him. He bent his head and their lips met. The kiss began slow and sweet, then turned passionate and deep. Weeks of pent-up emotions exploded between them. Ari's heart thudded. She wanted more, but knew they were playing off each other's wounds.

He must have come to the same conclusion. He broke the kiss but stayed close. "I must go," he whispered. His breath tickled her mouth. He kissed her once more, then stood to leave.

Chapter Fifty-Four

Monday finally arrived, and with it came torrential rains. "Just my luck," Ari groaned. "My last full day on the job, and I'll spend it cleaning up muddy footprints from workmen's boots." For the most part, the workers wore the footies Ari provided them, but inevitably, some of them managed to get by unnoticed.

A flagstone walkway ran from the street to the house, but the road itself was dirt—being basically a country road. In addition, flower beds with barely-blooming buds clustered on each side of the walkway. Little streams of muddy water trickled across the walk. That the landscapers chose to end their work with the flower gardens in front irritated Ari as she made her way from her car to the house.

Careful to wipe the muck from her own shoes, she entered the Somers' home. "Tomorrow—after the inspection—I will never have to see this place again." She blew out a breath, letting go of a portion of the burden which had increased daily over the months.

Fortunately, there were no more deliveries, so the mud was held to a minimum. The house still buzzed with installers, however. Ari had kept a detailed checklist of her weeks of work. She carefully perused each room every couple of hours to ensure every "t" was crossed and every "i" dotted. She couldn't leave anything to chance at this point. She just wanted to be done—finished with this job forever.

Everything appeared to be coming together in perfect order. No small miracle. She couldn't hide a satisfied grin. By tonight she'd be having dinner with Tasha. Her smile widened anticipating a friendly face far away from this horrible place. Two things to celebrate. Tasha would be driving in from Denver in preparation for the walk-through on Tuesday. Ari didn't know where they'd eat. Abby's was good. She shuddered at the memories of her and Tasha's last visit there. No, too soon. Maybe she should ask some of the workers what they'd suggest.

"Musso's or Pass Key," Jack said. "Or"—he scratched his head—"what was that other one? Oh yeah, Adolpho's. They're all unique to the area. And the food is great."

"Thanks, Jack." Ari jotted the restaurants' names down in her notebook.

As afternoon turned to evening, the workers began to disappear. There were a few muddy footprints, but she dealt with them easily.

Now, for her final stroll through the house to make sure everything was ready for tomorrow; then, she'd be off to her apartment, where she hoped Tasha would be hungry and waiting. Her stomach growled.

Darkness had fallen. She turned on lights as she passed from one room to the next. First, she inspected the main level, taking her time to make every detail precise. Other than some packaging materials scattered on the floor in the theater room, so far everything looked good. "Theater room," Ari snarled. "Four years ago, you didn't even know what a television was, Mr.

Somers." She gathered the trash and took it out to the garage.

When she entered the study, a dark foreboding sensation enshrouded her like a cloak. Shadows seemed to follow her as she moved. Taking a breath, she gave herself a mental shake.

Of course she felt this way—this house was haunted—not by spirits that once were, but by the evil spirit of one moving in. She shivered.

A door banged shut. Ari jumped a few inches off the ground and spun around. Everything appeared normal.

She wished she had cell phone service. Deep breath. Deep breath.

A creaking noise sounded like it came from above her. She stood frozen. *This feels so familiar*, she thought. *However, this time I'm supposed to be here doing my job, so there's no reason to be frightened.* The realization gave her enough courage to press forward.

Arianna headed up the stairs to inspect the game room and bedrooms. It was fully dark. She hadn't been to the upper level since the sun had set. Her heart rattled in her chest as she flipped the first light-switch, tamping down a childish fear that someone might jump out at every turn. The house, so quiet, felt eerie. Even the rain had stopped, ending the gentle pitter-patter she'd listened to throughout the day.

Clouds moved around the moon, generating ghost-like shadows in the activity room. Her flesh crawled with anxiety. She'd been pleased the Somers allowed for a game room in their Victorian mansion. At least there would be some entertainment for Joshua and Sarah. Guilt attempted once more to worm its way into her conscience. Helping them was imperative. She whispered a silent prayer for Christopher. Last she'd heard, he still waited for the analysis results. Everything hinged on those tests.

Moving to the air-hockey table, she lifted one of the pucks and twirled it in her hand, wondering if Josh or Sarah would know what do to with it. The disc slipped from her fingers, slamming onto the table. The noise made her jump, sending her nerves back to high alert.

She hurried on to the master bedroom. Once more she thought she heard something, stopped, and held perfectly still, listening. "Hello, is anyone there?"

Silence.

Shivering, she moved on. The master bath and closets all looked good. Wait; there it was again, a rustling noise. She paused, anxiety working its way through her nerves. She wondered if a window could be open, then realized that with the rain and her stern warnings nobody would have dared open a window. She proceeded quickly through the spare rooms.

Next came Joshua's bedroom. The baseball and glove were the only things out of place. With trepidation, she put them away. Was it her imagination, or had the ball quivered in her fingers? She shook her head. *I'm making myself crazy.* Her eyes landed on the family picture by Joshua's bed. Her thoughts nearly stole away with memories of her discussion with Christopher, when another noise pulled her from her ruminations.

I know that wasn't my imagination. Her heart beat too loudly now to hear anything else. Mentally retracing her steps, she was certain she'd locked up after the last of the workers had left the house. "Hello?" She tried to make her voice firm, but it faltered.

No response.

Only Sarah's room remained unchecked. She'd been turning the upstairs lights on as she'd inspected each room and off again when she'd left it. Sarah's light was on. Besides a few beams illuminating the main level, only Sarah's room remained lit. As Ari cautiously crept down the hall, the light cast a moving shadow on the wall, which chafed at her already tattered nerves. The extra adrenaline urged her to pick up the pace forward. She nearly sprinted the final feet to Sarah's room.

Before her foot connected with the wood flooring in that room, however, a beefy hand yanked her by the arm and tossed her to the floor. "M—Mr. Somers?!" she shrieked, barely recognizing her own voice. His beady, black eyes pierced holes right through her. She'd never seen eyes so full of venom. While he pinned her down with one hand across her neck, she recognized Sarah's journal in the other. A groan rippled through her.

"What gives you the right to come into my home and meddle, you sniveling upstart?" he roared. "You have no reason to communicate with my daughter." He threw the journal onto the bed and backhanded her hard across the face. His large, onyx ring dug into her flesh. "Speak up!"

"I—I was only trying to be her fr—friend." She could barely speak through her shock and terror—not to mention the fingers restricting her air passageway. Her cheek stung, and she felt blood trickling down her face. She clenched her teeth to keep them from chattering.

"Be her friend." He let out a grunt. "Sarah doesn't need you. Sarah doesn't need a friend. You should not have intruded in our affairs. Did your mother teach you no manners?"

Ari, still pinned between the floor and Mr. Somers' hand, winced at the mention of her mother. "She did. She—she did teach me manners."

He shook his head, his sneer deepened. "And yet you don't respect her memory enough to stay out of matters that do not concern you. You disgust me."

"I—I never told you she died."

His eyes flashed, and he darted a glance at the journal. "You didn't have to."

Tears escaped and slid down the sides of her face.

His features hardened, and he slapped her again. She recognized the demonic glint in his eye—the same glint he'd tortured her with in her nightmare. Her mother's, father's and Seth's warnings echoed through her mind now. Too late.

"It says in there"—he pointed to the journal—"that my dear son, Christopher, told you everything." He spat the venom-filled words at her. His bushy eyebrows arched as if waiting for her to deny it, his fingers tightening around her throat. She desperately clawed at his hand, trying to pry his fist from her neck. His fingers didn't budge.

"He—he doesn't know everything. He was un—unconscious," she finally managed to choke out.

"And why should I believe a solitary word that escapes from your deceitful tongue?"

Arianna coughed and attempted to draw in a breath. He loosened his grip just enough for her to gasp and think straight. She lifted a leg and kicked him hard.

Her foot met its target—a direct hit to his groin. Momentarily dazed, he lost his grasp on her. She sprang to her feet and took flight, sprinting as fast as her legs would go. Mr. Somers, who'd recovered remarkably fast, clipped at her heels. Groping in the dim corridor, she found the banister to the staircase and all but flung herself down the steps. She tripped at the bottom and nearly toppled headfirst, but somehow righted herself and managed to get to the front door. He wasn't far off. Swinging the door open, she ran outside, stumbled down the steps and into the flowerbed of mud—the very mud she'd been avoiding all day. She heard him grunting behind her. So close. Too close. He grabbed her hair; then she felt his icy grip around her neck again. "I should kill you right here," he huffed.

"No!" she screamed. "What do you want from me? I'll do anything!" The cool outside air cleared her head enough to at least get a coherent sentence out. "I'm leaving tomorrow; you'll never see me again. I won't tell anyone about the machine..." She gulped hard against the pressure from his thick hand.

"You know about the machine?" his voice boomed. He kept hold of her neck as he dragged her back into the house. "If you know about the machine, then you know I don't have to kill you here. I can kill you anywhere!" He dragged her—arms and legs flailing—to the study.

"No!" was all Ari got out before he yanked her into the room. Tears began to make their way down her swollen face. Mud was getting everywhere from her shoes.

Coughing and sputtering, she stomped hard on the beautiful Persian rug she had always taken such care to protect. Mr. Somers didn't let up. He yanked her out of the way like a ragdoll and flung the rug back with his free hand. As he jerked up the trapdoor, he adjusted his grip around her waist and pulled her down the ladder. The trapdoor slammed down behind them.

Once on the floor, he tugged a chain Ari hadn't noticed on her first trip down, which turned on the light. He pulled her to a chair by the desk and sat her down hard, always keeping an arm securely around her, then glanced to his right. She followed his gaze, which landed on a cord connected to his desk lamp. He gave it a yank and it broke free in his hand. Using the cord to tie Ari to the chair, he took care to make the knot unbreakable.

He'd take his time. No reason to hurry when no one knew about this room. The realization settled heavily in her heart. Wait. She'd told Christopher. Her memory was still fuzzy about their late-night conversation. Yes, she was sure she did. A small glimmer of hope sparked. She wiggled to try to loosen the cord, but it was fastened so tightly around her ribs she could barely breathe.

He opened one of his many books and thumbed through the pages. "Where would you like to die?" He said it casually, as if he were asking her favorite ice cream.

Ari didn't move or speak.

"Very well, then, I'll choose," he said. Consulting the book, he began mixing and measuring chemicals in beakers, then poured them into the vials on the machine—not the huge, rustic machine—rather, the one with a bin built for transporting large items, such as art. When he seemed satisfied with the amount of fluid in each vial, he said, "You're going to like the New York City of fifty years ago. And believe it or not, even back then nobody noticed a dead body on the pavement." He smirked, and his eyes blazed like a wild animal's.

Ari watched a crimson droplet splatter onto her leg and realized her face was still bleeding. She saw that it had mixed with her tears and had trickled onto Mr. Somers' fingers when he'd gripped her neck, rubbing off on the book and vials.

If Christopher—or anyone—found the room, she needed them to know where the madman had taken her off to. She leaned forward, letting the trickle of blood drop to the floor. Once enough had pooled, she dragged her shoe through it. She managed a mostly legible NYC and 50. Then she hid the letters and numbers by resting her legs above them.

The device apparently ready, she thought he would untie her and she could try to make a break for it. She eyed the ladder and took a breath in preparation to bolt. But instead of loosening the cord, he picked up the entire chair and hoisted it and her onto the machine.

"You'll never get away with this." She rocked the chair back—anything to stop him.

He caught it. "Oh, I think you know I will."

He turned the dials, then pushed the knobs. As the machine began to warm up, he made quick work of untying the cord around the chair, then shoved her off and into the bin—large enough to transport art, but too small for most people. Her head hit hard, and pain surged through her. She shrieked and grabbed the sides of the bin to lift herself out, but he slammed the lid shut, nearly taking off her fingers. "Let me out! You can't do this! Please!" A sob escaped her throat. Her body, forced to bend pretzel-like, spasmed.

The machine began to pulse, causing a hum; low at first, then gaining in volume as the vibrations increased. She pounded on the lid of the bin, but it didn't give. Pain seared her head, back and neck. She screamed again, even though there was no one to hear. Her voice echoed in the pitch-black box, overwhelming her senses. She gulped back sobs and pulled her knees to her chest. Hopeless tears rolled down the sides of her face, wetting her hair.

Either from the force of hitting her head on the bin, or from sheer panic, Arianna began to lose consciousness. The last thing she remembered was the loud hum as the odious machine buzzed and shook around her.

Chapter Fifty-Five

A number he didn't recognize lit Christopher's cell phone. His thumb hovered over the "ignore" button, then reconsidering, he answered. "This is Flemming."

"Thank goodness. I've made a dozen calls to find you. My name is Natasha Tate. Arianna Miller works for me."

"Yes, yes. We met." Fear clutched at him. Something had happened to Ari.

"I can't find her. I mean, I'm at her apartment and she's not. We were supposed to meet here over an hour ago. Ari's never late." Tasha paused and took a breath. "It's probably nothing, but she told me a few things about the owners of the house she's been working on that have me concerned. I wouldn't bother you, but I don't remember how to get out to the location, and she isn't answering her phone. I didn't know who else to call."

The more she spoke, the more frantic Christopher became. "I'm glad you called me. There is no cellular service at the Somers' home. I'll go out—"

"Can you pick me up?" Tasha's shrill voice cut in.

He thought for a moment. "Perhaps you'd best stay put, should Ari arrive home."

"I—I guess you're right. You'll bring her back safely, won't you?" she choked out.

Christopher's heart pounded in his ears. "Yes. I'll get word to you as soon as I'm able." He hung up and sped away in his squad car, thankful he could use his lights and siren to part the traffic.

He drove through Pueblo and to the outskirts of town in record time. As the house came into view fifteen minutes later, he spotted Arianna's little red car in front, where it always was. He ran to the door and, finding it unlocked, threw it open. He noticed mud on the floor. His eyes darted around the house, searching for clues as to where she might be. He called out "Arianna" several times but got no response.

Willing himself to be calm and think like a cop, he looked back down and studied the muddy footprints. They led to the book room. The Device. His heart raced like a rocket spiraling out of control.

Following the footprints, he could tell there had been a struggle. In fact, it looked as if Arianna had been dragged back into the house from outside. She'd been trying to escape. His heart twisted, imagining her fear and pain. The mud grew darker in the study—especially on the rug. He yanked it back, exposing the trapdoor. Any other time, this would have been cause for celebration. Not today. Not with Arianna's life dangling in the balance.

He descended the ladder in seconds and began frantically scanning the room. Seeing the light left on and a chair toppled over, Christopher knew he was in the right place. He'd studied Ari's pictures of the three machines so intensely; there was no question which one was missing. "If anything happens to her, Father, you will not live to see another day."

Discerning his next move, Christopher's heart dropped to his feet at the realization that with the aid of the device, his father could take Ari anywhere in the world in any time, kill her, come back and act as if nothing had happened.

He spotted Father's chemistry book lying open on the desk. In three large strides he was to the book, examining it for clues. Desperation seized him. Again, he had to take a deep breath and focus on the numbers and names in front of him. He'd studied the formulas. Surely he could figure this out. He used every bit of concentration he possessed to remember what he'd learned from the pictures. His eyes roved over words that were, until just days ago, foreign to him. Then he saw a red smudge. His gaze followed the scarlet fingerprints. Blood. She might be dead already. Anger boiled to the surface. He pounded the desk with his fist. But before he completely lost his presence of mind, he realized the prints could possibly serve as a guide if he followed the trail. Taking a deep, cleansing breath, he willed himself calm again.

The residue from the freshly mixed chemicals still clung to the sides of the beakers, indicating how full each had been before they were emptied into the vials. Referring to the book and opening the picture files Arianna had sent him, he began calculating how much formula it would take to fill each one to the residue lines.

It was no use. Father could have filled them up more than once.

He closed his eyes and stepped away from the books and beakers. There had to be something more concrete. Pacing, his shoes squeaked and felt tacky against the floor. More blood. It hadn't pooled. That was odd. He knelt to examine it. Although he'd walked through it, he realized it was more than just blood, it was a message. The number was clear. 50. Must mean years. The letters were too smudged to read.

Fighting down panic, he scanned the desk area until locating a map. Among other smudges, there was a fresh print next to New York City and nothing next to the others. He compared it to the blood on the floor to see if it could be a match. Yes, possibly. Relief gave him strength to go on.

Moving forward or backward fifty years—that was a guess, but an easy one. He knew his father hated uncertainty. *Father has undoubtedly gone back in time to commit his crimes,* he thought, reflecting on the valuables in the safe, and now would be no different.

Arriving somewhere completely unknown was unnerving, Christopher could attest to that. After all, landing in Denver had to have been a gamble for Father, since Colorado was known only as a western territory in the early 1800s.

That notion helped Christopher land on a decision. He'd go back first, then forward, if he couldn't find them.

He furiously mixed chemicals together—glad he'd spent some time memorizing the formulas. Christopher made a much larger amount than he would need—just in case he had chosen the wrong direction.

Packing the vest-like machine with the chemical formulas, as well as his own revolver, Christopher uttered a quick prayer, then followed his gut.

The vest hung loosely on his shoulders. After cinching it up, he carefully turned the dials to the appropriate notches. Immediately the vibrations and humming noises began. He braced for what he hoped would be a rescue mission through time.

Chapter Fifty-Six

Arianna woke to the hum of the moving device. She tried, but failed to stretch her cramped legs, and her head throbbed. Lifting a hand to massage her temple, her knuckles smacked on a hard surface. As she became fully conscious, reality crashed down around her. She gulped in an attempt to breathe. *I'm crammed in a bin on a time machine headed for my death in New York City. It may as well be my coffin.* Bitter angst for the man who put her there filled her heart. She wasn't sure how long she'd been unconscious, or when to expect to arrive. The bin would likely run out of air before then and Mr. Somers would simply dump her body. She shifted a fraction of an inch, which gave her burning spine some relief.

Every particle of her being wanted to beat against the box and scream. But she remained calm, realizing that her best chance of staying alive was to escape Mr. Somers' grasp once he opened the bin. She would hold very still and feign unconsciousness when—if—they stopped. Letting out a silent breath, she tamped her tears back, unwilling to risk Mr. Somers hearing so much as a sniffle.

Her stomach began doing cartwheels as the device decelerated, then came to a somewhat bumpy halt. Bumpy, but not hard enough to be a road. They must have landed on grass. She figured they'd just materialize somewhere. Surely someone saw them.

The lid of the bin creaked open. Dead of night—pitch black.

Ari was careful to make herself completely limp, no matter how her nerves jumped inside.

Something poked at her shoulder first, but she didn't flinch. "Miss Miller," Mr. Somers said in a low tone. Still, she remained motionless. Then a finger pressed against her neck.

He cursed, evidently unhappy her blood continued to pump beneath his fingertip. He shook her. Nothing. Once he seemed satisfied she was unconscious, he grabbed her arm and hauled her out of the bin; then, for whatever reason, he gingerly carried and placed her against something firm and scratchy. "Come now, dear, sit against this tree and you will feel better."

There must be witnesses.

Ari peeked at him through squinted eyes. He hoisted up the machine and shoved it behind a copse of trees, close to where he'd placed her. Hands fisted on his hips, he scanned the area. It looked like he was searching for the best place to kill her. His back was to her, but she still didn't dare move a muscle. A noise caught her attention, a couple sitting on a nearby bench—the witnesses. Thanks to them, he hadn't killed her yet. The man looked angry as he whispered to the woman, who rubbed her head. He pointed to Mr. Somers several times, then rose and pulled her by the hand until they were both out of view.

It was now or never. Keeping her eyes on Mr. Somers, she silently scooted close enough to the device to feel one of the dials. She yanked with all her might until it snapped off, then stood to run. Her legs wobbled, having been cramped for so long, but her blood pulsed, giving her a boost where her muscles failed her. She eventually took off, ignoring her pounding head pain.

Mr. Somers turned wild eyes on her. He lunged toward his machine. Her intuition paid off. She'd been certain that if she didn't take part of the device with her, he would be satisfied to leave her—dead or alive—and immediately head home. With an essential piece of the device in her pocket, however, there was a chance—albeit a small one—she'd make the return journey. Somehow.

This is Central Park, Ari realized as she dodged trees and spotted city lights. Where had that couple gone? She stared hard into the darkness but saw nobody. She'd just keep running until she found someone, or lost Mr. Somers and could circle back to reclaim the device.

Mr. Somers sprinted behind her. He huffed and grunted and huffed some more.

Her feet finally hit asphalt. Looking up and down both sides of the street, she didn't see very many people at all, let alone the sort who could help her. They mostly appeared homeless—slumped over, asleep, or passed out. She continued to run.

Even though Mr. Somers couldn't match her pace, each time she dared glance back, she saw him. Her hopes of ditching him dimmed. She knew, while *she* could be left in New York, he'd do whatever it took to get his device put back together. She needed to find help. Running faster, she passed some streets that looked hopeful, but he was still hot on her heels. She'd have to outrun him.

The clomping behind her faded; perhaps she'd lost him. A sharp pain shot through her ribs. Panting, she willed it to subside. She scanned her surroundings. Times Square. Her breaths slowed. There were lots of restaurants in Times Square; she'd just need to make it to one of them.

Ignoring the discomfort in her side, she continued until she stumbled into the first establishment she came to. It was a bar, or a club. It didn't matter to Ari; the neon sign blinked "Open."

Ducking inside, she recognized a Beatles song playing in the background. The strong smells of burning incense and cigarette smoke competed with each other, creating a haze that saturated the air and made it difficult to see—or breathe. She wove her way through tables and chairs, aiming directly for the bartender, who swabbed the Formica surface with a dingy cloth. A man nursed a cocktail in front of him and whined loudly about something—every once-in-awhile breaking into song with the Beatles. "I wanna hold yer haaaand…" He winked at a woman with ruby-red lipstick sitting on a nearby stool.

Ari caught her breath as she regarded the bartender, who shook his head and rolled his eyes at the crooner. Pieces of scraggly, long, brown hair escaped his low ponytail. He wore a colorful shirt bearing a peace sign in the center. Still panting, she had to get control before she spoke. "Please—" She let out a few breaths. "I need help!" More air escaped. "Someone is chasing me!" The bartender narrowed his eyes. He obviously didn't believe her.

She glared at him until he acknowledged her.

He threw the damp towel he'd been using to her. "That's some shiner." He motioned to her cheek. "But I can't have you bleeding all over my bar. Ain't good for business. Whatcha drinking tonight?"

Ari wanted to slug him. "I don't need a drink. I'm being followed. Please—"

He walked to the door, opened it, craned his head back and forth, then sauntered back behind the bar. Raising his hands to the surrender position, he said, "There's no one there."

She frowned. "He's there. I know he is. Do you have a phone I can use to call the police?"

He pointed to a payphone on the wall next to the restroom, then returned his attention to his musical customer.

Ari looked at the phone. She hadn't seen one of those in ages, and she didn't have any money. "Does anyone have a cell—" She caught herself before she asked the residents of the 1960s if any of them had a cell phone. That would plummet her credibility. No one even glanced up when she spoke. She blinked against the burning smoke and incense. They all seemed to be absorbed in their own worlds—or they were intentionally ignoring her. The lounge probably got a dozen crazies every night.

She turned back to the payphone and wondered if she pushed the "0," would the operator answer? It was worth a try.

"I'm looking for my daughter." A booming voice at the bar stopped Ari short.

Mr. Somers.

The only option that wouldn't expose her was the ladies' room.

She'd be a sitting duck in there, but maybe there'd be a window she could escape through.

She entered. Nope, no window. She paced, her brain working furiously.

Chapter Fifty-Seven

Arianna peeked out the restroom door to see Mr. Somers sitting at the bar sipping a drink, as if he were any other New Yorker. She looked down the hall past the men's room to see if there was a back way out. A door read "Exit." Her heart thumped faster as she glanced from the bar to the door and back again. Although Mr. Somers seemed contentedly drinking away his problems like everyone else in the room, she knew just a turn of his head would give him a perfect view of the ladies' room.

Maybe if she made a dash for it when he looked down, she could reach the exit unnoticed.

She cracked the door open again and had one foot out, when Mr. Somers stood. She immediately scrambled back into the restroom and locked herself in one of the stalls.

The door creaked open, and her heart stopped. If it was Mr. Somers, she'd be cornered.

She climbed onto the toilet to keep her feet from view. Peering through the crack of the stall door, she saw his black shoes—the very shoes that had chased her through the Victorian mansion and the streets of New York City. Her heart sank. She had hoped for a miracle—another woman needing the restroom.

"Miss Miller, I know you are in here. There is no way out." His voice was menacing. He opened the first of three stalls. Then the second. Through the crack she could see his arm reach for the door she hid behind. He yanked on the handle. Ari watched it jiggle, but not open—yet. She closed her eyes in anticipation of what would happen when he forced his way into the stall. He wouldn't let up. He needed the dial. She pushed it deeper into her pocket.

"I guess you wish to do this the hard way." She heard him take a breath, most likely preparing to break down the stall door. Laughter, however, cut in as she heard the restroom door fly open. High-heels click, click, clicked on the tile near the sink area. She could see Mr. Somers' shoes move as he flattened himself against the far wall, out of the girls' view.

"Shelly, let me borrow your lipstick. That color is far out." Silence. "Thanks."

"Oh man, that guy's hitting on you bad. Did you see him wink? It looked like he had something caught in his eye." A fluttery laugh followed.

"Ugh! He's not my type, Linda. But you're welcome to him."

"His shirt is groovy—love all that chest hair—and he wears those bell-bottoms well." More laughter.

"Wait"—shuffling noises—"there's a man in here, Shelly." Her tone was low now. The laughter stopped.

"What are you doing in here? This is the ladies' room. Are you some kind of perv?"

Ari could have kissed her.

While she couldn't see his face, by the grunting noises he made, Ari was certain Mr. Somers simmered. She watched his shoes pivot and flee the room.

This was her chance to slip out. She hoped that Mr. Somers' back was to the restroom. He'd surely be headed to the bar to formulate a plan B. ...Or, he could be waiting for her right outside the door. She let out a sigh and decided to hold off and exit with the two ladies—blend in, if that were possible.

"That man was twisted. Did you see the glare he gave me when I called him a perv?"

"Yeah. Let's steer clear of him. Maybe we should report him to Wally."

"Wally, the bartender? He's probably Wally's friend." Both ladies giggled.

The two continued to chat while Ari's anxiety level rose.

"You ready?" It sounded like the one named Shelly.

"Mmmm. Let's go."

Ari slipped from the stall and walked out, sticking as close to the ladies as she could. Except when they turned left, she kept going straight and dashed to the emergency exit door. Giving it a hard push, it opened. Sirens began to wail.

She took off at a run.

It didn't take long before she heard male voices—security guards. But Mr. Somers' voice rose above them all, verbally knocking them out of his way. "I'll get her! She is my daughter! She's always pulling these stunts."

"She might have stolen something," an unfamiliar voice said.

"Stand down, man! I will return anything she may have taken!" Mr. Somers barked.

Ari blocked out the voices and concentrated on running. The dark alley behind the bar backed up to several establishments and smelled of rotten food and sewage.

She yanked at a few of the back doors, but no luck. Panic rose and threatened to choke her as she heard Mr. Somers' heavy-footed clomping not far behind. She kept running. Central Park was in sight. Hiding places became scarce, and he seemed to have picked up a second wind.

She had to be careful not to trip over the legs of vagrants—some sleeping, some not. "What's up, pussy-cat?" A drunk ogled her. She ran faster.

Glancing back to see how far Mr. Somers trailed her, she smacked into a garbage can that had rolled into her path. Falling hard onto the road, she felt a sickening crack. She tried to get up, but the second she put pressure on her leg, she crumpled back to the ground. Agonizing pain shot from her hip down to her toes.

Squelching a scream, she used her arms and good knee to scoot, but the pain was unbearable. Fear ripped at her. She wanted to cry, but even her tears seemed too frightened to fall. She felt him bearing down on her.

"Help!" she yelled as loud as she could.

"Holler all you want. You'll get no aid from beggars." The moon lit Mr. Somers' black eyes. His evil glare speared right through her.

"Just leave me here. Go! Just leave me here! You don't have to do—"

"Shut your mouth!" He grabbed her arm and began dragging her toward the park. She winced at the intense pain that slashed through her limbs bumping along the gravel. Her leg bent at odd angles as it bobbed roughly along. She pushed her free hand against the road to slow his progress, causing asphalt to bite into her flesh. She clenched her teeth, refusing to cry out.

Finally, they reached the park. The grass, blessedly softer than the road, was at least bearable through which to be dragged.

Ari tried to pull away, but her injured leg caused her to whimper.

"Hush." Mr. Somers hauled her back and wrapped his arm around her neck, clapping his hand over her mouth. He felt his pocket with his free hand. "If only I had my gun, this would all be over by now."

She tried to scream, but nothing got past the hand over her mouth. She flailed her arms every which way attempting to free herself or attract attention. Searing pain shot up her leg. But the vacant park was still—no more witnesses to stop him from killing her.

"I guess I will just have to dispose of you the old-fashioned way—with my hands. Then I can search your dead body for the piece you broke off my machine." Mr. Somers sneered at her, a wicked gleam in his black eyes. She let out a choking sound as his hands tightened around her neck.

Her world began to fade.

"You looking for this?"

Chapter Fifty-Eight

Christopher cocked the gun he had trained on his father. Mr. Somers jerked around, swinging Arianna with him. The anguish on her face nearly undid Chris, and the odd angle of her injured leg fueled the fire already burning in his chest. He had to keep his anger in check so she wouldn't get killed as a result of his recklessness.

His father yanked her directly in front of him and slouched, making her a shield. "How did you get here?" he bellowed. His face contorted in a mixture of anger and confusion.

"Stop cowering behind Arianna and let her go." Christopher advanced toward them.

"If you come any closer, I will snap her neck." He had one hand covering Ari's mouth, while the other still closed around her throat.

Christopher stopped moving. "If you kill her, who will shield you from me?" His voice increased in volume. "Let her go!"

His father's eyes darted around, clearly searching for something. Christopher realized what it was. "Even if you find your device and take her to another time or place, you will not have enough of your chemical cocktail to get back, so let her go!" It was a bluff—any straw to cling to. He speared his father with a determined glare.

Mr. Somers' face twitched. His grip tightened around Ari's throat. "Where is it? Where is my machine?"

Christopher tilted his head and narrowed his gaze. "I stumbled upon your device, and it appears to be broken."

Arianna signaled with her eyes, which shot down and to the side. He dropped his gaze to where she looked. Something slightly bulged in her pants pocket. *Bravo, Ari.*

"I'm your father, Christopher. Put the gun down."

"You've not been my father for the past four years. Or is it two hundred and four years? I distinctly remember you disowning me in Denver."

"You know you'll not kill me. You don't have the stomach. You weren't even willing to help me when it was for your mother—we had nothing." Father shifted his weight and narrowed his eyes.

Christopher's voice rose again. "We had nothing because of you."

"How can you say that? I nearly worked myself into an early grave trying to provide for you, and this is how you show your gratitude?"

"An early grave would have been preferable to what you've become."

"I have become the wealthiest, most powerful man in the world!"

"To whom? To Mother? To Sarah? Or Joshua? Your prisoners? They think you are a monster! All they've ever wanted was for you to be a husband and father to them. Now they despise you. How long do you plan to keep them under lock and key? Until you die? Until they die?"

He realized he may have gone too far as he saw Arianna's eyes close, then crack open again. "Stop being a coward and let her go! She's not to blame for any of your failures!"

Mr. Somers' face glowed beet-red under light from the gibbous moon, his eyes wild. Christopher feared that pushing him any further would get Arianna killed. In this altered state, his father was not about to hand her over.

Keeping the gun trained on his father, he worked his way toward the devices. He used his foot to nudge each out to be within Father's view, then stepped in front of them. His father watched his every move.

Picking up the vest, he reached into one of the pockets and removed the extra beakers of formula. After he tossed them back toward the bigger machine, he held the vest in front of him.

"I have both machines in my possession. If you let Arianna go, I will give you the vest."

Confusion crossed Father's face as Christopher began to approach him. "Is this some sort of trap, son?"

Christopher winced at the word "son," but chose to let it slide. "No trap. I just need you to let her go."

"What is she to you? You risked your life coming here to find us—for what? Think of the money. We can leave her here and go home and share my wealth. Think about what you are doing."

"Do you really believe I'm searching for wealth and power? They've made you into a monster!" Christopher bit back the rest of the words he longed to say. "Now, if you let her go, you can have the vest."

Angry darts leapt from Mr. Somers' black eyes. His jaw clenched and unclenched. "You never answered my question. Why do you care about what happens to the girl?" He loosened his grasp on Ari ever so slightly. She gulped air, filling her lungs.

"Her name is Arianna, and the reason I risked my life to find her—" He glanced down and swallowed over the lump in his throat. He looked back up and locked eyes with Ari's. "The reason I risked my life is because I love her."

He watched as a tear slipped down Arianna's swollen cheek. His heart ached for her.

Mr. Somers blanched. He seemed genuinely surprised. "You—you what? How do you even know her? She's the interior designer—*my* designer."

Christopher, taking advantage of his father's shock, moved a few steps forward, holding out the vest. His father grabbed at it, but Christopher jerked it out of his reach. "First, release Arianna."

His father shoved Ari to the ground hard and charged at Christopher.

He held the vest close, but realized, too late, the vest wasn't what Father was after. Mr. Somers wrested the gun from Christopher's fingers and aimed it at him.

"No son should point a gun at his father. What kind of man did I raise?" He growled, then shook his head. "I must have taken temporary leave of my senses. I nearly forgot—you're not a man." He shoved the revolver into Christopher's chest.

Christopher closed his eyes.

With a deafening crack, the gun fired. His world went black.

"Christopher!" Ari's tortured voice rang out. "Christopher!"

A haze of confusion settled in his brain. "Ari?" He tried to move but found himself pinned to the ground. He worked an arm free and realized the complete darkness was his father laying prostrate on him. He pushed the bulk up and rolled out from beneath him. Propped against a tree, Ari balanced on one leg above them, wielding a bulky branch. Her eyes were huge with fear and pain.

"You're alive? I hit him, but the gun went off..." Her voice hitched into a sob.

Christopher picked up the vest. A bullet shook loose. "The metal—the vest saved my life." He raised his eyes to hers. "And you."

She looked at the piece of wood in her trembling hands and let it drop. "You—you should get the gun before he comes to."

"Right." He found the revolver and handed it to Ari, then tugged his father's arms through the holes of the vest. "Ari, I got word from Denver. It's good."

Her forehead creased. "What are you—"

His father grunted, rubbing the knot forming on his skull. He pulled himself to his feet and shot a baleful look at Ari. "You foolish girl!" Seeing the gun in her hands, his face contorted. "What business do you have meddling in our affairs? Do you really mean to challenge me, wench?"

"You—you killed my family." She held the gun steady.

"You have no proof of that."

"She doesn't, but I do." Christopher pulled an envelope from his pocket. "You're coming back with us to face charges for vehicular homicide." Christopher moved in behind him.

Mr. Somers sneered. "My son and the designer. Such a thing would never happen where I came from." He turned and spat, then grabbed Christopher by the shirt. His hand clamped around Christopher's neck. The foul stench of alcohol caused bile to rise in Christopher's throat. He tried to swallow it down, but his father's grip was too firm.

Ari raised the gun and aimed it at Mr. Somers' head. "Let him go." She cocked it.

He hesitated, then released Christopher, slowly lowering his hands to his sides. Ari kept the gun in place. "How dare you?" he hissed. "I'll go nowhere with you." He reached into the vest pocket and pushed the buttons to start a transport. The vibrations began.

With a jolt, Mr. Somers and the machine were gone.

"Where did he go?" Ari collapsed to her knees. "He needs to pay for killing my family!"

Christopher gathered her in his arms. "If he makes his way back, we've got what we need to arrest him."

She slouched in his arms and cried softly. He held her close, burying his face in her hair, he wished to weep with her.

He kept his arms wrapped around her for several long moments. Her fingers dug into his flesh as if he might disappear. "I'm so sorry, Arianna. I am so, so sorry." As he held her back to check her injuries, he shook his head at all the cuts and abrasions on her face, arms and hands. "Is your leg broken?"

"I think so."

He scanned the area and found a discarded sign protesting the Vietnam War, broke the wooden part off and formed a splint. She grimaced, and a low moan escaped her as he carefully straightened the crooked limb.

Once he'd done all he could to prepare her for the journey home, he gingerly lifted her onto the disc-shaped machine. She handed him the dial she'd hidden in her pocket. He found a compartment on the device containing tools and glued the dial in its place again. Picking up the wire, which had fallen and lay on the disc, he reattached it to the dial in the same manner as the other wires.

"What would you have done if you couldn't fix the device?" Ari asked. Her fading voice sounded weaker by the moment. He needed to get her home and to a hospital.

He caressed her cheek, taking care to avoid the open wounds. "Being deserted in a foreign place and time isn't exactly new to me. At least I'd be with you." He kissed her forehead. "Let's go home, love."

Chapter Fifty-Nine

The hospital hallway light flickered. Christopher shifted his weight, impatient to get to back to Arianna.

"Like I said, I had an arrest warrant for Mr. Somers, but didn't know where to find him. After receiving a call from Miss Miller's worried boss, I realized he might be at his new home. I drove to the Somers' house and found Mr. Somers—"

"Your father," said the uniformed officer.

"Yes. I found my father attacking her." He shot a glance at the room behind him.

"Sorry, Officer Flemming. It's, you know, for the report." Officer Barrett scribbled something on a clipboard.

"I know. I'm anxious to see how she's doing."

"I'll hurry this along, then. What happened next?"

"I pulled out my service revolver and told Mr. Somers to let her go. A tussle ensued. Mr. Somers got the gun, then Ari hit him with a tree branch. However, it only stunned him."

"You were in the yard, then?"

"Yes." Christopher hated to lie, but he didn't want to get into the whole time-traveling conversation. He especially wished to keep his mother and siblings out of the story—what a spectacle they'd become if anyone learned of their nineteenth century roots. They'd suffered enough. "Then Mr. Somers fled. I don't know where he is, but he is very much alive." Christopher finished his narrative of the events that had brought them to the hospital.

"I think that should do it." Officer Barrett handed the clipboard to Christopher. "Sign there on the bottom, then you can get back to Ms. Miller."

Christopher pulled a chair next to Arianna. More questions would surely arise about the attack, but for now, he wished only to be near her.

A nurse with a bulbous nose sashayed into the sterile room. "Would you care for a pillow, sir?" Her nasally voice pierced through Christopher's aching head.

"Thank you, no." He didn't intend to sleep while he watched over Ari.

"She isn't going to wake up any time soon. Not with the sedative Dr. Woodruff gave her. You may as well get some rest." She tapped her foot on the linoleum.

"Very well." Christopher took the pillow just to end the conversation. He wondered how the nurse expected him to sleep in a room filled with beeping machines, zigzagging lights and heavy smells assaulting his senses. Not to mention, the girl he deeply cared for lay bruised and broken on a hospital bed. His father put her there. If only he had stopped him sooner. No, Christopher didn't plan on so much as closing an eye. He tossed the pillow onto the sofa against the wall.

His gaze traveled the path from Ari's black eye across the gash on her swollen cheek, then down to the angry, red welts in the shape of his father's fingers circling her neck. He bent and kissed her hand, careful not to jostle her bandaged arm. The vision of the doctor painstakingly plucking gravel from her torn flesh made him shudder. He was relieved she'd slept through the procedure.

"She's lucky, you know."

Christopher startled. Why was the nurse still in the room intruding on his private thoughts? "How can you call her lucky?" He narrowed his eyes at the woman.

"She looks terrible now, but doc says she'll likely heal without much scarring. And, well, we won't know until the swelling goes down, but if her leg doesn't require surgery, she'll be out of here in a couple days." She pumped her eyebrows.

Christopher stared at her. He had no response.

She continued, "And those wretched welts on her neck"—she shook her head—"I'd say she's lucky to be alive."

Lucky or not, it sickened him to see Ari so bruised and battered. He would gladly take her place.

The nurse, silent in her soft-soled shoes, moved closer and peered down at Ari. "Who in the world would do such a thing to this poor girl? He must be a monster." She let out a groan. "I mean, look at her face—"

"Ma'am—"

"Peggy. Just call me Peggy." Her high-pitched voice grated like fingernails on a chalkboard.

Christopher took a calming breath. "Peggy, isn't there anyone else you should be attending to?"

"Nope. Not at the moment." She sidled even closer to Ari and let out a tsk. "I'll bet she was a beauty before—"

He closed his eyes to squelch the anger simmering below the surface. "I think I'll attempt a nap now."

Peggy's head snapped up. "You want me to leave?"

He said nothing.

"Humph." Peggy turned and stomped out of the room.

Exhaling a breath of relief, he reclaimed his seat next to Ari. With care, he pushed a lock of hair from her face. "I'm sorry you're here. Can you forgive me, love?" He kissed her forehead and watched the rise and fall of her chest, worried that if he took his eyes off her, she might stop breathing.

"Christopher?" He looked up to see Tasha in the doorway. She crossed the room, her eyes growing wider with each step.

"Tasha. I told you I'd stay the night."

"It's eight o'clock in the morning." Her lips curved up in a sad smile. "I'd say you should go home and get some rest, but I'm concerned about the Somers...er... your family."

A low moan escaped his throat. "I nearly forgot they were in Pueblo. I must find them"—he swallowed hard—"and deliver the news of my father's, uh, absence." He looked down at Ari, longing to stay with her.

"Don't worry, I'll sit right here with her. You go now." She squeezed Christopher's arm. "Thank you for saving her life."

He nodded. "Thank you, Tasha, for being here for Ari." His eyes lingered on Ari's face. "Take care of her."

Chapter Sixty

Two days later, Tasha helped Ari into her own bed, in her own apartment. "I wish I could stay until Saturday when the other three get here to help you move, but I have meetings I can't miss. I'll be back in a couple days." She leaned Ari's crutches against the wall near enough for her to reach.

Ari sank into the sheets, grateful to be out of the hospital.

"You seem to be getting around on these amazingly well, especially for having bruised ribs. Thank goodness your injuries weren't more severe." Tasha scanned the room. "There's a water bottle, your phone and some snacks." She motioned to the nightstand weighed down by things Ari might need. "Oh, and Christopher sent those." Tasha pointed to the dresser where a bouquet of yellow roses beamed like a vase full of happiness.

Ari sat up and sucked in a breath. "There must be at least two dozen."

Tasha nodded. "That man really cares about you." Her lips curved into a soft smile. "Are you going to be all right? Like I said before, I can call someone to stay with you."

Ari shook her head. "I've had enough nursing to last a lifetime—thanks to Peggy." She made a sour face.

Tasha chuckled. "My ears may never recover." Lifting a rose from the vase, she held it to her nose. "I have a hunch you're going to have company after I leave." A sly smile stole across her face.

Warmth spread through Ari. She ducked to hide the blush she knew reddened her cheeks, then quickly changed the subject. "Thank you for staying in Pueblo. I don't know what I would have done without you. You've been more than a friend to me; you've been like a mother—just what I've needed. Really, I can't thank you enough." She felt teary emotion rising as she choked out the last words.

"There is nowhere else I would have been." Tasha plumped the pillows before nudging Ari to lie back in her bed. "And, I could say the same for you. You're like the daughter I never had, but always longed for." She brushed a tear away, then bent down and kissed Ari on the forehead. Ari wrapped her arms around her, wincing a little at the pain in her ribs.

After Tasha departed, Arianna tried to sleep, but to no avail. Peggy, the badgering nurse, could no longer force pain pills down her throat. Even though her body still ached, she was finally clear-headed and didn't wish to return to the blurry haze she'd been living in for the last three days.

Instead of sleeping, she contemplated her upcoming move back to Denver. She experienced a jumble of emotions about leaving Pueblo. She shouldn't feel bad, but that house had been her baby for so long that she'd actually miss it. She paused, recalling images of Mr. Somers attacking her. Her body jerked, hurling knife-like pain from head to toe. Perhaps she wouldn't miss the house after all.

Then there was Sarah. She and Christopher had come to the hospital together on Tuesday afternoon. Ari had been amazed. Sarah became a different person once she could speak freely, without looking over her shoulder in fear of her father. Ari realized how much she would like to stay and get to know her.

But most of all, Ari would miss Christopher. The pain in her injured body was nothing compared to the pain shooting through her heart at the thought of leaving him. She had finally met someone she thought she could spend the rest of her life with, but she had to leave before truly getting to know him—that is, the Christopher without secrets.

Alone in her room, she could let her feelings free. Unimpeded by medication, she felt the impending loss acutely. His family needed him more than she did right now; they knew nothing of the twenty-first century they'd been thrust into. Ari was grateful they had him. Her gaze floated to the yellow roses that brightened her room. Denver wasn't so far away. Perhaps, once his family had become settled, a long-distance relationship would work.

Her phone rang, yanking her from her thoughts. She fumbled around on her well-stocked nightstand, finally locating it beneath her book. Christopher's name flashed on the screen. A bit shy after just admitting to herself the feelings she had for him, she answered in a soft voice.

"Hello, Ari. Are you up for some dinner?" His rich timbre gave her chills. "I'd love to bring some take-out."

She hadn't had the chance to speak with him alone since the end of the terrible ordeal. Either someone had accompanied him, the too-attentive, nosy nurse found a reason to be at her side, or Tasha was with her in the hospital. While she wanted to thank him for risking his life to save hers, her nerves jangled at the notion—there was so much to say, but she struggled with how to say it. Still, scheduled to leave in two days, she might not get another chance. "Uh, yes, that sounds nice."

After they decided on Chinese food, she ended the call and located the crutches. Her striped pajama shorts and pink T-shirt would have to do, but she could at least run a brush through her hair. She hobbled into the bathroom, wincing at the pain in her ribs.

The image staring back at her in the mirror was shocking. Her black eye had mutated into a strange bluish-purple now, but the swelling had diminished some, and the gash had begun to scab over. Scratches zig-zagged across her right cheek and neck. Her heart sank thinking this might be the last time Christopher saw her. Another tear leaked from her eye. She gave herself a mental shake and ran the brush through her hair.

She waited for him on the sofa. The bedroom felt too intimate.

"Ari, it's me." Christopher's deep voice sounded through the door a short time later.

"It's open. Come in."

He pushed through the entrance, bearing armloads of food. "I hope you're hungry," he said with a smile that melted her heart and sent shivers down her spine.

"Are you kidding? After two days of hospital food, I'm starving." Her eyes widened as she saw how much he'd brought. "Well, maybe not that starving."

He chuckled. "How about we start with these?" He held up two white boxes with red dragons outlined on them. "And I'll put the rest of the food in the fridge for you to eat later."

He brought enough for her to eat all week. A stab of pain pierced her heart at the thought of letting this perfect gentleman out of her life. "That was thoughtful. Thank you."

He assembled the food on a TV table Tasha had propped next to the sofa, unwrapped the restaurant-supplied chopsticks, and made sure Ari had everything she needed to eat comfortably. The aromas of cashew chicken and sweet and sour pork filled the room. "You will no doubt be happy to get back to your apartment in Denver, where the furnishings were hand-picked by you. I mean, this place is okay, but your apartment in Denver screams Arianna." He grinned.

"I nearly forgot you stayed there. It seems so long ago. I'll be happy to return, but there are a few things I will miss about being here." She straightened enough to make room for him on the sofa.

He sat down beside her and pulled the table close enough for easy access. "I doubt that. I should think that a place that has caused you so much pain and sorrow would have you running for home."

She didn't know what to say to that. "Shall we eat, then?" She readied her chopsticks.

They dined in awkward silence, only speaking about the food and his family.

When they'd eaten their fill, Christopher gathered the trash, cleaned and stowed the TV table, then rejoined her on the couch.

Finally working up the courage to say what was on her mind, she turned to him and began to speak. At that exact moment, he did the same thing. "Sorry," she said, "you go first."

"Okay then, Arianna, I just want to tell you how profoundly sorry I am for everything you've been through." He spoke in a low tone with more than a hint of sadness. "So much has happened that you neither asked for, nor deserved, and I cannot help but feel responsible." His eyes, misting, began to look like blue pools, but he kept his gaze fixed on her. "I—I just keep reliving it. I'll never forget…" His voice hitched, and he shook his head, unable to continue. "Can you ever forgive me?"

"Forgive you? You saved my life. Do you realize what would have happened if you hadn't come after me? And who, in their right mind, jumps on a time machine and guesses where his pernicious father may have taken the nosy decorator?" Her voice picked up volume as she spoke. She paused and took a calming breath, then continued. "No, Christopher, there is nothing to forgive. You tried to warn me, but I was too stubborn to listen, and it almost got us both killed. I owe you my life." She didn't try to keep the tears from falling. It broke her heart that Christopher had been blaming himself for his father's sins.

He located a box of tissues and tugged a couple out. "But if I had just told you earlier—"

"Then I wouldn't have believed you," she finished. "I understand now. I should have trusted you."

She watched relief wash over him as she said those words. His tight posture relaxed as he expelled a breath. He tilted his head. "You are a bit nosy, aren't you?" His dimples puckered. A throw pillow came his way. He dodged it. "Hey, you aren't playing fair. How am I to get even when you are," he paused and motioned to her injuries, "in tatters?"

"That sounds like a personal problem to me." She lobbed another one, gritting her teeth at the pain in her ribs. This time she hit her mark. She was determined to keep things light, now they'd gotten past the initial awkwardness.

His eyes twinkled. "Well then, if I can do nothing to win this battle, how about we watch some television? It is one of the inventions I have learned to particularly enjoy in this day and age—instant entertainment. Far better than impromptu concerts on the pianoforte."

Ari laughed and let out a contented sigh. They flipped through the channels until landing on reruns of *I Love Lucy*. "Mindless humor. Just what the doctor ordered." She let her head fall against his shoulder and breathed in his spicy scent. His cream-colored pullover showed off his muscular build and felt incredibly soft on her skin. He gently tugged her hand into his. Her skin sparked at his touch. "I wish we'd been spending our evenings like this all along," she whispered.

"As do I, my dear, as do I." He kissed the top of her head, sending warmth through her body. She snuggled closer to him.

After a while, he looked at his watch. "It's late. You need to rest."

He began to rise, but Arianna pulled him back down next to her. She took a breath and mustered her courage. "Christopher, there's something I need to know." She paused, second guessing herself before deciding she should continue. "If you don't want to answer, I will completely understand."

"What is it?" His brows lowered as his azure-blue gaze locked with hers.

Heat rising to her cheeks, she pressed forward. "Did you mean what you said in New York?"

His forehead wrinkled. "Ari, we barely spoke in New York. You were in a state of shock, as I recall. What do you mean?"

"Not what you said to me. What you said to your father"—she lifted a shoulder—"about me."

Understanding registered on his face.

Ari hurried on. "It's okay if you just said it to get us out of a nasty situation. It worked. I have just wondered, that's—"

Before she could finish her sentence, he put a finger to her lips. "Arianna." He paused and blinked back the moisture shining in his eyes. "I have never been more honest than I was in that moment. So, to answer your question, yes…I love you." He swallowed and whispered, "I only wish circumstances had been different and I could have told you sooner."

Arianna's heart overflowed with emotion, and tears spilled down her cheeks. She couldn't find her voice to respond.

Christopher gently cupped her face in his warm hands, tilted his head and kissed her lips. She melted into him. The physical pain pushed aside, all she could feel was warm electricity pulsing through her body. "I have loved you from the first day we met." His words vibrated against her mouth and tingled down to her toes.

She wrapped an arm around his neck. She knew he worried about hurting her in her fragile state, but she wanted more—she needed more. She kissed him hard and deep. His willing lips returned her passionate kisses. Her hands traveled to his hair, massaging his scalp. When she realized how carried away she'd become, she pulled back, afraid she'd crossed a line. "I'm sorry. Sometimes I forget what era you're from. You must think I'm terribly forward." She let out a nervous laugh.

He kissed her lightly, his lips warm with passion, then spotted her book on the end table next to him, picked it up and tossed it to the floor. "You really need to quit reading those books." He smiled as he gingerly scooped her into his arms and kissed her again. "I have a feeling we'll be putting a lot of miles on our cars, driving between here and Denver."

Ari thought her heart might burst. She burrowed into his embrace. "I love you, Christopher."